Operation Hoplon

The Joshua Booker Origin Story

Copyright 2024
Roger Willis Smith

All Rights Reserved

ISBN: 9798218539283

Independently Published
by RWSmith ETC, LLC.

Part 1

"There is no greater agony than bearing an untold story inside you."

~Maya Angelou

Believe me when I say I feel her pain. As I write this, I have many stories about my life that I feel the need to share. Some are inspirational, and I know that some were terrifying to live through. I don't see myself as a hero or exceptional in any way. We all have gifts, and I have been privileged to use my talents for what I and others believe to be the greater good.

This story follows me through the first twenty-five or so years of my life. Today, I am thirty-nine. Perhaps I will share more over time. I hope you – my readers – will grow to understand why I am who I am as you move through my story with me. I have included the moments and interactions that I believe molded me into the man I have become, but there is so much more I must leave out.

The dialog in the book is recreated as close to the original verbiage as I can remember it. I have been blessed with an incredible memory of past facts, figures, and events. I know the dialogue is not exact, but some of it took place many years ago. Know that even if I didn't remember the words exactly as they were originally said, the message conveyed is accurate.

I have changed names and locations for many reasons, including the safety of those I love and national security. Other names, places, and events are all too real, but you must decide which is which, for if I told you, it would create a maelstrom of trouble I would just as soon avoid. Regardless of the names and locations, the events are depicted as precisely as possible without jeopardizing my freedom or our nation's security and standing.

I don't know if this will ever be published or read. I am not interested in a legacy, yet something inside drives me. With all deference to Maya Angelou, perhaps it is simply the agony of bearing an untold story.

I hope you enjoy it.

Joshua

Chapter 1

I was born in the spring of 1984. The exact date is unknown, and as I have now reached the age of 40, it is inconsequential. My biological parents' names, occupations, and ethnicity are also unknown.

However, I would guess they were of Western European descent, with possibly some Native American thrown in somewhere down the line. I base my guess simply on how I look, my coloring, my body type, and the cut of my jaw, cheekbones, and forehead. Otherwise, I have no information on which I can rely.

What I do now know is this: my adoptive parents, The Reverend Rick Booker and his way-too-young wife Rachael, met an unknown man at a roadside park near Pickwick Lake, where Mississippi, Tennessee, and Alabama come together and they 'adopted' me. This unknown man, possibly my biological grandfather, placed me into the arms of the woman I would call my mother before he collected an envelope from my dad and drove off. My new adoptive father and mother drove away shortly after that as they continued southeast toward Birmingham, Alabama, where I would spend the next five years. Those five years are another thing about which I have almost no memory. At some point, they named me Joshua.

I learned these facts when I was 17, right after my mother died. A sealed envelope delivered with her last will contained a handwritten letter that filled in these parts of my past. In hindsight, I guess these facts and the events she shared significantly impacted my life, but I don't believe gaining knowledge of the things I never knew before has changed me. I share what I know of my background because perhaps it will help you, the reader, gain a little insight into what has been, by all accounts, my unconventional life.

My birthday was always recognized on the third day of March. Though I didn't know it as a boy, that was a guess, and I suspect "three-three" was an easy date to remember. My first real memory from my childhood happened soon after my fifth birthday when my parents informed me my dad had been "called" to a small-town church in northwest Mississippi. I had no idea what "called" meant at the time, but I remember my parents sharing this news with me because I didn't like the idea of going elsewhere to live.

Real memories from my childhood begin somewhere around age six or seven. Most of them are blurry, but some are burned so deeply into my soul that I will never be able to forget them. Dad was a Pentecostal pastor, and, it seems, not a very good one. Mom was a pastor's wife who wasn't allowed to be anything else: no job, no life outside the home, no say in any decision facing the family. The stay in north Mississippi lasted only a year or so before some scandal forced us to move again. I didn't care this time.

South Mississippi was the next stop. My father didn't have a permanent job, so we lived in our car for about a month before he convinced another small church just outside Yazoo City to give him a job. There was another scandal and another move. Louisiana and Arkansas followed, each with slightly longer stays than before. Dad was either getting better at preaching or better at avoiding scandal.

During these years, my father, a supposedly God-fearing, hellfire and brimstone Pentecostal preacher, began to drink. I was about nine when I realized the same man who preached about the sins of the bottle on Sunday was deep into one almost every night. That was also about the same time I noticed my mother's bruises. Typically, they were on her arms, defensive bruises, but the occasional black eye or swollen lip told me they were not caused by "clumsiness," as she told me.

By this point, my life had become a bit of a tragedy. My father never hit me with his fist, but switches and belts were always within reach. He was a stout man, probably five-foot-ten inches tall and 220 pounds, and he used his strength when he "applied the rod," as he called it. I

was whipped for making any grade less than an A in school (even daily quizzes), for failing to stand when a woman entered the room, for failing to offer the level of respect he required in speaking to any adult, for failing to quote a bible verse at the drop of a hat if he felt I should know it.

By this point, my mother, tall and thin with long dark hair, had begun to withdraw. She hardly spoke to me or anyone else. She no longer visited the parishioners with my dad, but in hindsight, I think he was okay with that because the bruises were getting harder to cover up.

Then, on April 6th, 1995, everything changed. I was getting ready for bed when I heard heavy footsteps on the porch, followed by loud knocking at our door. Like any curious child, I rushed into the den to see what was happening, only to be sent back to my room by my mom. But in that brief moment, I saw my dad, beaten and bloodied, carried through the door, and dropped on the floor without regard for how hard or soft his landing might be. After my hasty retreat to an adjoining room where I could listen, I heard a few words and phrases that were, I suppose, intended for my mom and not me. At eleven years old, I couldn't put all the information together, but I knew enough from talking to the other boys at school to understand what "adultery," "screwing my wife," "found him in my marital bed," and "I will take care of the whore as soon as I get home" meant.

Deacon Leland, a voice I recognized from its squeaky, nasal tone, told my mom that Dad was no longer the Christ Assembly Pentecostal Church pastor. He also said the family should move out of the house, which was owned by the church, by Wednesday. "Get him sober and get him packed," were his last words before slamming the door.

Mom called me out of my room to help get my dad into bed. She was crying and obviously both ashamed and scared. My father briefly regained consciousness and asked for bourbon, and for the first time, at least the first time I ever saw, my mom, without the slightest complaint, retrieved an almost full bottle of brown liquor from a high shelf in the kitchen and filled a large glass.

After delivering the drink to the bedroom, she led me back to the kitchen and washed Dad's blood from our hands. While the water was running, she leaned over and told me to quietly pack a couple of changes of clothes, a toothbrush, and anything else I could fit into my suitcase. My assumption at the time was that

I would need to pack before Wednesday, but she quickly added, again in a whisper, "We leave tonight."

While packing, I watched Mom tip the bourbon and refill the glass, almost emptying the bottle. When she turned around, I saw her smile for the first time in a long time. I didn't understand at the time.

Within thirty minutes, my dad had passed out on the bed. He was covered in dried blood and snoring loudly. Mom beckoned me from my room, where I had just finished packing, and we crept from the house to the family car, a 1977 Pontiac Bonneville. It was the first time I ever saw my mother drive and the first time I ever saw her not wearing a dress or denim skirt. She wore blue jeans, and her long, dark hair was in a ponytail—another first.

You may wonder how I remember the exact date we left Arkansas in the middle of the night.

The answer is that April 6, 1995, is the date on his tombstone. It's simply a name, Rick Booker, followed by the word "died" and the date. I never knew of any extended family members, so I doubt anyone else in the town knew anything about him. And since Mom and I had disappeared, they went with all they knew. I made my way through Arkansas a few years ago and found his grave in the town cemetery. I didn't shed any tears, and I didn't linger. I just wanted to confirm what my mother had passed along to me.

∞

After driving through the Arkansas night for thirty minutes, I quietly asked my mom, "Where are we going?"

"I'm going to try to find my brother, but I don't know where we'll end up," she replied in a slightly broken voice before adding, "Just know we are never going back."

"Won't he find us?" was my next question.

"No. I don't think so," was her only reply.

In the same letter where I learned about the meeting near Pickwick Lake where Rick and Rachael "adopted" me, I learned the bottle of booze my mother had hidden away in the kitchen was no ordinary bottle of liquor. It was a cocktail of Old Kentucky Tavern bourbon, some antifreeze, and a little rat poison for good measure.

I also learned that just before we left the house, Mom had taken the almost empty bottle and washed the remaining liquid down the drain. She rinsed the bottle with soapy water and poured about an inch of actual, untainted Old Kentucky Tavern into it before placing it back on the table beside the bed. She did the same with the glass from which he had been drinking. She was much smarter than I thought, which is why she was so confident my dad would not be looking for us.

On what must have been April 7th or 8th, 1995, we arrived in north-central Kentucky. I guess mom had saved – or taken – enough money to pay for gas and the occasional snack, but not a motel room. She drove through the first night, and we slept in the car the next morning before continuing. At dusk on Saturday, we reached the tiny community of Brandon, Kentucky.

Mom stopped at a gas station and asked if Samuel Rutland still lived over by Dowsing Creek. The man just replied, "As far as I know. I don't see much of him or Lucy."

"Who is Samuel Rutland," I asked her.

"Your uncle, my brother."

"So, you were Rachael Rutland?" I asked, thinking the name was funny.

"I was, but that was a long time ago."

Nothing else was said for about ten minutes until we turned down a long gravel drive.

"Joshua, I don't know how this is going to go. I haven't seen my brother for almost 13 years, and he wasn't too happy with me when I left town with Rick; sorry, with your dad. I had recently turned 15, and I thought I was in love."

I remained silent as we pulled up to a beautiful, white farmhouse. Beside it was a garden with small stalks of corn and a larger field prepared for planting.

"Come up to the house with me," Mom said. "Just stay by my side, and let's pray he will help out."

The walk to the house couldn't have been more than twenty yards, but it seemed like a mile. I am sure it seemed even longer for my mother. The white two-story farmhouse was in good shape, certainly bigger and nicer than any of the houses I could remember living in. It had a tin roof, and tulips and buttercups were growing near the porch. The steps creaked a little as we made our way to the screen door, which was allowing a cool breeze to blow through. I still remember Mom taking a deep breath before knocking, gently at first, then a little louder. Soon, a woman wearing a green dress and a white apron appeared on the other side of the door.

"Can I help you with something, dear?" she asked while wiping her hands on the apron.

"I hope so," my mom replied while the woman assessed the skinny, disheveled boy standing beside her. "I'm looking for Sam Rutland."

"He's out on the farm; he should be in before too long, though."

I noticed that her voice sounded suspicious of the strangers standing before her.

Mom hesitated again before tentatively saying, "I am Rachael," another pause, "Sam's sister."

Slowly, a smile began to spread across the face of the woman before us. "Okay, then," she stated matter-of-factly. "I'm Lucy. Come on in. We've been expecting you to show up for years."

Thankfully, Aunt Lucy didn't press Mom for details as we sat on a sofa in the living room, waiting for Sam to return to the house. After a bit, I looked out the window and noticed it had grown dark. I wondered if Sam was coming home, but Aunt Lucy didn't seem concerned. Occasionally, she would spring from her chair and say, "I've got to go stir dinner," before disappearing for a moment into another room. I wasn't sure what she was cooking, but after eating only gas station crackers and chips the past two days, I hoped she would share.

Lucy was slight in stature but attractive, with blonde hair cut short at her shoulders. I guessed she was around Mom's age, but she didn't look as tired. She also didn't look like any of the wives from the farm families back in Arkansas. Farm work, typically coupled with producing as many offspring as one's womb would allow, made for a hard life. But Aunt Lucy was different. She didn't suffer from the premature wrinkles, calloused hands, or stooped shoulders that were so prevalent. Later, given the gift of hindsight, I would understand why she held up better than others; she had no children and only rarely worked outside.

While we waited, Lucy continued an easy conversation about the weather and a dozen other topics. She never mentioned my dad. She asked me questions about school, favorite subjects, and things one would ask an eleven-year-old boy. She seemed nice enough, and that relieved some of my anxiety.

During one of her trips to the kitchen, I heard a screen door open and close, and I saw my mother tense and wring her hands before passing them through her hair. Another deep breath followed.

"Samuel Rutland, you aren't going to believe who showed up at our front door about half an hour ago," Aunt Lucy said with great cheer, loud enough to be sure we would hear.

The reply came in an intense voice that reminded me of an actor I had seen in a western movie at the small, one-screen theater in Star City, Arkansas. I tried, but I couldn't remember the actor's name. "I don't recognize the car." Then, in a lower voice, he added, "Is it Manning?"

"No, Samuel Rutland," That was when I noticed Aunt Lucy always called him by his full name, "It's Rachael...your sister."

No further sound came from the kitchen for close to a minute. Mom sat upright in her chair, still wringing her hands and bouncing her leg the way people do when they are nervous. After what seemed like an eternity, I heard the floor squeak and the shuffling of feet. The man I would come to know as my Uncle Sam, with his somewhat long and prematurely gray-streaked hair, stuck his head around the corner and looked at Mom, then me. Aunt Lucy appeared by his side, still smiling.

"Sis?"

Mom stood slowly and said, "Yeah, Sam, it's me."

In slow motion, they began covering the 15 feet between them until they were arm's distance apart. Mom stopped, but Uncle Sam continued and wrapped his arms around her. He held her while he looked over her shoulder, assessing me.

"It's really good to see you, Rachael. Who do you have with you?"

Mom broke the embrace and waived me over. "Joshua, meet your Uncle Sam."

I reached out to shake his hand like Dad had taught me, but he stepped forward and put his hands on my shoulders. "It is nice to meet you, Joshua. I think we all have some catching up to do."

"First, we eat," Lucy chimed in. "Then we can get you two settled in a bed."

"I can't ask you to do that," Mom said, but the remark confused me since I knew it was what she was hoping for.

"You two got anywhere else to stay tonight?"

"No, we don't," Mom replied.

"Then why don't we go with my plan."

We sat down to a dinner of ham, cornbread, and peas. Aunt Lucy poured me a glass of milk and fixed tea for everyone else. I would have preferred tea—sweet, the way Mom made it—but I didn't say anything. The dessert was lemon pound cake, and Aunt Lucy gave me an extra piece.

Mom and Uncle Sam talked all through dinner. Even at eleven years old, I knew what was not said at the dinner table provided more information than what was said. They talked about the farm, the food, a new movie theater, and Super Walmart, which was being built about forty minutes away just south of Lexington. What was not discussed was family history, my dad, or any other subjects I would have asked about if placed in the same situation.

After dinner, Uncle Sam suggested we get the bags out of the car, so I followed him out the door. That was the first time I studied him. He was strong, with broad shoulders and a small waist. His biceps stretched the fabric of his flannel shirt, and he moved like a man in control of himself and his surroundings. I compared him to my dad; while it had never occurred to me before, Dad was weak. He spoke loudly and often. He was animated in his movements; he commanded attention in a room by controlling the action and the dialogue. Sam was different. He didn't say much. Nothing was done to attract attention. Nothing was said in an effort to impress his audience. I wasn't sure how old he was, but I later learned he was three years older than my mom, who had just turned 29.

I opened the car door, and we pulled the two suitcases from the back seat. Walking back to the house, I paid attention to the face illuminated by the single porch light. It may sound strange, but the face was simultaneously gentle and terrifying. The piercing blue eyes were intense, but the rest of his face seemed friendly and welcoming.

Inside the house, Sam turned left and ascended the staircase. Upstairs, he seemed lost for a minute before shouting, "Lucy, where do I put young Joshua?"

"Blue," came the reply echoing up the stairs. "Show him where the bathroom is."

Sam and I continued to the end of the hall, where he opened a door on the right-hand side. Before entering, he looked to the end of the hall, less than a step from where I stood, where there was a full bath. "I'm not sure how you could have missed the bathroom, but Lucy said to tell you where it is, so there you go."

My thoughts entering the bedroom were split between fear and comfort. I know those two things seem diametrically opposed, but that is what I remember. For some reason, the room gave me comfort. It had a full-size metal bed with several quilts neatly folded at the foot. I touched the bed and realized the top mattress was full of feathers, and there was another mattress and springs below. I had never had a real bed that I remembered. Maybe I had a crib, but I doubt it. In recent years, I slept on a small mattress on the floor with a sheet and blanket on top. I was young and could have slept on anything, but that bed looked glorious.

The room was painted light blue, and it smelled fresh. A small closet in the corner had only a rod and a couple of shelves, but it was more space than I needed.

Something about that room fit my idea of "normal." It seemed like what the kids I met back in Arkansas had. I had never had a room like this before, and knowing I wouldn't have to spend the night in the car was nice.

The fear part was simply the unknown. Aunt Lucy and Uncle Sam seemed nice enough, but even my dad could act civil when it suited him. I was supposed to be in school on Monday; what would happen with that? If we left here – which mom had given mixed signals about – where would we go?

I also worried about Dad finding us. Over the years, he had made so many threats about what would happen if Mom were to leave him. I guessed that if he had to come all this way to find us, he wouldn't stop the beatings until someone died. Now, I know that wasn't a worry, but I didn't know it at the time.

Mom came by and commented on how nice the room was and told me to thank Uncle Sam and Aunt Lucy for letting us stay for a few days. "A few days." That answered one question. I went back downstairs and thanked them. Aunt Lucy hugged me, and Uncle Sam clapped me on the shoulder and said, "I know you can't understand this, but you're family. To us, that means something." He was right; I didn't understand.

Returning upstairs, I saw Mom had unpacked my clothes and put them in the small chest just inside the door. She handed me my pajamas and toothbrush and told me to go into the bathroom, brush my teeth, and get dressed for bed. When I returned, Mom was sitting on the bed with her face in her hands.

"Joshua, I don't know what to tell you," she said without looking up. "For now, we can stay here with Sam and Lucy. I need to find a job but don't know where to start. Maybe I can work at a restaurant or the new movie theater. I will find something. After that..." She trailed off, and I could tell she had no idea what came "after that." After a moment, she looked up at me and smiled. "I love you, Joshua. Let's say our prayers."

We knelt by the bed, just as Dad had insisted for as long as I could remember, and asked Jesus to watch over us. Mom would pray, and occasionally, I would add something I thought was important. On this night, I asked Jesus to watch over Aunt Lucy and Uncle Samuel (I knew the name Samuel was in the Bible, so I used the whole name). I never mentioned or prayed for Dad, but I thought about how I last saw him. I didn't think he deserved my prayers.

After I climbed into bed, Mom told me she was going to visit with her brother for a bit. I snuggled under the warm quilts and wiggled deep into the feathers of the mattress. I could hear muted conversation downstairs but couldn't make out any words. Soon enough, I fell into a dreamless sleep, interrupted only by the sunlight streaming through the window.

When I awakened, I experienced momentary confusion about where I was. It has happened many times since as I traveled the world. Those five seconds of disorientation while you try to remember where you are and why you are there. Believe me, as you read my story, you will understand more about why I am very familiar with this feeling, but that morning may have taken the longest to resolve.

I didn't know what time it was, but I got out of bed and followed my school morning routine. I had always been forced to make my bed – such as it were. I wasn't sure what to do here, but I pulled the covers up, smoothed some wrinkles, and fluffed the pillows. Good enough, I decided. I dressed in the same clothes I wore the day before and the day before and went into the bathroom to brush my teeth. Sitting on the edge of the sink was a washrag, a bar of soap, and a towel. I assumed it was a hint, so I undressed, showered, brushed my teeth and hair, redressed, and descended the stairs.

Aunt Lucy was cooking in the kitchen, and it smelled wonderful.

"I'm cooking bacon and pancakes this morning," she said. "Your mom said you like pancakes."

"Yes, ma'am," I replied.

"Uncle Samuel has gone to the barn, but he'll be back shortly. Just picking us up some eggs. Have a seat."

Aunt Lucy turned the gas on the stove to low and let the bacon keep cooking. Then she stirred the pancake batter before sitting down at the table beside me. She took my hands, and I noticed they were not as soft as the rest of her looked. They were kind hands but those of someone unafraid of physical labor.

"Joshua, I'm not sure what I need to say here, but I'm guessing you are scared and a little confused."

I wanted to say, "I'm not scared," but it would have been a lie, and she would have known it, so I said nothing.

"Your Mom, Uncle Samuel, and I talked for a while last night. We have some things to work out but know that you are safe and loved, and we will all stick together. I am sure you have many questions, and we will answer them the best we can, but for now, trust me when I say everything's going to be okay."

Again, I didn't say anything. But for some reason, I remember nodding my head. It wasn't a timid nod; it was a confident nod. Her words hit me, and I, for the first time since those men dragged my dad into the house in Arkansas, felt that I really was safe and loved.

Before anything else could be said, Uncle Sam entered the kitchen through the back door with a small basket of eggs in his hand, and Mom entered from the hallway. I could tell Mom had not slept as well as I had, but I also saw hope in her eyes. She was very different from the night before when we prayed for Jesus to watch over us.

After breakfast, Uncle Sam guided me out to the back porch.

"Joshua, you go explore this place a little bit. Head out to the barn and climb around on the hay bales if you want. You'll find a small pond if you keep going past the barn. We'll go fishing soon. Maybe we can catch enough catfish for a nice fish dinner with hushpuppies and coleslaw. There's another barn, an older black one, that you'll see on the other side of the field when you top the ridge. That's where we used to cure tobacco. It isn't used for that now, but I occasionally put the horses up in it. For now, stay away from the tractors and equipment. You will learn about them soon enough. Just stay within sight of the house, and we'll call you later."

So off I went. During the last couple of years in Arkansas, we lived in a house owned by the church, and it was right in the middle of town beside the sanctuary. The lot might have been 60 feet by 60 feet. When I went outside to "run around in the yard," there wasn't much yard to run around in. This was different.

When we arrived the evening before, the light was almost gone from the sky. Darkness and probably fear of the unknown had prevented me from noticing there was not another house to be seen. There were a lot of trees to my left, and what I considered at the time to be an enormous mountain towered before me. I now know it was simply one of the smaller Appalachian foothills, but compared to the Arkansas delta, this was Mount Everest.

The big red barn was built into the side of a hill. The walk from the house to the barn is about 60 yards. I remember looking in every direction, trying to take it all in. Several tractors and equipment, one of them big and green, were arranged around the barn, but as instructed, I avoided exploring there.

As I approached the structure, several scents almost overwhelmed me. Even today, I still distinctly remember every one of them. Is that because of that first entrance into the barn or the time I spent there afterward? I don't know. I know there was the scent of hay and manure, the leathery smell of tobacco, and the smoky scent of burning wood all blended together. Strong and intense, but somehow comforting. It smelled like Mother Earth.

I did precisely as Uncle Sam had suggested. I climbed on the hay bales and even began building a small hiding place – a fort in my mind – where I would go if my dad came looking for us. I planned to make it big enough for me and my mom. But a gray rat snake, which I would later describe as eight feet long, changed my plans. I rolled over a hay bale, and there he or she was. The snake slowly crawled off while I sat, paralyzed with fear. The snake put an end to my fort building for the day. If Dad came to find us, I would just have to fight him.

Behind the barn was a chicken coop. I saw about a dozen hens and a rooster that would not shut up even though the sun was far above the horizon.

From the barn, I moved on toward the lake. I remember watching every step for another snake. It was a beautiful "pond," as Uncle Sam called it, about six or eight acres in size. There was a small green boat turned upside down on the shore. I hoped we could take the boat fishing.

Below the levee was an older barn. It was painted black at one time. There was a lean-to-shelter on one side over a couple of tables. Between the lean-to and the levee were assorted pieces of plywood and other materials attached to posts in the ground. The far side of the barn had stalls for horses.

I continued to explore and walk around. As I approached the "mountain," I found a series of washed-out gullies and exposed rocks. There was a pasture nearby with three horses and about a dozen cows. I had never ridden a horse, but I wanted to. We never had a TV, but my friends had some "Rawhide Kid" comic books, and cowboys seemed like the most incredible people on the planet to me.

While gazing at a tree with a platform nailed about 12 feet in the air, I heard footsteps and turned to find Uncle Sam approaching.

"I see you found my deer hunting spot," he said with a smile. "I killed three bucks from that one spot this past winter. They come down from the trees on the hill to eat the grass each morning and evening. Maybe I can get Lucy to cook some venison tenderloin for breakfast tomorrow."

"Is it good?" I asked.

"Yep," he said, "If it weren't good to eat, I wouldn't kill it. God put animals like deer, ducks, turkeys, and the like on the earth for several reasons, and one is to provide food. We never kill what we won't eat. And we eat what we kill. Always remember that."

"Okay," I said. It made sense to me.

"Let's get back to the house. Your mom and Aunt Lucy need to talk to you about some things."

Chapter 2

Mom and Aunt Lucy were still sitting at the table where I had left them a couple of hours before. Mom held a cup of coffee, and Aunt Lucy sipped on water. Uncle Sam pointed me to one chair and filled a glass with tap water before sitting in the last chair. I could hardly breathe.

Uncle Sam started. "Joshua, I'm going to tell you a couple of things before I have to leave. Your mom and Lucy will fill you in on the rest. Years ago, before you were born, your mom and dad fell in love. I was protective of my kid sister, I guess I still am, and I told her I didn't like your dad and that she was too young. I regret it in one way, and in another way, I wish I had done more. Soon after your mom left with your dad, I joined the Marines, and we kind of lost touch. I regret that to this day."

I could see the pain in his rugged features, which made the hurt he felt stand out even more.

"After I got out of the Marines, I tracked down your mom and dad. But your dad was preaching at a church, and your mom seemed okay. I had no reason to believe she wanted to talk to me, so I came home and got on with my life and work. Fresh out of the Marines, I took another job, came home, and met up with Lucy here. I finally convinced her to marry me, and we've worked for the last couple of years to get this place back in shape. Everything here belongs to your mom as much as it does me."

"You grew up here?" I questioned. Mom nodded.

"You two can stay as long as you like. Your mom will look for work to help with the groceries, but that's at her insistence, not mine. I still do a little work for an importer, which takes me away on occasion. She takes care of things while I'm gone," he said, tilting his head toward my aunt.

"Lucy's degree is in education; she can teach you since there isn't much school left this spring. Then we'll decide what to do next year. After school, you'll have chores but nothing an eleven-year-old can't handle."

23

He walked back to the sink and washed his glass carefully before placing it upside-down on the drying rack. He took a deep breath, let it out, and said, "You and Rachael got dealt a bad hand, but it is all going to be okay."

I believed him. We made eye contact, and we nodded a little before he walked out of the room. Thinking back, I was already taking on some of his traits and mannerisms. They would later serve me well.

Lucy took over. "You gotta tell me exactly what you're learning in school. I will find some textbooks, and we'll figure out the rest. Anyway, don't worry about that."

"Your mom or I will get you up at six each morning. I want you dressed and downstairs by six-fifteen, and your first job will be to go to the hen house and collect the eggs. I will show you where and how this afternoon. Just watch out for the snakes. They won't hurt you, but they will scare you sometimes. They like the eggs as much as we do."

I spent the next five minutes explaining my experience with the snake in the barn, and I heard my mom laugh for the first time in a while—really laugh.

"I think Samuel Rutland calls him Pete," she said. "He has been living in the barn for so long I don't even notice him anymore. We have the snake but no rats or mice. We prefer the snake, so just ignore him, and he will ignore you. There are a few bad snakes in this part of Kentucky, but we don't see them much. I am sure Samuel will teach you which ones are which.

"After you gather the eggs, we will eat breakfast and do schoolwork until lunchtime. In the afternoon you can go out and work with your uncle. Shower and put on clean clothes before dinner. Your mom and I will go to town and get you more clothes, boots, and other things this afternoon."

Mom took over, but she just told me she expected me to behave and do what my aunt and uncle said. "No backtalkin' and no sassin'" were her exact words. I can still hear them today.

When they were done, I went back outside and sat on the porch until lunch was served. They called it "lunch," but my mom and dad always said "dinner." It didn't matter to me. Aunt Lucy gave me a roast beef sandwich with a lot of mayo and potato chips—one of my favorites.

That afternoon, Uncle Sam and I went into a small structure covered with clear plastic on the south side of the bank barn. He called it his hot house. There were a couple hundred plants in small containers growing there. He began touching the soil around the plants and urged me to do the same. "This is the tobacco we will plant in the field in a few weeks. Feel the dirt carefully. It doesn't need to be completely dry, but it can't be too wet either."

I did as he said.

"I think it is about right for now. We will check it every day and decide when to water it again. When we do water, it'll be just a good sprinkle. Not too much because we can always come back and do more. Tobacco doesn't like too much water. That's your first lesson for the day."

I tried to remember how the soil felt. How it crumbled but did not turn to powder between my fingers. I was determined to contribute. Next, he suggested we visit the hen house, and he would show me how to collect eggs because Lucy said it would be my job. I confirmed that was what I was told. As we arrived at the hen house, I told him about my run-in with "Pete" earlier. He simply laughed, shook his head, and said, "You and Pete will get used to one another soon enough."

From there, we made a couple of other stops, and he showed me where he kept his tools, like rakes and shovels. There was a wheelbarrow, and some other things I assumed were needed on a farm. I asked him what crops he farmed.

"Well," he said. "I grow some tobacco and sell that. There are 70 acres of hay. I use some for the horses and cows and sell the rest. We grow our vegetables. We don't need much, and the import company pays me pretty well when I work for them, so we have plenty if we need to buy something."

Being an 11-year-old kid, I had to ask, "What is your job with the import company?"

Uncle Sam tilted his head to one side and said, "Let's just say I take on special projects and they require me to go many places. Maybe we will talk more about it later."

That is how things went for the next three years. Mom found a job working in a truck stop restaurant from three until eleven, so I saw her when she got up and again at lunch. After I was older, my chores expanded. I never minded doing them. Helping harvest the tobacco was hard, but it only took a couple of weeks each year. Working in the garden in the afternoon was often hot, and putting out hay for the cows and horses in the winter was cold.

I noticed early on that Uncle Sam was rarely in the home at breakfast. He would come in most mornings at about 8:30 wearing sweatpants and a tee shirt. And no matter the temperature, he was sweating. I would ask what he had been doing, but he always replied, "Just keeping old age away." After a quick bite, he was off to start on the day's work while I did my schoolwork.

One afternoon, about three weeks after our arrival, Uncle Sam suggested we stop work early and go to the range. He was talking about the smaller black barn below the lake.

"I come over here a couple of times a month and shoot my guns," he explained. "This old barn used to be for curing tobacco, but now we sell it right after harvesting. I like to shoot, and this keeps me sharp."

I would later understand why this was necessary.

He pulled the barn door back, revealing a metal shipping container inside, like the ones the trucks and railroads used. "I keep most of my guns and extra ammunition locked away in here. Don't tell anyone about it."

There was peg board on the left wall, and about a dozen handguns hung from hooks. Another half-dozen rifles of assorted sizes and shapes were further down. On the right was a table and several boxes of rags, tools, and bottles of liquids. In the back were stacks of boxes. I recognized 12-gauge and 30-06 on some of the boxes. Other numbers and descriptions were not as familiar. There were a lot of boxes and green metal cans with 5.56 NATO and 9MM stenciled on the side.

He handed me a set of earmuffs and some glasses that were too big for my face, but they stayed on.

"I am going to shoot targets for about an hour. We will get you shooting soon enough, but I want you to watch me for now. I have a chair somewhere in here we can drag outside. Do not get up unless I tell you. Understand?"

"Yes, sir," I replied. "Why do you have so many guns?"

"Guns were my specialty when I was in the Marines. I enjoy them. I like the precision required to hit a target quickly. Around here, I just use 'em for sport."

Uncle Sam grabbed two pistols and a short rifle from the wall, a canvas bag full of ammunition, several rolled-up pieces of paper, and a staple gun. We walked out to the shelter built on the side of the barn, and he placed everything on the tables.

"There are a lot of fundamental rules when you are handling a gun," he said. "First, even if you know it is not loaded, treat it as if it is. Second, never point it at anything you don't want to shoot, even if you are certain it is not loaded. Third, never put your finger on the trigger until you are ready to shoot. Fourth, always know your background. Bullets don't always stop when they hit the target, and we don't always hit our target anyway. We shoot here below the lake for several reasons. This valley blocks most of the sound, so we don't bother anyone down the road, and the lake levee is a good backstop. If a bullet continues through the target, which they all do here, it hits the levee. No harm."

We both went out and stapled some of the paper targets to the plywood I had seen earlier. It was about 50 yards to the levee's base, and we put targets at different distances.

As we were walking back, he explained that sometimes he would shoot on the other side of the barn, where he had over 700 yards of open field, when he practiced with his hunting rifle. I wasn't sure how far 700 yards was until he said it was as long as seven football fields. That gave me a point of reference, and it seemed like a long way.

For the next 45 minutes, I sat and watched as Uncle Sam fired a pistol, dropped the mag, reloaded, fired, dropped the mag, and reloaded once again. He must have fired three or four hundred rounds split between three pistols. He almost always hit near the bullseye, no matter the target distance or how fast he shot.

Eventually, we returned to the container, and he turned on a light over the table. I noticed it was wired to a car battery. As he broke down the pistols, he taught me what each piece was and showed me how he cleaned each part before reassembling them and placing the gun back on the wall. As we returned to the house, I couldn't wait to shoot with Uncle Sam and hit the targets like him.

After several months, I got my first opportunity to shoot. Uncle Sam had a German Sport Guns GSG .22 caliber pistol built on the 1911 platform. He also had a Ruger Mini-10 .22 caliber rifle. I practiced with those until I was about 14 when he let me start shooting the larger caliber 9mm Glock and H&K handguns he liked. He also had a Beretta Model 92, which was my favorite. My mom bought me a Remington Model 700 hunting rifle for Christmas, and Uncle Sam and Aunt Lucy bought me a Remington Model 1100, 12-gauge shotgun. I still use both for hunting today.

∞

Not long after we arrived in Brandon, Aunt Lucy registered me with the state as a homeschool student, which gave her access to state-approved textbooks. After the first year or so, a new personal computer showed up at the house. I still don't know who bought it, but I guess it was Lucy and Sam. Uncle Sam set it all up and helped us connect to America Online. The first time the modem dialed out, the screeching carrier wave sounded like the world was ending, but most folks younger than me don't remember that sound.

Lucy insisted I study a foreign language, but she only spoke English. One day, UPS delivered a box with computer disks and a workbook inside. The workbook said, "Speak Spanish Like a Native."

"Maybe we can learn Spanish together," Lucy said. We will spend 30 minutes a day and see what we can pick up."

It turned out we both enjoyed learning Spanish. Within a couple of months, we had completed the course and were speaking basic phrases to each other around the house. I couldn't use it with Uncle Sam, though. He would look at me and growl. "I know some Spanish," he told me more than once. "But this is America; speak English." He smiled when he said it, but I felt he was only half joking.

Lucy ended up ordering the intermediate and later the advanced "Speak Spanish Like a Native" programs. We completed them all, but I had no idea if I could actually speak the language because there were no Spanish speakers with whom I could practice anywhere in the county.

During my free time, I explored. I climbed the trees, fished in the lake, and tried to keep my mind occupied. Over time, I quit wondering if my dad would find us. I should have missed him, but I never did.

Over those first three years, Uncle Sam left the home over a dozen times. Most times, he was only gone for about two weeks. One time was for three weeks. On two occasions, it was over two months. When he returned, he never talked about where he had been or what he had been doing; he just asked how I was doing and picked back up right where he left off. I asked questions but only got "taking care of something for the importers" as an answer.

He and Aunt Lucy were always good to me. I had spent my first ten years following orders from my dad without question because I didn't want the switch, so I continued being compliant as I got older. I knew my job, and I did it. That discipline would go a long way later in life.

I continued with homeschooling. I think having one-on-one instruction helped me focus, but there is no doubt I have an aptitude for learning. By age 15, I had worked through all the high school textbooks Aunt Lucy could round up. Each evening after dark, I would read novels. Aunt Lucy and I would go to the library in Richmond every two weeks and borrow everything from classic literature to modern-day thrillers. I read them all. Louis L'Amour and Tom Clancy were my favorites. Cowboys and government agents took me to places I never expected to visit. After Aunt Lucy became convinced I had mastered everything in the high school textbooks, she began to order college textbooks in math and history, which were my two favorite subjects.

Sam and Lucy had a television, but it only got turned on if the Cincinnati teams – the Reds or Bengals – were playing. Lucy loved the Reds. We got the newspaper out of Lexington, and part of my daily assignment was to read stories Lucy had marked and write a short synopsis or tell her about them. I learned a lot about the world that way. Between exploring the outdoors, the books, the work, the shooting, and school, I never thought about the TV.

On Saturdays, Mom and I would go into town. I saw other kids and remembered playing with friends and classmates in Arkansas. Those were good memories, but I never really missed having friends to run around with. Uncle Sam and I did almost everything I would have done with a bunch of kids, with the notable exception of getting into trouble. Uncle Sam was 36 years old, which was ancient in my mind, but he was still spry, and we had a lot of fun when we were not working. When he went out of town, I would sometimes be asked to do extra work on Saturdays to help pick up his load. Aunt Lucy would pitch in, and Mom would help if she had time. A couple of times, Lucy insisted we skip school to finish some work, but that was fine with me.

Life was good.

Chapter 3

I turned 16 on March 3, 2000. My voice had deepened over the past few years, and other physical changes became noticeable. There is no need to cover the details. You all know what happened.

The work on the farm had been good for me. I stayed lean and grew strong through work and long hikes in the foothills during my spare time. I had learned to swim and would often spend time in the summer swimming from one end of the lake to the other. On occasion, usually on Sunday, when we didn't do any more work than was necessary, Uncle Sam would take me hunting or on a hike through one of the many state parks in the area.

I was growing rapidly; having blown past my mother's height in the past year, I was now bumping six feet tall.

After lunch that day, Uncle Sam left the house in his truck and returned a few hours later with all kinds of assorted exercise equipment: a barbell with 220 pounds of steel plates, dumbbells in pairs of five, eight, ten, fifteen, and twenty pounds, a couple of kettlebells, and elastic exercise bands.

"Happy birthday, Joshua. You're starting to sound like a man and grow like a man. It's time for you to look like a man. Plus, I need to work out too, if you don't mind me joining you."

I replied with a quick "thanks," but honestly, I wasn't too excited. I worked enough around the farm as far as I was concerned. I didn't need extra work.

"Lucy tells me she is rounding up college books. Are you interested in college one day?" he asked.

"I've never really thought about it," I said.

Mom, who had been quiet up to this point, chimed in with, "I want him to go to college one day. I never even got to finish high school. I think it's important."

"Yep," Uncle Sam said, "But there are many kinds of education. I never went to college, but the Marines taught me skills I used then and still use today. Plumbers, mechanics, and electricians make great money, and they typically either go to a trade school or hook up with someone as an apprentice. There are a lot of ways to gain education and life skills. If he wants to go to college, I suggest he keep studying whatever books Lucy can round up. Then, when he'd normally have been graduating from Brandon High, we will see what we can do about getting him enrolled."

"But I won't have a diploma from high school. Can I go to college?" I asked.

Mom replied, "Let's see how it goes between now and then. You are registered as a homeschooler, so you gotta pass the state test to get your diploma. Aunt Lucy says you'll have no problem with the test."

Uncle Sam moved us back to the subject of turning me into a man. "As you know, I leave the house to exercise each morning before you get up. I do what I did in the military. They called it PT, also known as physical training, but we called it 'pain and torture.' After a while, it gets in your blood. I still do it because I like to take care of my body. I like to stay strong. And occasionally, I need to be strong. Why don't you join me every morning for the next month? We'll exercise together. This time of year, I leave the house at six. What do you think? Can you keep up with this old man?"

I didn't know much, but I knew I was being baited. I had seen Uncle Sam swinging an axe or splitting maul with his shirt off. His flat stomach, broad chest, and sinewy muscles had already told me he was in great shape and exceptionally strong. Scars on his legs, chest, and especially his back told me he had been through a lot. But I felt the new sensation of testosterone flowing through my body, and I accepted his challenge.

"See you at six," I said. "See if you can keep up with me."

I am a dumb ass.

The following day, I came bounding down the stairs wearing sweatpants, high-top tennis shoes, and a tee shirt, like I knew

Uncle Sam would have on. He was leaning on the counter with an apple in one hand and a banana in the other.

"The body needs a little fuel before a workout, apple or banana?"

I pointed, and he tossed me the banana. We walked to the barn in the cold and dark, eating along the way. We stopped south of the barn, and he led me through stretching and calisthenics. Jumping jacks, push-ups, sit-ups, squats, lunges, and more. This went on for 45 minutes. I was already winded and sweating.

"Next, we will go on a little jog," he said as it started to get light, "but I will ask two favors. First, calling me Uncle Sam sounds patriotic but silly. How about we stick with a simple Sam and drop the uncle part? Second, I ask that you do your best for these thirty days. You're a good athlete and strong, but you are not in shape or nearly as strong as you could be."

I wasn't sure what to say, so I just nodded once, and he took off on a slow jog northwest toward the river, a direction I had walked but never explored. As far as I knew, it was heavy woods and game trails. It was the area where the deer stayed before they came to the field to graze.

After about a quarter mile on a narrow path, we intersected an old logging road. It was a winding path with a consistent descent for nearly a mile. By the time we reached the bank of the Kentucky River, I was several hundred yards behind and barely able to breathe. Sam, as he was now to be known, waited for me beside the river.

"You surprised me," he said. "I didn't think you could run all this way with no training. We have another half-mile or so along the riverbank. Watch your step. It's pretty flat, but there are holes and roots and other things that will turn an ankle in a hurry. I'll wait for you at the trail's end before we turn for home. Keep pushing. You can slow down, but never stop."

And with that, he was off.

I tried to keep up, but it was no use. I was soaked with sweat, and my legs and lungs burned, but I plodded on at what I would now describe as a slow jog. I also fell three or four times. I don't remember the exact number, but my battered, scraped, and bruised body caught up to the waiting Sam. He just looked at me and said something about not making it home by 7:30 that morning.

The final leg was up and down hills, mostly up. I followed the path and made it home at about 7:45. Sam had been home for 25 minutes. When I could breathe again, I mentioned that he did make it home by 7:30, as usual. I was feeling pretty good about myself. He confirmed he did make it home on time before adding, "But I skipped about 40 percent of the run."

I apologized for messing up his workout. "Not to worry," he said. "You'll not do any better tomorrow or the next day. But soon, you'll start to improve, and as you do, we'll make it harder and harder until you're doing what I do."

He was right about almost everything he said. The next day, I was so sore I could barely get out of bed. My finishing time was even worse. The following day was just as bad. But after three days, I began to progress, shaving a few minutes off my time each day.

By the end of the 30 days, I was mostly keeping up, though I was far more winded at the end of the run than Sam. He said he was proud of me for making it through the 30 days, which I was pleased to hear, and asked if I wanted to continue. His earlier comment about "it kind of gets in your blood" was correct. I did want to continue. I wanted to get faster and stronger. I wanted to beat him on that run.

We also began working out with the weights. Each evening after dinner, Sam and I would go to the barn for weight training and other exercises. My 16-year-old body responded, and that would continue for the next couple of years. At just over 16, I was approaching 6'1" and weighed in at a lean but muscled 185 pounds. By 17, I would grow to 6'3" and 205 pounds.

Mom insisted I spend time with other teenagers. She said I needed to be "socialized," as if I were a wild animal. Sam and Lucy agreed. To accomplish this "socialization," I needed a driver's license, but first, I needed a birth certificate and a social security number. This fact was discussed around the dinner table. I assumed the documents were left behind in Arkansas. Maybe my dad had them.

Sam said he would make some calls, and I later heard him asking Mom questions regarding my place of birth and the hospital's name. I couldn't hear Mom's answer, but she and Sam stepped outside for a while. When she returned, she said, "Sam is going to see if he can get you what you need."

About a week later, Federal Express delivered a package, and Lucy pulled a birth certificate and social security card from within. She handed it to me. It said I was born to Rick and Rachael Booker at North Mississippi Medical Center in Tupelo, Mississippi. At the time, I assumed it was all true.

I easily passed the written test and got my license two weeks later. On Friday and Saturday nights, we would skip weight training so I could go to North Fork or Richmond and just be a teenager. I tried to socialize and make friends, but I found most of the people I met who were my age to be silly kids, only worried about where to buy beer or how to get their hand into some random cheerleader's bra or panties. We never connected socially or intellectually.

The North Fork football team kicked off their season in August, and I drove into town to watch the Friday night game. Sitting beside a group of recent graduates, all eighteen to twenty years old, I decided I had more in common with them than those my age. They sized me up and eventually asked where I was from and if I was a student. I told them I was from the Brandon area but had been home-schooled. I didn't mention that I was 16 and still in high school because a cute brunette, Kathryn – "but call me Kate" – McDonald was sitting with them. I immediately discovered I wanted to hang out with this group, or at least the beautiful Kate. However, it was not to be because Kate and the rest were headed off to college the following week at places like the University of Kentucky, Georgetown College, Louisville, and Berea College. Additionally, one "traitor" was going to the University of Tennessee, or at least that's how everyone in the group described his enrollment.

I never saw them again, but I decided I wanted to attend college, wherever Kate was enrolled.

Another thing that is apparent now but wasn't obvious then is that Sam was grooming me. I spent less and less time doing schoolwork and more and more time going on extended adventures with him. What started as just physical training became something more.

We would go to state parks to camp. Sam would teach me how to survive in the woods for days or weeks, if necessary, though we never stayed too long. We camped in the summer and winter and during heat, rain, cold, and snow. No matter the conditions, we entered the woods with whatever clothes we wore; plus, I had begun carrying a multi-tool, and Sam always had a hunting knife. Beyond its six-inch blade, the only thing special about the knife was it had a striker in the handle that made fire starting pretty easy if one could find dry wood and some tender.

We also began spending more time on the home shooting range with military-style rifles. Sam had a pair of M16A1E1 rifles manufactured by Colt. Thousands of rounds of ammo don't last long when firing full auto or three-round bursts. It never occurred to me that the fully automatic M16, the military version of the now popular AR15, was illegal for a private citizen to own.

We practiced tracking and discussed hunting strategies. I never considered tracking people until the conversation turned to finding a person. We didn't call it tracking, but that is what it was.

Sam also began to open up a little more about his time in the military. As we would shoot, he would talk about his training in the Marines and eventually with special forces. He spoke about being sent to Qatar before making his way across Saudi Arabia and into Kuwait ahead of Operation Desert Storm. He sent encrypted intel reports back to his team leaders across the border.

I remember asking about the others on his team, and he said that during his five weeks in Kuwait, he never saw another team member. He was on his own, as were they. Each with a mission.

He traveled at night and tried to hide in the shade all day. He never said the words, but I gathered he preferred to work alone.

As for me, I was "living my best life" – words my mom often used. I occasionally made the trip to town for a football game, and I still read textbooks, biographies, and fiction. I had exhausted the works of Louis L'Amour, so I continued reading Clancy and added Dale Brown and W.E.B. Griffin to my list of favorites. By early 2001, I was running beside Sam each morning, and that initial 3-mile cross-country run was back up to his original five-mile path. We ran rain or shine, hot or cold, except on Sundays, always wearing sweatpants, high-top tennis shoes, and a tee shirt.

Then, suddenly, my life changed.

Chapter 4

Beginning in early June of 2001, three events happened in quick succession, and living my best life was suddenly out of the question.

Late on June 4, Sam and I were in the barn working out when a black Chevrolet Suburban pulled up to the house. A man emerged from the rear seat and started toward the house before Sam whistled and motioned for the visitor to join him. It was getting dark, and I guess I was hidden in the shadows.

"Do you know him?" I asked.

"Yep, I do," he replied. "I've known him for a long time."

Sam was quiet for a few seconds. After a moment, he turned to me and quietly said, "I'm not sure what will happen or be said in the next few minutes, but you sit right there and don't move unless I say so. Don't say a word. Okay?"

I nodded, totally confused about what could be happening.

The visitor was dressed like a man trying to fit into the rural Kentucky lifestyle but failing to do so. For one thing, his skin was pale as a ghost, and the population in our part of Kentucky spent enough time outside to be tanned to some degree. He wore a pressed and starched flannel shirt in 85-degree weather. His jeans had creases down the front, and he wore black shoes that reflected the light from the string of bare bulbs in the barn. If we had seen this man under other circumstances, we would have wondered who the tourist was and how he got lost in northern Kentucky.

When he reached Sam, he extended his hand but spotted me sitting on the weight bench before the handshake connected, causing him to stop short.

"Who is this, Sam?" he asked.

"This is my nephew, Joshua," Sam replied. "Joshua, meet..." A pause ensued before the visitor jumped in.

"I am Mr. Smith. Jack Smith," the visitor completed the sentence, but I didn't believe that was his name. Sam just rolled his eyes.

"Sam, I need to speak to you in private," Smith said while taking a few steps away from the barn.

"We can talk in here. I think it is time Joshua knew a bit more about what I do."

If Smith could have gotten any paler, it would have happened at that moment.

"But," he stammered, "this is all highly classified. We can't talk in front of someone with no clearance." At this point, his voice had gone up an octave, and he sounded more like a boy than I did.

"Not a problem," Sam said. "You take care, and don't mess those shoes up on the way back to the car."

"But we have to talk. This is a matter of... national security." He whispered the 'national security' part, but I could still hear him as if we were standing side by side. The exasperation was evident.

After a moment, Sam told me to go to the chicken coop and grab the eggs to give them privacy. I did as he instructed, but I also knew my visiting the chicken coop would not accomplish the goal of giving them privacy. From the coop, one could hear every word said in the barn. In fact, the coop was constructed against the barn wall on the high side, placing it almost directly above where they were standing. The acoustics were perfect. I quietly moved into the coop, sat, and leaned against the wall above their heads. Suddenly, I saw Pete Jr., a younger rat snake that had taken up residence in the barn after the original had disappeared. We ignored each other, and I peeked through a small crack between two boards.

"What the hell was that all about Sam?" Smith said after he was convinced I had enough time to be clear of earshot.

"Smith? Really? Is that the best you could do, Manning?" Sam said, ignoring the original question.

"Caught me off guard. You should have sent him away when you saw me coming."

"It's time he knew the truth. And you must be getting slow to let a 17-year-old catch you off guard."

"Seventeen? He looks older."

"Acts and thinks older, too. That's why it is time. Lucy knows. He's family too, and when I am gone off on one of your little assignments, he's the man around here."

"You know that breaks every protocol we have, Sam. We can't include him."

"He's smart. He'll figure it all out soon enough. Better to get out in front of it."

"Can we talk about this later? We have a problem."

"Have a seat," Sam instructed as he settled on the weight bench, with Manning taking a folding chair.

Pulling an envelope from his back pocket, Smith passed it over and began a long narrative. I found it all fascinating.

"Sam, something's happening, and the government is in the dark. The NSA, CIA, DIA, and that whole alphabet soup of other agencies agree something big is planned for this fall, but we don't know what it is, where it is, or when it is." Sam opened the envelope, withdrew a single sheet of paper, and scanned it but said nothing. "We think it is tied to a terrorist group called Al Qaeda and likely Osama Bin Laden, but we have no direct links."

"What's the confidence factor?" Sam asked.

"The reports I was provided indicate the CIA believes there is an 80-percent chance something is planned for this fall, likely on US soil, and the FBI and others pretty much agree with that number. The other 20 percent is the possibility they sent messages they knew would be intercepted to yank our chain. The biggest disagreement, however, involves scale. The CIA doesn't think anyone will try something as big as blowing up the Twin Towers again after failing to do so last time. They believe it will be a series of smaller attacks, possibly on the power grid or bridges—some kind of critical infrastructure. However, the FBI behavioral analysis experts think it will be something big. I flew to the Supermax prison in Colorado last week to interview Ramzi Yousef, the mastermind of the 1993 attack on the towers. He told me nothing new, but he said the people of Islam chose the towers for a reason, and the reason remains. Those two towers are seen as the symbol of American greed and decadence. That's a quote."

"Maybe you didn't ask the right way," Sam said.

"My hands are tied when a prisoner is on US soil, you know that, but I doubt he has any useful information. He has been held without communication with the outside world for too long.

"The Jordanians have indicated they have intelligence pointing to an airborne attack. That makes me think of small planes hitting nuclear power sites, bridges, or something similar. But they have no details."

"Why are you here, Manning?"

"You know our operational group is very small. Me, plus three operatives. You are the only one with any experience in the Middle East. I am asking if you have any thoughts or suggestions."

"I suggest you find out what they are planning."

"No shit. And how do we do that?"

"Assuming you can't cut the head off of this serpent, do you know where to find any members of Al Qaeda?"

"We can locate a few known associates, but that doesn't mean they know anything. These groups are very compartmentalized, and everyone is strictly need-to-know," Manning replied.

"I suggest you do that and ask them some tough questions - off of U.S. soil."

"It sounds like you suggest we employ enhanced interrogation techniques, Sam. You know that isn't reliable."

"Yep. And if you had two years to lock 'em up, build trust, and question them daily, I would say do it the right way. But if this event is scheduled for later this year, as you said, I think it's time to stop cutting bait and start fishing."

"That's what I thought you would say. Sam, as you see in the letter, I received instructions to execute an undefined fact-finding and intelligence mission. That can mean almost anything, so I have great latitude. Unless you have a better suggestion, I will instruct each of my three operatives to get their hands on one known associate and use whatever means necessary to get some information. I need you in Washington tomorrow. I need you back in Islamic territory – the middle east or one of the 'stans' – by early next week. We might be able to get a little help with logistics and securing the targets, but after that, you will be on your own. From your previous answer, I am guessing you agree that this is the best way to proceed. I'll get you details shortly."

And with that, Manning turned and made his way back to the Suburban. After the vehicle was out of sight, Sam said, "Joshua, let's finish our workout."

I returned to the bank barn, but we didn't finish the workout. I spent the next hour asking questions. Sam told me that after tours in Iraq, he was recruited for a special program very loosely tied to the government. Sam explained there are overseas missions suited for special forces teams like Navy SEALS, Army Rangers, or Marine Recon. There are also jobs where a team would jeopardize the mission, but a single, highly trained operator, sometimes CIA and sometimes not, could be successful.

43

After agreeing to work with this group known as ACXN – which stands for absolutely nothing but is pronounced "action" – he went on to train for a year with the SEALS, Army Rangers, Israel's Shayetet-13, and Germany's KSK Special Forces Command. He was officially discharged from the U.S. Military and became a private citizen—but one who was highly trained, effective, and no longer a part of any government organization. Manning had been his contact from day one, and Sam said he assumed the Central Intelligence Agency was involved somewhere up the chain of command but that he didn't know for sure. His pay came through a company set up to import and export electronics worldwide. That was sometimes also part of his cover, but he didn't know if they imported or exported much. He was shown in their books as a contractor, and payment, a monthly amount and special payments when given an assignment, went into an overseas account from which he occasionally transferred money to his bank in Lexington. He would then declare it as income and pay the taxes.

"If something happens to me, Lucy can access the accounts and get whatever she needs. There is plenty of money to last us all into old age."

As far as I know, he left nothing out.

When I ran out of questions, he showed me one more thing.

"While I am gone, this time and the next time, for as long as you are here, I expect you to protect your mom and Lucy." As he spoke, he motioned me a few steps to the wall near where he and Manning had stood. It was just below the chicken coop on the outside. He reached up and pulled an old farm tool hanging from a rope. As he did so, I heard the click of a latch, and a section of the wall swung open. Behind it was a solid steel door.

"How did I never know this was here?" I asked. "I have spent hundreds of hours in this barn."

"You weren't supposed to know," he said as he lifted the latch on the metal door. "The barn was built pretty much by just me and Lucy, at least through the point we could hide this. I hired help to put the rafters and roof up, but this was all completed and hidden before help arrived. That is why I built a bank barn when I could have built a regular barn just 50 feet over. We dug out the bank for the barn and then dug out the area for this shipping container. We waterproofed it and added drainage. The chicken coop above also helps keep water away. It should last a long time."

"I had wondered why there was a wood section in the stone wall," I said.

"I couldn't figure out how to build a hidden door in a stone wall," Sam replied. "It's very much out of place if you think about it, but most people don't think about it."

As the door opened, lights came on. Inside were several additional weapons – M16s and Beretta Model 92s, folded cots with blankets, and stacks of Army surplus MREs plus cases of bottled water. In addition, there was an odd-looking telephone and a computer much like the one in the house.

"It is simply a hide if you ever need it. I don't think anyone will ever come here looking for me. In truth, I am a nobody, and when I travel or work, it is under a different name and address. But, in my Boy Scout days, we always said, 'Be Prepared.' Just get in here with Lucy and Rachael and use this crank to close the door. It is heavy because we welded on ballistic steel. Then, pull this rope to move the barn wall back in place. You are now the third person who knows this room exists. Protect that knowledge."

He demonstrated the process and later reversed it, allowing us to step back out. We pushed hard on the door to latch it before resetting the barn wall to cover it. Even knowing it was there, I couldn't see it.

"So," I asked, "you will be leaving tomorrow?"

"I imagine so. They will arrange my flight to Washington, but I will likely leave out of Lexington tomorrow afternoon."

"This sounds dangerous."

"I'm not going to lie to you. It is. But I've been well trained, and someone's got to do it. I'll have a plan before I head out. It won't be a good plan because there isn't time, but each of us will have a way in, a mission, and a way out."

"What if you die or get captured?"

Sam hesitated before saying. "If that happens, Mr. Manning will let you know. Just get on with your life."

"You said Lucy knows what you do. Does she know it all?"

"More or less. She knows nothing more than she needs to know. Mission details aren't important. She understands. Yes, before you ask, I have killed as a part of my military time and in this job. But everything I did was to make this country safer for Lucy and everyone else. Truthfully, this all probably sounds more exciting and dangerous than it is. Do you remember last July when I was away for a few weeks?"

"Yes, it was hot, and I had the garden to tend and grass to mow," I grinned as I said it.

"I was in Italy, Rome to be exact, and for a week, I walked around to all the tourist sights hoping to run into a specific person, who we knew to be in town vacationing with his family. Well, his family and his security detail. I knew where he was staying but didn't know his schedule. I couldn't follow him from the hotel because his security would have noticed me. Each day, I picked a tourist sight and hung out. For eight days, I chose the wrong place. On the ninth day, I was waiting at the Trevi Fountain, and luckily he showed up. I was positioned in the perfect place, so he had to approach my position to see the fountain. Just a note: always make them come to you, never go to them; it is a dead giveaway you are up to something if you appear to make the first move. As he approached where I stood, I said, 'I love a day in Rome.' He replied, 'It is best if you have someone to share it with.' That was it. Message delivered and confirmed. I do not know what it meant, but other people up the food chain apparently thought it was important. I still don't know why they needed me to do that, but I saw most of Rome. Nice city."

"That was it?" I asked.

"That was it for that assignment. Sometimes it is different, like this next one."

"Who was he?"

"They gave me a bio for him. He sold off a software company a few years back. Billionaire now. Probably not a name you would know."

We had returned to the house and were about to enter when Sam said, "I will let Lucy know that you know, but let's not tell your mother right now." I nodded my understanding. "And if Manning comes back, call him Smith. I know I can trust you not to tell another soul because it could threaten the life of everyone on this hill. But he doesn't know that and is simply doing his job. We will keep him in the dark for a while."

The next day, Sam was gone when I woke up. The wheels of the government turned fast overnight. Lucy just gave me a smile and a hug. I headed out the door for my run. Alone.

Chapter 5

Sam returned to the farm on July 3, 2001. I remember the date because he brought fireworks to shoot the following day. Except for gathering eggs, we always took a break on Independence Day. Following my discussion with Sam and during his absence, I had decided to abort my plan to pursue Kate McDonald. I wanted to follow in his footsteps and join the Marines. I had hinted at this to Mom, who was now managing a convenience store and working days, but I had not flat out told her that was what I wanted to do. I decided to wait until Sam returned to tell her because I felt he would support my decision.

During the previous fall, in preparation for college, I drove to Lexington and easily passed the GED exam. In the spring, I sat for the ACT and SAT exams, which colleges used to determine if you were intelligent and educated enough to give them a lot of money for an advanced education. After getting a 34 on the ACT, I started getting letters from colleges and universities nationwide. After scoring 1520 on the SAT, the flood of requests to apply for admission increased, along with scholarship offers contingent on my acceptance.

During our next workout, on July 5th, when Sam and I were alone, I asked him about the latest mission. He ended up in Yemen, he told me. Per his cover story, he entered the country as a contract employee of British Petroleum on an assignment to take soil and air quality samples as a part of BP's environmental responsibility efforts.

After clearing customs under the name Tanner Raines of Rosharon, Texas, he took a taxi to an address two blocks south of an address he had been provided before departing. From there, he hopped on and off a bus, walked several blocks, and eventually hired a car to continue to a hotel just north of the target address. Three hours after landing in Sana'a, Yemen, carrying only a small backpack and a small case containing soil and water testing equipment, he walked to a street-level building entrance and pressed a call button. A brief coded conversation with someone inside followed, and he entered after the lock clicked.

At over 7,000 feet above sea level, Sana'a was comfortable compared to much of the country. The thick stone walls kept the inside temperature in the mid-seventies as highs outside moved to around 90 degrees.

He told me that after entering the apartment, he was met by an older man who smelled of, like everything else, Turkish tobacco. We would grow and cure about a half-acre of tobacco on the farm every year, but Sam hates the smell of cigars and cigarettes, so this was an observation he pointed out with obvious irritation.

The man, whom he knew only as Nabil, handed him a third bag containing a Glock 19 compact 9mm pistol with two double-stack 15-round magazines. The bag also contained bundles of Yemeni Rials, 200,000 of them worth about a thousand United States dollars but about six months' wages in Yemen. Other items included about fifty feet of paracord, a small med kit with a syringe, and a vial labeled as Insulin. There was also a multi-tool, a cloth mask used in the desert during sandstorms, and a change of clothing that matched what every male in the country wore. The only other thing he received was some verbal instruction.

Nabil instructed Sam to buy a bus ticket to Ma'rib, about four hours away and near the oil fields and the country's only refinery, hence the cover story. Sam would be met at the bus stop by a man wearing a white shirt and a bright green vest. That is all Nabil knew.

The bus ride was described as uncomfortable but uneventful. During the journey, elevation dropped to just over 3,000 feet, and the temperature soared to over 100 degrees. Due to the sand and dust in the air, the windows on the bus were closed, and Sam described it as "like a freaking oven full of body odor."

"Sure enough," Sam told me. "I got off the bus, and immediately, a young man with a green vest and a BP identification badge approached me and acted like a fool. He was shouting, "Mr. Raines, Mr. Raines," and telling me he was to be my escort for BP. He always screamed BP. It was not the way these things should be handled. At that point, I assumed any cover I had was blown."

Sam said he continued with the man, also named Nabil according to his ID badge, to a small but clean and well-maintained car where he screamed in highly accented English, "Get in, I'll take you to BP."

"I just shook my head and said a prayer for my soul at that point," Sam told me. "I figured I would be followed and at least interrogated. Since my knowledge about soil and air testing is non-existent, my odds weren't good."

"When we got in the car, Nabil sped away. After we were clear of the bus station, he stuck his hand out and said, in the purest southern accent I have ever heard, "Call me John. Let's see if we can get you what you came here for."

"At that point, I called him every name in the book and asked if he was trying to get us killed," Sam said. "He grinned and told me he really is an in-country host for BP, among other things, and he greets everyone that way at the bus stop. My greeting was no different than a hundred other greetings over the past year. 'Tradecraft comes in all shapes and sizes,' he said. I wasn't sure about that but hoped he knew what he was doing."

John took Sam to a car rental facility. "He told me to go in and ask for a BP car and a map to the facility. He also passed me an envelope and a BP identification card with my picture. John just said I was on my own from this point forward, but the information in the package should get me near my target. And good luck."

"So, who was the target?" I asked.

"Joshua, I'm going share more than I should. There are things I normally don't tell a soul. I will tell you because it lets you know what I do and how it sometimes happens. I would prefer you not to know these little details for several reasons. One is these missions are highly classified for a reason. Another is that you can't let something slip one day if you don't know. I don't think anything I ever do can be traced back to me by anyone. Our government is damn good at covering things up, but they are also horrible at keeping secrets. It isn't impossible that someone could find out who I am and what I do. Do you fully understand this can never, ever be shared?"

I nodded, yet here I am sharing the story with you.

"Here is the short version. I had a target and a location in the envelope. A photo, a name, and GPS coordinates for a house. I assume that was provided by some intelligence service, maybe the CIA or one of the partner agencies like the Brits or Israelis. He was thought to be a close associate of a guy named Osama bin Laden, who is from Saudi Arabia. He was also suspected of training a guy named Ramzi Yousef who built the bombs that were detonated in the parking area at the World Trade Center in New York in 1993."

I recognized the name from when Mr. Smith came by.

He continued. "I located him and, after a couple of days, neutralized him and dragged him into the desert away from his family. I don't like involving families, and I will tell you that they are alive and well as far as I know."

"And him?" I asked.

Sam paused before responding with, "He is neither alive nor well. I had put some water, food, and other provisions in the rental before I headed out. He lived east of Marib in a small house on the outskirts of town. One night, he walked out to the outhouse, and I was able to quietly incapacitate him and get him into the trunk of the car before driving about 30 miles out into the desert on what might or might not be described as a road. The vial I picked up contained Ketamine, not insulin. I grabbed him from behind and injected him as he left the outhouse. He was out in about 15 seconds. As I drove, we dropped another 500 feet in elevation. According to the rental, the temperature was 27 degrees Celsius, about 80 degrees here in the States, and the sun was just coming up. It gets cool in the desert overnight. But I knew the temperature would reach nearly 120 degrees during the day. Maybe even 125."

"I eventually exited the road and found some rock outcroppings where I could hide the car. Everything over there is brown, orange, and tan. These rocks were dark brown and surrounded by light tan sand that reflected the sunlight. Locals wear these loose-fitting robes and cover everything but their faces to protect themselves from the sun for a reason. I stripped him and staked him to a couple of small scrub trees about three feet tall. He was spread eagle, on his back, on a rock. I pulled a bottle of water from the car, opened it, and placed it about three feet away so he could see it but not reach it. Then, I headed to a shady spot in a crevasse between two boulders and slept. I knew he would let me know when he woke up."

I stared but remained quiet as he told the story. It was somewhat surreal.

"His file said he had attended college in England, so I knew he spoke English well enough. He tried to play dumb for a couple of hours, but after 12 hours of cooking in the sun and so dehydrated he could barely speak, he at least started playing dumb in English. His skin was covered in blisters. I sat, asking him questions while sipping on a bottle of water. Eventually, I let him drink most of a half-liter bottle to give him hope.

"The cool night may have been worse than the day's heat. He had a high fever by the end of the first day, and he shivered all night. The next day, I offered another water bottle if he would admit he knew Osama Bin Laden and Ramzi Yousef. He did, though if I weren't already confident he knew them, I would have doubted that he was being honest. Under certain conditions, people will say anything for relief.

"Later that day, I began trading sips of water for information, promising that if he talked, I would drive him back to Marib and drop him off. He told me enough of what I knew to be true that I believed the rest, which wasn't much. In the end, I didn't get anything of great use. He said bin Laden had told him two years before he would attack America's heart. He never told him what, when, or how. He said that was the last time he had spoken to him."

"And then?" I asked.

"I ended his suffering and the threat he posed. He was a bomb builder for terrorists—end of story. I got back in the car, drove to Marib, got a room and a shower, returned the rental, and caught the bus to Sana'a the next day. I flew back to DC, met briefly with Manning, and came home."

I wasn't sure what to say.

"Look, I know the details may shock you. I probably shared too much. There are bad people in the world, and a few of us have the means and willingness to hopefully do some good. At least, that's how I justify it. I have never regretted anything I have had to do. I have never lost any sleep over it."

Sam let out a short laugh. "When I returned to the bus station, John was greeting a couple of men in suits. He was screaming that he was from BP and he would take care of them. I guess if you set a precedent, it doesn't matter what you do."

"I have decided to join the Marines," I said abruptly.

Sam paused, "Don't think what I did in the military or what I do now is in any way glamorous. Military life is hard, and the pay is lousy. However, when you get out, you should have some marketable skills. If the Marines is what you want, I recommend asking to specialize in something technical, like computers, or maybe become a pilot. You can talk to a recruiter about your options. After basic training in Parris Island, South Carolina, they will typically honor your request. Get a skill that will let you get a good job when you exit, be it after a single enlistment or after multiple re-ups."

"What if I want Special Forces, like you?" I asked.

"I was never exactly in special forces, but I was allowed to train with them for a year. Manning worked it out. But if that is what you want, you can request it after you get your MOS certifications and gain rank. Only a small percentage of the people who enter the program make it through, but you are smart enough and tough enough. It just takes a certain mindset. It isn't the strongest people who make it; it isn't the most confident who make it. It is the people who are mentally tough and willing to work alone or as a part of a well-oiled machine, always focused on the mission and the men beside you."

I heard Mom's car coming up the gravel drive. "I need to let mom know," I said. "That may be tougher than getting into special forces."

Sam just laughed and nodded. "Tell her soon, get it over with. She will be proud and supportive, but it will scare her."

We headed toward the house. It was warm, and the night sounds were loud. There wasn't a cloud to be seen, and even with the ambient light from the bulb on the back porch, I could see millions of stars overhead.

Stepping onto the back porch, I heard something I had never heard before. My mother was sobbing. Lucy held her tight as they sat at the table and rocked gently back and forth. Minutes later, after Mom regained some measure of control, I was hit with my second life-altering event.

Chapter 6

I haven't talked much about my mom following our arrival in Kentucky. Sam and Lucy were more like my parents, and I spent hours each day with them, but Mom was still Mom.

We never spoke about anything that happened in the years 'BK.' 'Before Kentucky' was only mentioned as a line of demarcation. For example, she once said, "BK, I never had a job, so I have to work my way up from the bottom."

She worked as a cashier and part-time waitress at the truck stop for about a year. Sam and Lucy, as far as I know, never took any of the money she earned. They told her to put it into a college fund for me. Eventually, a man who owned several convenience stores but ate at the truck stop occasionally offered her a job as a store clerk with a promise of a store manager position. His name was Henry. I didn't know his last name. He treated Mom well, and she moved into a store manager position after about six months. Eventually, she managed four Richmond and North Fork stores, hired and trained new employees, and ensured everything remained in working order.

She had also met someone. She was a pretty woman when she wanted to be, but I think she found the no-makeup, disheveled look prevented advances from drunken customers. She never really talked to me about her relationship, but I know she told Lucy about it. Mom had also studied on her own, many of the same textbooks I used, and she earned her GED. My father had not allowed her to continue school or work after marriage, so she was only formally educated through the ninth grade. I remember the smile on her face when the certificate came in the mail. I will never forget it.

Occasionally, she wouldn't come home until morning, when she would shower quickly and return to work her shift. She seemed happy. I never asked any questions.

But her smile was gone on the evening of July 5th, 2001, and it never returned. A thousand things ran through my mind as I came in from the porch. The first thought was, 'Who has hurt her, and whom do I need to kill to fix this?' No joke. I don't know if my recent conversation with Sam spurred the thought, but that was where my mind went.

Lucy told us to sit down and gave us a look that said more than words. Something was very wrong, and we needed to sit and be quiet for a minute.

After what seemed like 30 minutes but was probably closer to five, Mom suddenly sat up straight, took a deep breath, and, from somewhere, summoned the courage to deliver her first words. "Joshua, Sam, I have cancer, and it's bad."

I simply sat there. What exactly did this mean? What kind of cancer? How do we fix this? All these thoughts bounced around, but no words came out.

Sam cleared his throat. "Rachel, I'm so sorry. Tell me what we can do for you."

I still said nothing. I didn't move. Mom reached across the table and took my hand. "Joshua, I love you. You have grown into a man, so I will tell you what I know."

I moved to sit beside her.

"It's pancreatic cancer. I have been having pain and losing weight for a couple of months. I went to the doctor, and they checked me out in May but found nothing. This morning, the pain got so bad I couldn't work. Henry came by the store and saw me. He took me to the hospital. They ran tests and did a CT scan. The next thing I know, there is an Oncologist, um, a cancer doctor, talking to me and saying he wants to run additional tests. I have stage four cancer, Joshua."

I thought I knew what that meant, but I asked the question anyway.

"According to the doctor, I have three to six months with you. Likely, sometime soon, they will have to put me in a hospice care facility, where they will manage the pain. He said I likely won't be awake much after that. Joshua, I am so sorry."

And with that, she put her head on my shoulder, and we cried together. Sam and Lucy were also hugging, and both had tears rolling down their cheeks. Seeing Sam cry helped with my slight embarrassment over being, in my mind, weak. I realize now that I wasn't weak; it was love for the woman who had probably saved our lives when we skated out of Arkansas years before.

I will not cover the details of the next several weeks, but suffice it to say the doctor was off on his prediction. On August 1st, Mom was sent to a hospice care facility, and on August 5th, one month after the diagnosis, she mercifully died. We arranged for her to be buried on the family property, atop the hill, overlooking the open hay field and the house and the valley below.

She said she didn't want a marker. She didn't want anywhere anyone felt they had to visit. Before she went to hospice, she gave us a list of people to inform of her death. Henry was the only name on it, and I wondered if Henry was that 'someone' she had met. I wondered if those nights she didn't come home were spent with him. But I didn't care. She had seemed happy.

I met Henry and, I should note, his wife at the small ceremony. Three of her coworkers, Lauren, Matt, and Shalane, showed up, and all told me she was a great person. I smiled the best I could and nodded in agreement.

I had stopped my daily exercise and workout while mom was sick, and Sam never said a word. I never told her about my plans to join the Marines either.

On August 8th, the day after the funeral, I was downstairs at 5 a.m., our summer starting time, eating an apple when Sam stepped out of his bedroom, dressed in sweatpants, high tops, and a tee shirt, despite the

almost 90-degree temperature and suffocating humidity. He grabbed an apple, and off we went. Things would never be the same, but the routine helped with my emotional health. I would learn later in life that when things seem too big to deal with, rely on what you know. I didn't realize it then, but routine is my coping mechanism.

When we returned to the house at about 8:30, someone was sitting at the table with Lucy. She introduced him as Mr. Berry. He shook my hand and said he was an attorney in North Fork. I replied with the traditional "Nice to meet you, sir."

Lucy got water for Sam and me and put some bacon and toast before us, our usual post-workout breakfast. We ate while Mr. Berry talked. He told me my mom had approached him about two years ago. She wanted to prepare her Last Will and Testament. Later, she entrusted him with an envelope. He laid two things on the table. The first was a two or three-page document, legal size, with light blue paper stapled to it that served as a cover when folded.

The other item was a letter-sized white envelope. 'Joshua' was handwritten on the front, along with the words, 'to be opened in private, only after my death.'

"Let's start with the testament. I will need to do some paperwork, and there will be a short court hearing, but I will take care of everything. Your mom already paid for my services. In this situation, everything should be done in about six weeks. She also provided that Sam and Lucy become your legal guardians until you turn 18. As a 17-year-old, you can appeal that if you want.

"No, that is fine," I told him.

"The will states," he continued, tilting his head back so that he could read through his glasses, "that all of Rachael Booker's assets now belong to you, Joshua. This includes a 1996 Honda Accord, assorted clothes, electronics, miscellaneous items, and a North Fork Farmers and Trust checking account. Joshua, do you remember signing a signature card?"

"Yes, sir," I replied. "Mom took me to the bank three or four years ago, and I signed some things." Throughout my reply, I watched Sam and Lucy for their reaction. I am not sure why. I imagined that if they were okay with this question, I was too. I knew 'civics,' as Lucy called it, but nothing about estate laws.

"Well, you were a joint account holder with her, so now that is simply your account. When you get the death certificate, I recommend you go to the bank and remove her name from the account. It will save you trouble down the line. When we set up the will about two years ago, she told me there was almost one hundred thousand dollars in the account." That was a surprise to me.

"I will also take care of filing her final tax return," he said.

"She said the car title is in a box in her bedroom here at the house. Lucy, maybe you can find that, and after I get through with the legalities, we will have that retitled in Joshua's name. Finally, your grandparents jointly left this property to Samuel Rutland and your mom. That includes structures and property. Mr. Rutland, I assume all the other assets are yours."

"This property and everything we own will go to Joshua when we die," Lucy said. "In the meantime, this and everything here is home to Joshua for as long as he wants. Hopefully, that'll be long after we are gone."

I had not said much up to this point. "Aunt Lucy?" I asked.

She looked at me and took my hand. "We never had any children, so when you and your mom showed up, it filled a void for us. You are family and like a son to us, and we want this land to stay with the family."

I remember squeezing her hand and the look of pure love and joy in her eyes. No one said anything for a while.

Sam spoke for the first time. "If Rachael owed anyone money, I would be surprised, but if there is a legitimate claim against the estate, we will take care of it."

"Understood." Mr. Berry said, rising from the table. "The only other thing is this envelope; you can see what she wrote on it. She called me about three weeks ago and asked me to hold it. I am going to leave it here. Read it when you're ready."

We all stood, shook the attorney's hand, and Sam walked him to the door. I sat back down with the envelope in my hand, studying the writing.

Lucy pushed my unfinished bacon and toast closer and touched my shoulder. With a gentle squeeze, she said, "You need to eat. Read the letter whenever you are ready."

I must have sat at the table for an hour. I wasn't thinking about anything; I was just sitting. Eventually, I walked out into the woods and sat on a fallen tree, and, for the first time since her death, I cried. I cried hard. I screamed, stomped my foot, and pounded on the tree until my hands bled. All the emotions, the love, the anger, the confusion, leaped forth right then and there.

I eventually burned myself out, returned to the house, and resumed doing what was needed around the farm. That night, I walked to the gravesite with the letter in my hand, but I didn't read it then or the next day. I think I was saving the letter as a final moment with my mom. I also think I believed that as soon as I read the letter, my last ever interaction with her would be over, and there would never be another.

A week after her death, I was in my room reading and was overcome with the need to know. What did she have to say to me that she couldn't say while alive? What message did she want to deliver to me from beyond the grave?

I carefully slit the envelope open with my pocketknife and removed two sheets of paper torn from a legal pad. The note, handwritten front and back, said:

> My dear son, Joshua.
>
> *I don't know what to say or how to say it, but there are some things you need to know.*
>
> *First, I made a mistake when I ran off with Rick. Sam was right. He was not a good man, but you know that. The thing is, if I had not married him, I would never have met you. We all have secrets, and you were our secret. Joshua, I was never able to have children. I lost two, one when I was 16 and another when I was 17. I was told I couldn't get pregnant again after that. Rick met someone and arranged to unofficially adopt you when you were born. I have no idea who your real parents are. We picked you up from your biological grandfather at a rest stop near Pickwick*

Lake. Rick had been offered a job preaching in Alabama, so when we showed up there with a baby, everyone just assumed you were born to us. Your March 3 birthday is a guess, but it is very close.

We spent five years in Alabama. At first, everything was good, but after about a year, Rick started drinking, and when he drank, he lost control. It was occasional at first, then more and more. After a time, the church fired him. We all moved to Batesville, Mississippi, but that only lasted a year. We spent six months in south Mississippi, two years in Bastrop, Louisiana, and three years in Arkansas. Rick's drinking got worse and worse, but he got better at covering it up. The more he drank, the more he beat me and whipped you. I was terrified he would kill one or both of us.

Joshua, I believe in Jesus, and I know murder is wrong, but I likely killed Rick. I hope Jesus understands.

The night we left Arkansas, Rick had once again been caught with one of his church members. He would get these women alone and tell them that God told him they should be together. How wrong is that? The woman's husband rounded up a couple of neighbors, and they beat Rick within an inch of his life. They dragged him to the house and dropped him just inside the door. He was barely conscious, but you and I managed to get him to bed. All he asked for was a bottle, so I poured some of his favorite, Old Kentucky Tavern.

I had already saved a bottle of bourbon and put some antifreeze and poison in it. I read a story in a magazine about a woman who killed her husband, and that was what she did. But she got caught because she didn't rinse out the bottle. I am still not sure why, after all the drunken nights and all the beatings I took, I chose that night. But when those men came in and dropped him on the floor, I knew that was it. I never questioned it or panicked.

I thought your dad might die anyway; the beating was so bad, but I didn't want to take a chance. He drank a big glass of poisoned bourbon; then I brought him more, but regular bourbon in a clean glass this time. I washed the first glass and the poisoned bottle with soap and water, and then I poured in a little pure bourbon from another open bottle. I didn't want to get caught like the woman in the magazine.

The thing is, I don't think there was even an investigation. When we left, he was alive, but he must have died overnight, and I imagine the law just said good riddance. It might have been the beating, the poison, or the alcohol that killed him. Doesn't matter. I made some calls to the local paper and learned he was found dead in the house the next day. The police said he died from a combination of injuries and alcohol poisoning. I don't know if they ever wondered where we went. I loved Rick once, but I never cried over his death.

I am telling you this truth for a couple of reasons. First, you deserve to know. Doctors will ask you about your family history. Don't give them my medical history. We simply don't know yours.

The second reason is Sam and Lucy see you as a son, and they are far better parents than Rick or me. I tried, Joshua, I really tried. But Rick had broken me, and all I knew to do was run to Sam and see if he would help.

I told Sam the truth the first night we were in Brandon. He never said, "I told you so." He never judged me. He just said the farm was mine as much as it was his and to stay as long as needed. After a couple of months, it became home again. You were doing well, and I had nowhere else to go, so we are still here. I won't be here much longer, though.

Sam says you should stay at the farm until you go to college. They haven't let me pay for much, so almost everything I have earned, aside from some gas money and insurance payments, has gone into the checking account at North Fork Farm and Trust. I bought the Honda with cash, so that is ours too. If you are reading this, I guess the lawyer has already told you that. Hopefully, it is enough for you to get a degree. Probably not, but it's a start.

My final words to you are these. Always know that I love you. No matter how you came into my life, you are my son. When I am gone, don't live your life for me. You have grown into a good man. Go and live your best life. Do great things.

It was simply signed, *Mom.*

Chapter 7

I didn't sleep much that night. I laid the letter on the table when I went down to join Sam for the run the following day. "We can talk about this after," I said. "You and Aunt Lucy need to read it."

When we walked back into the house, both hot and sweaty, Sam and I grabbed a glass of water, toweled off, and sat at the table. Lucy had sausage, egg, and cheese biscuits for us that day. Sam picked up the letter and looked my way. I nodded, and he began to read.

"Did you read it, Lucy?" I asked as she sat down with a biscuit, jelly only.

"Yes, I hope that's okay. Since you left it on the table, I figured that was the purpose."

"Yes, I wanted you both to read it."

Sam flipped the page and kept reading. Finally, he looked up.

"The last part is all that matters. She loves you. She wants you to be happy."

"Where did you get the birth certificate?" I asked, somewhat abruptly and possibly accusingly.

"Remember Mr. Smith?" he said. "There are other people like him that help with various things we need to get our work done. If I need a driver's license with my picture but a different name and address, they get it for me. If I need a different passport, like one from Canada or Chili, or just another name on a United States Passport, they get it for me. Getting you a birth certificate and social security card was easy enough. Both of those documents are in the system; by the way, that's

something else they do. They are not fake documents; they are real enough. If you ever need to contact the state of Mississippi for a replacement birth certificate, give them your name, date of birth, and county of birth, along with your mother's name, and they can send you a new one. Smith's contacts injected all the data into the state's computers, created a birth record and then requested a replacement birth certificate. Same for the social security number."

"I never told Mom I wanted to join the Marines. She thought I was going to college. I know she isn't here anymore, but for some reason, I want to do what she expected, especially with the money she left."

Lucy spoke up this time. "Joshua, she wanted you to follow your dreams, whatever they may be. I remember when my mom died, Samuel Rutland and I asked the preacher about something, what it was isn't important, and he said, 'Mrs. Rutland, we must live for the living, not for the dead.' You do what will make you happy. Joshua, live for you. Not for your mom. Suppose you go to college because that's what you want to do, that's great. If you want to go into the service, that would be great. It would also be great if you chose to stay here and work on the farm. Follow your dreams."

Even though I was almost certain the Marines were in my future, I would wait until the end of the year to decide. Then, I would either apply to several colleges in hopes of getting accepted or talk to a recruiter and take the ASVAB.

I looked at them and said, "But I am not true family. Not by blood."

Lucy replied again. "Not only are you family, you are the only family we have. Family isn't all about blood. I don't ever want to hear that again."

With that, she stood up and started washing dishes. I guessed the conversation was over.

By the end of August, my routine had returned to close to normal. I still ran with Sam every morning and worked on the farm during the

day. In the evenings, we lifted weights out in the barn. I had continued to get stronger, and one Saturday, Sam and I drove to Dick's Sporting Goods in Lexington, where he bought six additional 45-pound plates for the bar and about all the ammunition they had. We still tried to shoot at least once a week, and we burned through ammo in a hurry. I still couldn't outshoot Sam, but I could bench press more weight.

I say close to normal because two things were different than before. First, I walked up the hill each night before bed to say goodnight to Mom. I don't know why, but it made me feel better. The second was that Lauren, Mom's co-worker who came to the funeral, came to see me. I thought she was older, but she was only 18. She had worked at the store in North Fork after school for two years. She said she thought my mom was great, and she talked about how good she was at running the stores and training new people like her. Lauren was attractive, with long brown hair, green or blue eyes depending on how the light hit them, and a quick smile.

We sat on the steps the first night she came by and talked for about an hour. When she left, she said she just wanted me to know what my mom meant to her. She gave me a quick hug before she turned to leave. Talking to someone close to my own age was nice, and I enjoyed her company. I never really thought about anything romantic until I walked into the house. Lucy was sitting in her chair reading a book, and she looked up with a silly grin on her face.

"She seems like a nice young lady for you," she said. "Cute one, too."

My experience with girls was pretty much non-existent, though somewhere deep down inside, I agreed with Lucy's assessment.

"She just came by to tell me about how mom helped her," I said. "She's nice. It was good to talk to her."

"That isn't why she came by, Joshua. You can keep telling yourself that, but I assure you she came by to see you. You're a good young man—smart and handsome, too."

I felt my face flush. I didn't know what to say, so I walked up the stairs and put on some workout clothes. I guessed Sam was already about done with his workout. I would have to catch up and then walk up the hill.

Oddly enough, the next day, I felt the need to drive the Honda to North Fork to buy gas. I had not bought gas a half dozen times in my life. Sometimes, when I was with Mom or Sam, I would pump, but that was about it.

Lauren was working when I went in to prepay. I handed her thirty bucks and told her I would fill up. It only took eight gallons. When I went back inside to get my change, I asked her if she wanted to get dinner sometime, and she said, "Yes, tonight."

From then on, I saw Lauren three or four nights a week. Thankfully, she was patient with me. My social skills were unpracticed and unpolished. She guided me along as I met her friends. Our relationship would continue to grow and mature over the months and years. Lauren was my first and only true love.

∞

The third event that would profoundly affect my life was the terrorist attacks on September 11. Our home phone rang just as Sam and I stepped back into the kitchen following the morning run. I could hear the panicked voice of "Mr. Smith" telling Sam to turn on the television. "Any channel," he screamed. "The bastards are attacking us."

I could hear the whole conversation, so I walked over to the TV and turned on the NBC affiliate from Lexington. We watched a jumpy, low-resolution video of an airplane hitting the North Tower of the World Trade Center. Soon, reports and video of a second plane hitting the South Tower were shown. Moments later, we began hearing of two other aircraft that were not following their designated flight path and were out of contact with air traffic control.

Lucy, Sam, and I sat there for several hours. New information trickled in and was shared with the world. After the tower attacks, a plane flew into the Pentagon, and another crashed in

Pennsylvania. Rumors stated that passengers took over that flight and caused it to crash instead of allowing it to reach its destructive destination. Speculation was that the target was the Capitol Building or White House.

At about six o'clock in the evening, the phone rang, and Sam instructed us to ignore it. "That will be Manning. He is going to put me to work again. I need a minute to think about this. He will call back."

The phone rang every 15 minutes until Sam answered it at about 7:30. When he rose, Lucy did as well, reminding me we had not eaten since breakfast. As Sam picked up the phone, she started making sandwiches.

I got up to listen to the conversation, but Sam waved me away and stepped onto the porch, stretching the phone cord to its limit. I helped Lucy with the sandwiches.

After about 10 minutes, we were again seated in the den with our sandwiches.

"I am going to DC tomorrow. The plan right now is to catch up on some things that aren't public, and Manning doesn't want to talk about them over the phone. I should be back within a week, ten days at the most."

He looked at me before continuing. "Joshua, you know what needs to be done around here. Do what you can. Lucy can help a little, but you know what must be done. The hay we cut will be dry enough to bale in a couple of days. See if you can get that done and the hay in the dry. It will be hard for one person, so Lucy can drive the tractor and pull the trailer. I don't want it to rot, so just get it in the dry. We can stack it later. Take care of the garden. The horses and cattle will be fine."

I nodded, then asked, "We are going to go fight them, aren't we?"

"Yep, but the problem is we don't know who to fight. That was half the conversation with Manning. This attack didn't come from a country; it came from some misguided people within a religion. I know we will go after those people, but it probably won't be a war in the typical sense unless some country is stupid enough to protect them. Bin Laden is from Saudi Arabia, but Al Qaeda is based primarily in Afghanistan. Saudi Arabia presents a bunch of political problems if we go there. They are considered allies but only cooperate when it is in their best interest. We will have to see what the President and Congress decide to do.

"Planes are grounded and will be for a while. I am going to drive to Arlington to meet with Manning. His other operative is based on the West Coast, so it will take him several days to get there. We will see what we can figure out while waiting on him."

"You said 'other operative,'" I pointed out. "I thought there were two others."

"According to Manning, one of them didn't make it back from our last trip. He was sent to Pakistan but never met his contact. That's all I know. No one knows if he bugged out, got captured, or was killed. I am going to bed, and I suggest you do the same. I have a nine-hour drive tomorrow, and I will start early. Be careful baling the hay and take care of your Aunt Lucy. You know not to tell Lauren anything, right?"

"If she asks, I'll tell her you went to check on some friends in Washington. Given the Pentagon strike, that should work."

"Lucy, that's the story. Sounds plausible, and there is a lot of truth in it."

Lucy and I sat and watched the TV for a few more minutes before turning it off and going to bed. I didn't visit the grave that night. I didn't want to tell Mom about the attack.

The next morning, I thought Lucy looked more worried than usual. Perhaps the gravity of the situation weighed on her.

Sam called twice while he was in Virginia. He rarely called if he was out of the country but would call at least once a week while working in the States. We chatted once. He asked about the hay, the garden, Lauren, and other mundane matters. I assured him all was well on "Rachael's Ridge."

"Rachael's Ridge?" he asked. "I like that. I know your mom would like it."

"I like it too," I said before passing the phone to Lucy.

Sam had been gone 18 days when he drove up the gravel drive. I stopped mowing and walked over to say hello. After a short greeting, he took me to the back of the truck. Under a tarp were several shrink-wrapped Pelican shipping cases.

"Manning sent some new toys he wants me to have. I get some computer training each year. Not all my trips are mission-related. This is all new stuff. I spent ten days getting up to speed. I don't necessarily understand how it works, but I know how to operate it. Drive the mower back to the barn and open the safe room. We need to put this in there. I am going in to say hello to Lucy."

I went to the barn and pulled the big, ballistic-steel-lined door open. The inside looked the same as when I last saw it.

When Sam returned, I noticed he had something hanging from his belt. Lauren had a new cell phone, but this one looked different.

"It is a Blackberry," Sam said when I pointed at the device. "If there is any service up here, I can get calls and emails sent to this thing. Manning wants me to have it with me all the time. He said it is a special encrypted model."

We rounded up two sawhorses and a sheet of plywood to create a table, then put much of the new equipment on it. Sam was efficient in setting up the computer. He told me we would need to run another phone line from the house to the safe room, and we would need to hide it as well. There was also a fax machine, and Sam installed a switch

between it and the computer. He also sent me to the top of the chicken coop to install a small satellite dish. After we got it pointed due south and at a specific elevation, Sam yelled that it was working. We hid the wire so it would not give away the location of the safe room.

"We have a computer," I said. "Why do we need another one?"

"Good question. This one has some special programs on it."

"And what do they do?"

"They mostly allow secure communications. Manning can send me documents and messages no one else can read."

"What did you learn about the attacks?" was my next question.

"They know bin Laden was behind it. I'm sure you have watched the news. The President has started attacking known Al Qaeda training sites, and we are shutting off the flow of money as best as we can. We have already captured a couple of dozen known terrorists and sent them to a military prison in Cuba."

I asked what I wanted to know. "Are you going to be leaving again?"

"At some point, I probably will," he said. For now, I am going to work from here. There are some things Manning thinks I excel at. Gleaning information from interrogations is one of them. They will email me transcripts from interrogations in Cuba, and I will review them and provide additional questions for them to ask. It's gonna take up a lot of time, but it is important. Can you keep up the work here?"

"I will get it done. You take care of this. And for the record, unless you tell me not to, I am joining the Marines next spring."

"It is a dangerous time, but anything worth doing has an element of danger," he said. "I am proud of you. You will make a damn fine Marine."

"I do have one concern. If I am away in the Marines and you are working for Manning, what about Lucy? She can't do all of this herself."

"That's true, but we can either just not do it or hire someone to help. As I said earlier, we have money. Most of the work we do around here is to keep me occupied. Lucy made it fine before you and your mom showed up, and she will be fine now."

Chapter 8

To help prepare me for Marine training, Sam suggested I wear a backpack with extra weight inside during our morning run. We started with a single stone, about nine pounds. Then, each day, Sam would add another rock, just a piece of gravel from the driveway, but by November, the backpack had grown to thirty pounds. He suggested I get it up to at least 45 pounds before I headed to basic training.

After our morning run, I would take care of things around the farm while Sam sat in the shipping container with the doors open and a fan blowing. He would often work until late at night. After reading dozens of transcripts from interrogations, he would put together a couple of notes and send them to Manning through the encrypted email. I guess Manning forwarded them to the interrogation team. On two occasions, he had flown to Washington and on to Guantanamo Bay in Cuba, aka Gitmo, to deliver information and interrogation strategies in person.

Something seemed strange about Sam's work. Later, I identified what was bugging me and asked him about it.

"There is one thing I don't understand," We often talked about his work by this point, even though I knew he wasn't supposed to share half of what he did. "You are a private citizen. You are 'off the books,' so to speak. I understand that sometimes, someone, somewhere, needs something done, and it needs to be handled in a certain way. That's when Manning is contacted, and he calls you. But hundreds of people in the military and intelligence communities must be experts on interrogations. Therefore, how did they know about you, and even then, why you?"

"That's two questions. First, how did they know about me? The answer is they, the President and Congress, are at least attempting to create a new cabinet-level position that will oversee everything regarding the country's intelligence and defense. I don't know what departments will be included; likely the FBI, CIA, Customs and Border Patrol, maybe Treasury. They have already pulled many people in to discuss fighting back and defending against another attack. Whoever is pulling Manning's string asked him to help. The President decided to move captured high-value targets to Gitmo, and we need to know what they know."

"Because if they are on American soil, they have additional rights to attorneys, speedy trial, bail hearing, all of that?" I asked.

"Exactly," he said before continuing. "During one of those sessions, the President expressed concerns about waterboarding and other enhanced interrogation techniques used at Gitmo. He knew that if those rumors were true, and they were, they would eventually leak out and cause problems. Someone suggested several prisoners be segregated and that someone apparently also knew Manning had a resource: me. I guess whoever Manning's boss is sits in with the President."

"Manning hired some retired FBI Special Agents to go to Cuba and question the prisoners every day. Those agents tell the prisoners they report to someone named "Elijah," and they feign fear at the mention of the name. It's just a mind game. Occasionally, I, as Elijah, show up and sit in on the interrogations. I never say anything, but the interrogators act nervous, and after I leave, we carve one person out and move them to another area. The rest are left to wonder what happened. Their interrogators never provide details, only acknowledging that the missing man was 'not cooperative enough' or promising that he had 'cooperated and been returned to his home.' Our methods are for those men on site to build trust while I play the part of sole judge and executioner or the grantor of pardons. We never physically harm them, but the unknown can be more intimidating. The prisoners eventually believe those agents are the only ones who can help and protect them from me, but only if they participate in their own survival. It takes time, but it produces better intel.

"As for the second question, Lucy knows part of this story, Manning knows most of it, and maybe some people in other agencies know some details, but I doubt anyone knows the whole story. I didn't give Lucy all the details, and I will not give you all the details either."

Sam took a couple of bites of food and drank some water.

"My second job for Manning, the first after Lucy and I were married, didn't go as planned. I was sent to Mexico to eliminate the leader of a human smuggling cartel. A man named Cortez. He was kidnapping girls from all over the world and auctioning them off to the highest bidder. Arabs usually bought them, but it certainly wasn't only Arabs. They housed the girls and held the auction in an old dairy barn.

"I did what I was sent to do, but as I left the scene, I was in a motorcycle wreck and captured."

Sam gave a half laugh as he thought back. "You see these people in the movies pull off crazy stunts. Crash, flip three times, and shoot five bad guys while flying through the air. Then, they walk away. That isn't how real life works.

"The next thing I knew, I was waking up in a hospital bed, but I wasn't in a hospital."

The story enthralled me. "So, what happened when you woke up?"

"I spent five weeks as the victim of enhanced interrogation, which is the new way liberals say torture. I had nothing on me when I wrecked to give away my involvement, but they believed they had gotten lucky and captured Cortez's killer. I am not going into the details of the torture. The Marines trained me for capture and torture, but that training was useless. Let's just say Manning chose me because I am one person with first-hand experience regarding what happens to a person mentally when they are questioned and, potentially, tortured."

"Is that where the scars came from? Before you escaped?"

"That is where most of the scars came from—the wreck and what happened in the old dairy barn. But no, I didn't escape. Eventually, someone pressured the Mexican government enough to raid the farm. They didn't even know I was there. I was locked in a concrete closet when the shooting started. It was over in seconds, and the Mexican soldiers who found me took me to the hospital in Monterrey. After I recovered enough, they called the U.S. State Department and told them they had a victim of a motorcycle wreck who was American but had no identification or passport. The State Department worked it out for me to return. I was just Samuel Rutland, an American citizen and motorcycle rider to them. That is 'why me.'"

"Why do you keep doing this?" I asked. "You said you have plenty of money."

"I was offered the opportunity to serve my country in a special way. It allowed me to come home to Kentucky, get married, and settle down, but still do my part and use the training the military invested in me." He continued. "It doesn't have insurance or a retirement program like the military, but as I said, they pay me well."

"In short," I said. "You get to serve."

"As you will. And you will understand that feeling more after you enlist. There really are greater causes. I hope I have taught you that over the years."

∞

In late October, Sam, Lucy, and I visited a Marine recruiter, Sargeant Logan Raynes, in Lexington. Sam wore a 'United States Marine Corp, Retired' cap I had never seen before. He said it wouldn't hurt for the recruiter to know he served.

Sam and Lucy were my legal guardians until I was 18, so they had to sign off on my enlistment. The recruiter said I could choose an MOS (Military Occupational Specialty) after basic training. He also said I didn't have to take the ASVAB test because of my ACT and SAT scores but suggested I take it anyway. I arranged to do that on November 12. The following day, I would take the physical and conditioning tests.

We agreed that, assuming my testing was acceptable, I would report to the recruiting office in Lexington at 8:00 a.m. on January 5, 2002, for the ride to Parris Island, South Carolina, and basic training. That would mean I would be just past my 18th birthday when I went on active duty. Over the next two weeks, I studied and refreshed myself on math and physics before taking the ASVAB.

On November 14, the recruiter called the house and told me I scored 129 on the General-Technical section and 125 on the Skilled-Technical section of the ASVAB. Overall, I had 95 out of a possible 99 points. I didn't know if 95 was good or bad, but he said the scores were good enough that I could pick any MOS I chose, and I could be 99 percent assured I would get it. He also said my physical conditioning scores were among the highest he had ever seen.

Fall meant there was a little less work required around the farm. There was no garden to worry about; the hay was cut, baled, and in the barn for use over the winter months. Being cooler in the mornings meant I could push myself on the morning runs. I continued adding weight to the pack but never weighed it again. Just one small rock each day was hardly noticed, but as I ran farther and faster, I knew I was gaining the strength and stamina I would need at Parris Island.

I also spent even more time with Lauren. I often did my weightlifting at around noon so I could spend the evenings with her. Sam was always sitting in the hidden container reviewing transcripts, but we could talk while he worked and I lifted weights. He began to talk to me more about how he had been trained with Marine Force Recon, the Navy Seals, and the German special forces. We talked about methods, strategies, and tactics. He also talked to me a little about the tradecraft used by ACXN. I found it fascinating. Again, I was not supposed to hear these things, but at this point, our trust in each other was absolute and unconditional.

Lauren's mom had abandoned the family years ago, leaving her and an older sister named Jolene with her father. He was a successful plumber and electrician, and they lived in a nice home. For the most part, Lauren and I visited with her friends at Eastern Kentucky University in Richmond. Sometimes, we would go to Lexington to eat and watch a movie.

After spending several months dating, Lauren and I had grown close, and yes, we were in love, but we were also mature enough to know I wouldn't be around much longer, and the relationship was likely to dissolve. One night, we discussed that fact and agreed neither of us should hold the other to any commitment. We would be together until I left for basic training, and maybe we would see each other when I came home on leave, but otherwise, we were free to date. I never did.

Holidays were never a big deal for us. Sam and Lucy described themselves as 'spiritual but not religious' Christians. We exchanged small gifts at Christmas and always ate a special Easter lunch, but otherwise, each day was pretty much the same as others. I struggled that year because it was my first Christmas without my mother. Lucy picked up on my mood and suggested we "walk up the hill."

By this point, there was a well-worn path to her gravesite. Over the late summer and early fall, the dirt on the grave had settled, and the grass had returned. I could still make out the spot, but I knew the gravesite would be hard to find by next summer, likely by the next time I was home. That was okay; It was how she wanted it. In my mind, Rachael's Ridge was all-encompassing of the 800 acres owned by Sam and me. That was my home. That was mom's home. Forever.

"You know Rachael and I talked all the time," Lucy began. "You were her favorite subject. During those first couple of years, when she was hardly ever home and awake, she demanded I give her a minute-by-minute review of your day."

I didn't say anything. I knew she loved me.

"I can tell you she was so proud of the man you have become. You are strong, but you can also be kind and gentle. I am proud of you, too."

She turned, leaned into me, and hugged me. "God didn't choose for me to birth children, but He blessed me when you showed up on my doorstep. I know I have said this before, but I mean it, Joshua."

When she moved away, a tear rolled down her cheek. "This has been a hard year. It has been hard for everyone. It has been hard for this country, but people like Sam make a difference in so many ways. You are going to do the same."

We stood there for a while as the temperature dropped. A cold, dry north wind signaled an approaching cold front. After a bit, we headed back to the house.

Sam met us halfway with a bag over his shoulder.

"Manning called," he said, pointing at the Blackberry device attached to his belt. "I'm scheduled on a flight out of Lexington at 6:30 this evening. Manning has arranged a private jet this time, so I'll be in Cuba before midnight. We may have a line on where Bin Laden is hiding out."

"Joshua, I know you plan to see Laura tonight, but would you drive me to the airport first? We need to talk a little more before you head out in two weeks. I may not be back."

"I'll call Lauren. I can still be at her house by 7:30. It's no problem,"

On the ride to the airport, Sam was more serious than usual.

"I've told you what to expect at basic. Just follow orders. Training will be hard, but it will be harder for everyone else. You are in great shape. You are mentally and physically strong. Training will be the easy part.

"Always remember that you are part of a team. A successful Marine thinks about his team before himself. Your training officers will be looking for leaders; be a leader. They are going to push you, whether you perform better or worse than everyone else. Take care of those on your team, and always know that you can do more than you believe you can."

After a short pause, he continued. "The odds are you'll have to go fight these fanatical Islamic bastards because I don't see this being over any time soon. They've been programmed from birth to hate anyone who doesn't believe as they do, and they hate America and Americans even more. Your instructors will get you ready; rely on that training. Trust that training. It is the best in the world."

He was quiet while I considered what he said. Then, as we arrived at the airport, he simply said, "I am proud of you. Lucy and I will be fine. You worry about you and your brothers in the Corps. Don't worry about us."

And with that, he climbed from the truck and headed to a plain white jet parked at the FBO. I saw Manning standing by the steps.

I returned to North Fork and visited with Lauren until almost midnight. I gave her a gold chain and a sweatshirt. I had purchased the sweatshirt a few weeks before when Sam and I went to Lexington to buy ammunition. It said, "Back off. I belong to a Marine." I think she liked it.

As 2001 changed to 2002, Lauren and I made love before promising that no matter what, we would always be friends. We knew our relationship would never be the same. I could never ask her to wait for me. At this point, I regretted my decision to enlist, but I also knew it was what I was meant to do.

I ate with Lauren and her dad on the night of January 3, knowing it was the last time I would see her for several months. I had already told her I planned to spend the evening of January 4th with Lucy before rising early to head out to Lexington. She understood.

Chapter 9

Nothing is ever as one expects. Basic training was mentally draining and physically challenging, but I made it through relatively easily.

The first thing we all learned when we arrived at Parris Island, or what I was reminded of since Sam had already prepared me, was that we were the lowest form of life and unworthy to be there. We were told we were not even deserving of a rank and we were never to call ourselves or another recruit Marine.

We spent the first several weeks working on discipline and physical training, learning how to march, dress, eat, speak, and tie our shoes. There was more school and classroom-style education than I expected. Our subjects included the history of the United States Marine Corps, first aid and basic medical training, core values, leadership, and teamwork. Tactics, we were told, would come later.

When I arrived at Parris Island, I had never been in a fight, so the hand-to-hand combat training was new to me. It was not something Sam and I worked on. That was both good and bad. Good because I didn't have any bad habits to break. Bad because I simply had no experience fighting someone. Most of the training was based on a variety of martial arts. It took me a while, but in the end, I learned to use my strength and stamina to my advantage. I would never be as quick as some in my class, but I learned to overcome that by leveraging my size, strength, and other learned skills and tactics.

The Corps taught the Marine Corps Martial Arts Program, or MCMAP for short since everything in the military must have an acronym. The program pulled from various disciplines, like judo, karate, taekwondo, and jujutsu, and combined those techniques with traditional Marine Corps hand-to-hand and close-quarter combat training.

I was good in the gym. I typically scored early and often in sparing sessions, but no one knows how they will respond in the real world. As fighter Mike Tyson said, "Everyone has a plan until they get punched in the mouth."

Week four was called swim week. Our instructor constantly called us "chum" as we learned to swim and operate in the water. I thought I was a decent swimmer, but I truly believed I would drown the first time I jumped in the pool wearing a full battle uniform, boots, a loaded backpack, and twenty pounds of other equipment. The instructors pulled me – and several others – from the pool just before we lost consciousness. I think that was the only time I was terrified in basic training.

After the fourth week, we took our first physical fitness test, and I finished second by a single point to a guy who weighed forty pounds less than me. I vowed it would be different after the next test four weeks later.

Week five was a chance to recover. We still worked on physical fitness and drilled, but most of the time was spent working in teams to complete simple missions. Unloading trucks, for example. Dear reader, I can tell you there is a right way and a wrong way to unload a truck. There is also the Marine Way, and that is the only way that matters.

Weeks six and seven added weapons training and live-fire target training. While water week almost killed me, this week was the easiest of all. Years with Sam had thoroughly prepared me.

After two weeks of weapons basics, I qualified as a marksman. Week nine challenged everyone with the combat fitness test. This consisted of running in full uniform, lifting, maneuvering, and operating under simulated live fire. I did well and finished first this time.

Then came 'The Crucible."

Remaining awake and functional for over 48 hours is difficult under the best of circumstances. Doing it while constantly facing physical and mental challenges is hard for anyone. I made it through, but many didn't.

I will never forget the ceremony after The Crucible, where the survivors were awarded their Eagle, Globe, and Anchor pin, signifying that we were now worthy of being called Marine. I was finally a Private (E-1)

The final two weeks at Parris Island were largely ceremonial. For the first time, we were treated as men who were supposed to be there. We spent time with our instructors and discussed the different jobs in the Marines. Many of my fellow new Marines entered with a predetermined Military Occupational Specialty as part of their enlistment. I was glad I chose to wait.

On March 15th, 2002, I met with Gunnery Sergeant Quinton Biggs. He had been one of our weapons training instructors. Biggs was a very big black man with a shaved head, a small mustache, and the most intimidating baritone voice on the base. I was waiting in his office when he entered with a smile I had never seen before. He carried a box with a small cake inside. I rose, but he immediately said, "Have a seat, Marine."

"You were experiencing the crucible on your 18th birthday. You missed it. We aren't big on birthdays around here, but I wanted cake, and you were a good excuse."

He pushed the cake, a few napkins, and a plastic knife over to me. "Cut us a couple of pieces while I review your file again."

When I set a large piece of cake in front of him, he looked up from the file and asked. "Who is Samuel Rutland?"

"He's my uncle," I said. "But truthfully, he is more like my father. My mother and I were alone when I was growing up. I have lived with him since I was eleven. Mom died last year, and Sam and his wife, my aunt, Lucy, became my legal guardians." It suddenly hit me. "I guess that doesn't apply anymore. I didn't even think about turning eighteen."

"Well, you are now a Marine and a legal adult. Welcome to the real world. I served with a Sam Rutland back in the day; he was also from Kentucky. I think we joined at almost the same time. Is he about thirty-six, maybe thirty-seven?"

"Yes, sir," I replied. "He turned 37 in February."

85

"We lost touch after he was reassigned. I have no clue where he ended up. I have always been an instructor. Tell him I said hello."

"Yes, Gunnery Sergeant."

"Now, what do you want to be when you grow up? You have excelled in your testing. Excellent recruit. All positive performance reports. We usually let the best recruits in the class pick from the available careers first; then, we work our way down. You were the highest-scoring recruit, so you get to pick first. If it is available, it is yours."

"Sir, my ultimate goal is to go into special forces," I said, "but that's three or four years away. I have been considering careers that would prepare me for Marine Recon. I am leaning toward intelligence."

"Excellent choice," he said as he stood and closed the file. "You are wrapped up here in three days. Report to Camp Lejeune on April 1, and enjoy your week off."

That is exactly what I did. Many fellow Marines headed south to Jacksonville or further down to Miami for a week of partying. I bussed to Charleston, South Carolina, and called Lucy before buying an airline ticket on Delta to Lexington. She promised to pick me up.

When I exited the Lexington concourse, Lucy and, surprisingly, Lauren were waiting for me. It was a good day.

I ended up with six free days back on the farm. It was cold and wet that time of year, so there wasn't much work that could be done. I spent a few days with Lauren, but she had to return to school. While on the farm, I didn't run or lift weights. I relaxed, talked to Lucy, and read books. As far as Lucy knew, Sam was now at the Embassy in Doha, Qatar. He had been gone for almost two months. She said he called weekly, and they talked for a few minutes. He wasn't allowed to say anything about his work. She said she didn't ask after he made it clear the telephones were not secure on his end.

I offered to help her start the tobacco in the hothouse, an annual ritual I enjoyed, but she said they had decided to skip the tobacco planting for the year.

One day, we drove into Lexington. The Marines have a saying, 'If we don't issue you one, you don't need it.' That is somewhat true, but I needed new clothes for when I was off base. Most recruits gained muscle and lost fat during basic. I weighed the same as I did the day I walked on base, but my body was reshaped.

I mention this trip for one reason. For the first time in my life, I was personally challenged in a non-training environment. I wore a tee shirt under my jacket with "USMC" stenciled across the front. We were leaving The Olive Garden restaurant when a man, probably 45, walked up and got in my face.

He was obviously drunk. He kept screaming about how the Marines were nothing, and he had words for me and Lucy, who he called my "skanky mom." I assume he didn't know I was immune to that sort of thing. He was nothing compared to the drill instructors at Parris Island.

I told Lucy to ignore him and keep walking to the truck, but he grabbed my shoulder and spun me around. I again told him he needed to move on. Lucy moved to my side, and the man shoved her to the ground.

We were told this could happen. We were told to rise above it. We were told never to engage a civilian unless our life was threatened. We were told there would be consequences if we were arrested. I didn't care.

Within seconds, the MCMAP training kicked in. I didn't even think about what I did. I sent a blow to his chest below the sternum that took the wind out of his sails and doubled him over right into my rising knee. He was out before he hit the ground, and it was over.

Lucy's hand was cut where she hit the pavement, but otherwise, she was okay. I helped her up, and we continued to the truck. When Lucy took her first step, she intentionally stepped heavily on his folded hand. I heard the bones break. I smiled.

I never heard another word about the incident. I know people were watching, but apparently, no one reported it.

As I said, that was my first real-world conflict. It wasn't much, but it gave me confidence.

∞

I arrived at Camp Lejeune on March 31 and went to work the next day. Training continued, but much of my time was spent learning the intelligence trade. This included informational analysis and information gathering, electronic intercepts, physical document intercepts, and human intelligence.

After a year at Lejeune (yes, I drank the water for those of you wondering and who understand the reference), I transferred to Quantico, Virginia, where I served as a liaison between Marine Intelligence and the recently formed Department of Homeland Security. DHS, as it is usually referred to, was built to bring resources from all federal agencies under a single umbrella, eliminating information silos and leading to better information analysis. It was good in theory. I can tell you today, many years later, it still doesn't work as it should because people, people who are more worried about advancing their careers than protecting this country, still don't share much of the information they collect. But that is a conversation for another time.

I spent a year learning Arabic and Farsi. I mastered neither, but I knew enough to struggle through a conversation and could translate from either into English relatively well.

Then, I served two one-year tours in the Middle East. One in Kuwait and another in the United Arab Emirates. In each case, I helped analyze, scan, and catalog every piece of physical intelligence that came into our facility. This included documents, computer data, photographs, and electronic video and audio records.

I had reached Sergeant (E-5) when I asked for and received permission to apply for MARSOC, the Marine Special Forces Operations Command. After submitting fitness reports, medical reports, and a dozen other items, I returned to Camp Lejeune for the Assessment and Selection Phase and to begin training.

It was more challenging this time. The Marines who had served in infantry units had remained in shape, with daily physical and weapons training, and they had the advantage this time. I had spent 12 hours a day studying documents, maps, and photos for the past three-plus years. I had stayed in good shape, but not Marine shape. Thankfully, the conditioning and skills came back quickly.

My biggest struggle during the eleven months of intensive training was once again the water activities, which almost washed me out of the program. I was fine with swimming but hated diving. Eventually, I grew more comfortable underwater and made it through.

Sam and Lucy were at my graduation. I had not seen them in almost a year. I called them and Lauren about once a month, but I had not been home. The meeting and conversation were brief but nice. Aunt Lucy said they hadn't seen or heard from Lauren in a while. I wasn't surprised. She had graduated from college and started a job at a bank in Cincinnati, Ohio. I assumed she had met someone else. It hurt, but I hoped she was happy.

After training, I transferred to Camp Pendleton as a full member of MARSOC. Within five weeks, I was sitting on a rock in Afghanistan, talking to a tribal leader about supporting the United States and the new Afghan government that was established after the fall of the Taliban. We were there for nine months, from October of 2007 until July of 2008. By then, many United States citizens and most politicians had lost their taste for the fight. President Barack Obama sent 17,000 additional troops to the country, but Al Qaeda and the Taliban, terrorist groups we had once decimated, began to build strongholds once again.

Our unit was attacked several times, and we lost four of our small number to improvised explosives or ambush. Often, the attack came from groups we thought to be friendly. It was my first taste of real war. I performed well and was proud to serve.

On the trip back to the United States, I wondered how the rest of my enlistment would go. I still had four years left.

I returned to Brandon on a four-week leave and spent time with Sam and Lucy. I called Lauren, and we met for dinner. As she matured, she grew even more beautiful in my eyes. I was still in love.

She told me before I asked, "Yes, I have dated. No, I am not dating anyone special." I told her I had not dated but added that I hadn't had time to date. I didn't think it would be fair to tell her the truth; I didn't want to date anyone else.

∞

Sam updated me on his work. The farm was only a home place now. A small garden Lucy could take care of and the chickens. They still had a couple of horses, Emma and Frank, plus one bull and six heifers. Each year, they sold off three or four young cows and kept a couple to slaughter for food.

That was it.

Sam talked about the new challenges ACXN was facing. For example, so many countries were putting in facial recognition software at airports that getting in and out of countries was getting increasingly difficult, even using the legitimate passports Manning provided him.

"If I enter a first-world country as Tanner Raines this year, then go back with Steve Grossen on my passport later, the software matches my face, and they start asking questions. It is something Manning and I are working through. He has six operatives in ACXN now; one is a woman, so we have room to rotate people. That's all we know to do. Again, this isn't like the movies. We don't have a magic bullet to fix the problem.

"I've only met a couple of the new operatives. We are off the nine-eleven response and back to doing missions on occasion, so no more time is spent with interrogations. The assignments, however, are getting more complex and time-consuming. I spent two weeks in Argentina last month asking an arms dealer some hard questions. Everything went smoothly. I was sent to eliminate him, but we worked out a deal that I hope he will remember. He wasn't the big fish. The big fish is in Venezuela, we think."

I caught him up regarding my last two years. It had been that long since we had talked for any length of time. He listened intently and asked questions occasionally. I figured I could speak freely because, while not technically a government employee, this citizen held 'Top Secret/SCI' clearance—two levels higher than mine. Since 9/11, gaining that clearance level has been difficult for a government employee and almost impossible for a private citizen, and one must have a high-ranking sponsor to start the process.

I enjoyed my month in Kentucky. I saw Lauren three straight weekends, and we spent them in her apartment in Cincinnati. Returning to California was difficult.

Chapter 10

Back at Camp Pendleton, our unit resumed training. We had been told to expect a return trip to Afghanistan in December or January, and we were preparing for that deployment when, early on the morning of September 20th, I received an order from the base commander to report to his office immediately. I passed the note to my unit leader and headed off.

When I entered Major General Thomas Fowler's office, he put me at ease but left me standing before him. I knew it would be a short discussion.

"First of all, Sergeant Booker, congratulations. I have approved a promotion request to Gunnery Sergeant."

I was somewhat stunned.

"Yes, you too noticed that you skipped Staff Sergeant altogether," he said as he sat and picked up a sheet of paper. "A gentleman entered my office today and presented me with a letter from the Secretary of the Navy. It was upon his recommendation that you receive the promotion. Staff Sergeant, I might understand, but I verified its validity, and I do not question the Secretary."

He continued. "The letter also states you are to immediately meet with a man who says his name is Mr. Smith and then report back to me. Following that, you have three days of leave if you choose to take it. I don't like where this is going, Gunnery Sergeant Booker. But again, I don't question the Secretary. Mr. Smith is waiting in the conference room at the end of the hall. Please fill me in after you meet with him."

I stood in stunned silence. A thousand thoughts were going through my mind. The first one was that Sam had been killed. He had told me that if anything ever happened, Mr. Smith - Manning - would let me know.

"Do you know this man? Mr. Smith," General Fowler asked.

"I have an idea about who he is, sir. But that's about it."

"Any idea how he has enough juice to get SECNAV to write me a letter?"

"Honestly, sir, no, I don't."

"You are dismissed, Gunnery Sergeant; let my secretary know when you have finished your conversation with Mr. Smith."

I made my way to the conference room at the end of the hall. I was certain that Manning was not in the military, so I neither saluted nor addressed him as sir. He was standing, looking out the window at the parade grounds.

"Mr. Smith," I said, entering the room. "You asked to see me."

"Yes, Gunnery Sergeant, I did. Please have a seat. Do you remember me?"

I hadn't paid much attention to his appearance in the bank barn that night, but Manning was much older than I thought. His previously dark hair had grayed at the temples and beyond. He also seemed thinner, as if time had worn him down. I guessed he was in his mid-sixties, probably six feet tall, but a skinny 165 pounds.

"Yes, I do. Did something happen to Sam?"

"No. He was good when I saw him yesterday. How much do you know about what Sam does, about what I do?" he asked.

I wasn't sure what Sam had told him. I didn't want to step on a mine here.

"I know some. It is hard to live on a farm and in a house with someone and not figure out what's going on," I answered. "I don't know who you work for or what agency, for example, but I am guessing it's the CIA. Sam seems to do your bidding, but he just states that he 'does some work for an importer.' Based on his training regimen, the hundreds of rounds he fires every week, and the fact that he doesn't make any money on the farm but has plenty of money, I am guessing these are covert missions. Again, it sounds like CIA, but he never confirmed anything."

Mr. Smith just nodded and looked at some notes.

"Your fitness reports are outstanding," he said.

"Yes, I've worked hard to be a good Marine. What does this have to do with Sam?"

"And you have 'Secret' clearance. Know that everything we will discuss today is sensitive, compartmentalized information. Do you understand?"

I answered in the affirmative.

"May I call you Joshua?" he asked.

"May I call you Manning?" I replied.

He grinned. "Not much gets by you, does it?"

I said nothing.

"First of all, I do not work for the CIA. I am employed by a shell company that is possibly owned by the CIA, the DIA, the DOJ, or another one of those other alphabet agencies. I honestly don't know for certain. My orders are delivered secretly and securely. I am sure the CIA and other agencies within Homeland Security are involved, at least indirectly. Still, I haven't been to Langley since eighty-eight. I do have contacts who can help with documents – like your birth certificate – and arrange travel and alternate identification. They can point an operative to weapons caches, in-country human resources, etc. I don't have their names and I don't know who they work for."

"Anyway," he continued, "The group I lead is referred to as ACXN. A computer randomly chose those letters, but we pronounce it 'action.'

"ACXN is a small collection of people with the skills to carry out what are typically solo missions worldwide, but never on U.S.

soil. None of us have any currently documented ties to the government. We are import and export consultants as far as the IRS and every computer in the world is concerned. After the 9/11 attack, Washington was

scrambling to find people who could help in the war on terrorism, so we assisted as anonymously as possible. I assume you figured out what Sam was doing regarding interrogations. He is good at getting in people's heads and extracting good intelligence."

"Anyway, while everyone was focused on preventing the next attack, other people and groups were getting on with their business unmolested. Illegal arms traders were, and still are, supplying both sides in many conflicts. Sometimes we don't care. Let them kill each other. But in Afghanistan, they supply the remnants of Al Qaeda, the Taliban, and the tribal leaders we are fighting against. I am sure you understand the players."

He paused to let me say something, but I remained silent.

"Officially, the US government doesn't carry out extra-judicial justice and never sanctions assassinations of foreign government officials. But that doesn't mean they don't do it through back channels. We are often the back channel. Certainly, not every assignment we get involves assassination or even foreign governments, but sometimes it comes to that."

I wondered where this was going, but I continued to say nothing. I learned in Afghanistan that the best way to get information is to create space for the other person to speak.

"Joshua, I have two critical pieces of information to share. Then I will let you consider them for a day. It is essential that you think about them before we continue.

"Your uncle has indicated he intends to retire. He said he just wants to be a 'gentleman farmer.' He can certainly retire at any time. I asked him for six years when he started with me in 1990. We were both a lot younger then. He more so than I. He has given me what, 18 years? But he is also deeply invested in his current mission. He needs help with this one and has asked that you assist in completing the mission and then be given the option to join my team to replace him. Your fitness reports, test scores, Marine training, and minimal family make you a perfect fit.

"I will ask you for a six-year commitment. We will continue to train you in our ways; call it 'tradecraft' if you want to sound like a CIA spook. Much of that will happen immediately.

"Two more notes. I am going to be upfront with you," Manning became even more serious. "If something happens on a mission, no cavalry is coming to save you. You are simply a citizen. We will help where we can work with the State Department and urge them to use their leverage to get you home, but we don't officially exist in Washington and have no official government ties or backing. Finally, our shell company pays well. Far better than what a Gunnery Sergeant makes in the Marines. It's even better than what a two-star Major General makes. Plus, we pay bonuses for missions and time out of the country. Call it hazard pay. You will clear well over a quarter million dollars each year."

Money had never really interested me, so that information was superfluous. But the opportunity to maybe live the life Sam and Lucy led was appealing.

"I still have about four years on my Marine Corps obligation," I said. "Can we talk about this after I complete my commitment?"

"No, we can't. This is very time-sensitive. Sam started this mission several months ago, and we need to see if we can cut the head off this snake soon. He is working to break up a weapons cartel selling to Al Qaeda and other terror organizations."

After a pause, he continued. "I have another letter from the Secretary of the Navy, signed by him and the Marine Corps Commandant, granting you an immediate honorable discharge from the Marines and releasing you from future obligations to the reserves. If, after six years with ACXN, you wish to return to the Marines, it will be as a Gunnery Sergeant, just about where I would expect you to be by then."

My mind was racing. I needed to speak with Sam.

"I need to talk to Sam," I said.

"As expected," he replied. "I have a jet waiting just down the road. You will be home tonight and back here the day after tomorrow."

"I need to grab some things and speak with General Fowler. Can you give me an hour?"

"Let's see if we can speak to the General together."

And that is what we did. Fowler didn't seem very happy that 'Mr. Smith' had gone over his head to SECNAV, especially when he didn't know what was happening, but he sent us on our way. I told my unit leader I would be gone for three days and that General Fowler had already signed my leave request. Then, I headed to my on-base housing to grab a change of clothes. We were in the air fifty minutes after walking out of the General's office.

Chapter 11

Manning handed me a stack of papers and documents as the Gulfstream G150 leveled off at 37,000 feet above the California desert. I wanted to think, but Manning wished to talk.

"Listen, Joshua," he said. "You have been through the cesspool that is Afghanistan and come out on the other side. If you choose to join this cause, I will send you to places just as bad or worse on occasion, and you typically won't have a team with you. There will be some limited logistical support, but nothing close by or ready to fight."

"Is that your sales pitch?" I asked.

"I want to be upfront with you. I don't want people like you, or your uncle for that matter, pissed off at me. I was a CIA operator for a very short time, but I never had the training or skills you two have."

I imagine I raised my eyebrows at that statement. He sighed and continued, "I was recruited to the CIA out of college. Dartmouth, if you care."

I didn't.

"I spent several years training to be a CIA operative. I was going to go all over the world and work behind the scenes to make things happen. Stir up trouble here, calm things down there, and spread money around somewhere else to pave the way for a new military base—that type of thing.

"My first mission was in the Philippines, nineteen eighty-five and eighty-six. I was working both sides between representatives of the Marcos family and the people who wanted to spark a revolution. The United States openly said they wanted the Marcos family out one week and then openly supported them the next week. In late February of eighty-six, the Marcos family was out, and people on both sides got to talking. The new government started looking for me, and they had a great photo of me that ended up on television. I got away on a freighter bound for Taiwan but was forever useless as a field agent. Get your face on the news as a person of interest, and you're finished."

"So, how did you land this job?"

"I went back to the CIA and took a desk job. One day, the director told me to meet with the chairman of the Senate Intelligence Committee. The senator told me they were looking to start an off-the-books operation to address occasional 'special and specific problems.' It would be completely non-governmental, and I knew what that meant. We talked for about 30 minutes; then he told me to return to my office. I had four weeks to present him with a plan, but I couldn't speak to anyone about what I was doing. He told me to explain exactly how I would accomplish his goals."

"So that is what you did," I stated.

"That is what I did. I never saw him again. He had given me a contact number – just a number, no name – to call when I had a plan developed. He hinted that perhaps others were also offering plans, but he never said. Shortly after I called the number, a courier arrived to transport the document. Three weeks later, I was fired by the Agency. That isn't unusual for outed agents. I went through the exit process, and they reminded me that sharing certain information I possessed would land me in prison or worse. After that, I went home and started thinking about what I would do with my life. Two days later, I was unlocking my front door, and two bruisers grabbed my arms and threw me into a van. Cliché, isn't it? I was taken to an unknown location, and over the next twelve weeks, the details were worked out for the ACXN group. I never left whatever building I was in during that time. I never talked to anyone outside. There were four other people there. Their names were John, Paul, George, and Ringo. I have never seen nor heard from any of them again," he paused, "unless they are the faceless people I contact when I need something. I will never know."

"Is there any way ACXN is legal?" I asked.

Manning shrugged. "Borderline at best. But I have every correspondence I have ever received as insurance."

We were probably passing over northern Arizona when the co-pilot exited the cockpit and started unwrapping sandwiches and passing them to us. She passed me a Coke and a bag of chips to go with it. We were quiet until she returned to the cockpit.

"Who owns the jet?" I asked.

"Rolle Imports, headquartered in Nassau, on the island of New Providence, Bahamas. Rolle Imports also has offices in San Diego, Savannah, London, Singapore, and Athens."

"Why the Bahamas?"

"That was a part of the original plan. Create a legitimate company, not just a shell, based outside the United States as primary cover, allowing us to do a few things. First, it creates separation. It moves us further from being a U.S. government agency. Second, some entity, yes, it is probably the CIA, manages to move millions of dollars into Rolle Imports each year to pay us and pay for our operations.

"Rolle has a working staff and several salespeople who import, export and sell extremely high-end audio equipment in about fifty countries. The CEO knows the enterprise is a front, but she also knows to run the business and ignore the rest. We have a couple of agents there to answer the phone and respond correctly if the caller asks for one of our operatives. Last year, they moved about eight million American dollars in audio equipment and profited about two million after expenses. Our total available budget, however, is over one hundred million, though we usually don't come close to spending it."

If I had not known that Sam had worked with this group for almost two decades, I would have asked many more questions and been far more skeptical.

"What is all of this?" I asked, holding up the documents he had handed me earlier.

"Just brochures for Rolle, gives us legitimacy."

I looked over the stack of documents. There was some general information about Rolle Imports, brochures about theater surround sound units, and big, beautiful speakers. Many of the systems were priced in the six-figure range. A couple were seven figures. Who the hell would pay that much for a home audio system?

I spent most of the remaining flight time thinking about how this could affect my relationship with Lauren. It was evident that if I continued down my current path, marriage and a life with her were at least five years away. I could never ask her to marry me now when I would be gone ninety percent of the time.

If I took the position with Manning, I would still be gone some, but it shouldn't be that often. Sam was, last I heard, averaging about four months a year away from home. That number was higher than it had ever been except right after nine-eleven. Maybe if we married, we could live on the farm at Rachael's Ridge. Lauren would have Sam and Lucy and be close to her dad and sister when I was away.

But would she be willing to give up her career and move back to middle-of-nowhere Kentucky? Could she be happy just tending to a house and some chickens? Possibly a baby - or two - as well?

It was a lot to consider.

∞

We arrived at Central Kentucky Regional Airport just south of Richmond at dusk. Sam's pickup was parked near a small hangar.

"I left the truck here yesterday. Sam was confident you would come to talk to him, so he told me to leave it here. If I didn't return, Lucy would bring him to get it."

I tossed my bag in the back of the GMC Sierra and stood by the driver's door. Manning hesitated before tossing me the keys.

We were silent on the ride to Rachael's Ridge. We passed within a half mile of Lauren's family home, and it was all I could do not to stop by and ask her father or sister how she was doing.

As I drove the gravel driveway, I saw lights on in the barn and knew that was where we could find Sam, so I continued beyond the house to the open barn doors. Sam was sitting on the weight bench.

Exiting the truck, I grabbed my bag and walked to the house. "You go ahead and catch up with Sam. I am going to say hello to Lucy."

Manning said nothing; he just waved a hand over his head.

Lucy saw me enter and immediately came to hug me.

"I didn't know you were coming," she said, moving toward the refrigerator. "I would have cooked for you."

"No problem, I am here with Manning."

She stopped immediately and turned to me.

"I will explain later. And I had a couple of meals on the flight over. You can fatten me up tomorrow."

"Are you here for a while?"

"No, I imagine I will be heading out the day after tomorrow. Probably early."

As I said that, I saw the pickup truck heading down the driveway. Sam came in right after, his face serious.

He walked over and put his hands on my shoulders, just like he did the first time I met him.

"Joshua, I am sorry," he said. "I wanted to talk to you first and give you a heads-up, but Manning insisted on doing it this way. He is giving us some privacy until noon tomorrow; then, assuming you go through with this, he is coming back for us all to talk. We need to discuss this, but we can wait until morning if you wish."

103

"Well," I replied, "The clock says eight fifteen, but I am on California time. It is early for me. You make the call."

He paused. "I still plan to run tomorrow. Let's plan to talk at about nine o'clock. That will give us three hours before Manning comes back."

"Enjoy your run," I told him. "Nine o'clock is six a.m. on the left coast. That is early enough for me to get started. I won't sleep for a while."

∞

I descended the stairs at about 7:30 the following morning as thunderstorms dumped torrential rains. Sam was sipping coffee and sitting with Lucy in their regular spots at the kitchen table.

Lucy immediately got up and started cooking breakfast. I poured a cup of coffee, hot and black, 'the Marine way,' and pulled up a chair.

"There was a time I would have run in this," Sam offered, "but not today." Weather should be better tomorrow."

"This is one of the few days I have seen you miss; rain, snow, sleet, it didn't matter."

"I'm in my mid-forties. I'm now more worried about breaking something on that slick hill than I was fifteen years ago."

Lucy spoke up. "Joshua Booker, fill me in on how you have been doing."

General 'catching up' conversation continued until she placed three plates of food on the table. Each had a slab of country ham, a couple of fried eggs, and two biscuits. "More biscuits are staying warm in the oven when you finish those," she said, adding three jars of various homemade jellies, plus butter and sorghum molasses, to the table.

"When I said you could start fattening me up, I didn't mean in a single meal," I joked, but Lucy became serious.

"Sam has finally," Lucy said while staring at my uncle across the table, "told me what he wants to do and what he wants you to do. I will support your decision, but I hope you say no. Finish your service, get a real job, and settle down with Lauren."

I grinned. "What makes you think Lauren will be there in five years?" I asked.

"She will. Trust me."

No matter what choice I made, I hoped Lauren would be there. The rest of the conversation revolved around cable television and cable Internet having arrived on Rachael's Ridge. After breakfast, Sam and I helped get the dishes to the sink, grabbed jackets, and headed to the bank barn, which Sam now referred to as 'my office.'

Sam opened the door to the safe room, and I saw that he had upgraded his equipment since my last visit a month ago. Two tables had been added. On one table sat a flat-screen television, plus there were two more computers; one was a Panasonic Toughbook, like I used in my unit, and the other was a small Dell tower with two flat-screen monitors.

"Sam embraces technology," I said with both a smile and some amazement in my voice.

"Yep," he said before adding, "Times change. We have to change, too. I was also an early adopter of modern conveniences like the automobile, electric power, and air conditioning." He grinned as he said it. "Don't think this old man can't change."

"There is nothing old about you, Uncle Sam," I said, throwing the 'uncle' in for effect. "You are in better shape than ninety-nine percent of the men half your age."

He spent a few minutes booting up a computer and quickly visited a Hotmail account.

He turned on a small fan and rolled his chair closer to where I sat near the door. "Start hitting me with questions. I know you have 'em. But hold off on anything mission-specific until you get your other answers."

"First question," I said. "Can Manning be trusted?"

"All I can tell you is this: I have worked with him for 18 years, and as far as I know, he has never once lied to me. There have been times I asked a question, and he told me he couldn't answer either because he didn't know or because he attempted to compartmentalize information, but at least he gave me a plausible reason for not answering. He didn't just make something up and lie to me."

"Now that we are deeper into this, is this the CIA? Manning says he isn't sure. Let me note that my experience with the CIA in Afghanistan was not positive."

"I can't answer you with certainty, but the odds are high the CIA and probably the DIA have a controlling interest, with multiple layers of cutouts and separation between us and them. I think I can guarantee ACXN is nowhere to be found in any documentation in Washington and certainly not within the CIA. However, I also know federal funds are placed into an account each year with no earmarks. That money is covertly distributed to any number of shadow projects and agencies. It could be building a listening station in Taiwan to intercept Chinese communications. It could be for a new satellite used for whatever some scientist might dream up. It could be for ACXN to run completely off-the-books operations through a shell company in the Bahamas."

I considered his answers for a minute.

"Manning said there is support in the field, but it is limited. We have already talked about this, but explain exactly how limited we are talking about."

"Given time, Manning's contacts can get you about anything you need, about anywhere you need it, except for trained, fighting assets. But it requires time. In short, once you are deployed, he can help out with some things on short notice, but you are pretty much on your own.

"Let me give you an example. Back in, I think it was ninety-seven, I was in Kyiv, Ukraine. It was a simple mission gone wrong. A Russian named Morozov lived there and claimed to have viable nuclear material for sale. In this case, highly enriched uranium left over from the old Soviet Union days. Someone in some random agency picked up on the offer. Finding out if it was true was the first question. That task was assigned to ACXN and, ultimately, to me. Manning established my credentials not as a buyer but as a verification expert who, on behalf of an anonymous buyer, would certify that the seller possessed fissionable nuclear material. I went into Kyiv with the test equipment Manning had procured. According to the agreement, I was to test the material and then report to the buyer."

"Let me guess. The seller had no nuclear material and couldn't let you report it."

"Very accurate. I was picked up at the airport as planned and driven to a warehouse on the edge of town. The only things inside were four identical Benz Sprinter vans. All had blacked-out windows. I was put in one van with a driver and two big military types. All four vans left the warehouse. At the first intersection, two of the vans went right. Then, one took the exit at a major interchange while we stayed straight. Manning was supposed to have satellite coverage, but he had no idea which van I was in. He guessed, and they followed one to a nuclear plant to the west in Varesh. I, however, continued southwest for five hours to Volya.

"A quarter mile from the gate, the van slowed and pulled off the road. One of the military types, a tall blond bruiser in the back seat with me, drew a weapon and started screaming in Ukrainian or Russian or some other Slavic language I didn't speak. When the van stopped, the heavy in the front seat jumped out and opened my door. He reached in and grabbed my collar to pull me from the van. I wanted space, so I went easily. He was thinking about me and not the Veresk SR-2 machine pistol he held in his other hand. Since I didn't resist him pulling me from the vehicle, I went by him faster than he expected, and I was able to grab and twist the gun free. There was a strap around his neck, but enough play that I could turn the gun and pull the trigger as we both went toward the ground. He took three rounds at point-blank range and was dead. But he landed on the gun and on me.

"The driver never left the van, but Blondie came around and fired twice. One round hit his partner. The other hit the ground right beside my hip. About this time, the van started moving, distracting the blonde and giving me a second to get some leverage. I lifted the dead guy just enough to adjust the gun and fire a short burst. One round hit Blondie in the ankle, and he dropped to the ground, putting him in my limited firing arc. I pulled the trigger again, and he took two rounds at least. I wasn't sure about the van and driver, but with those two out of the fight, I pushed the big guy off me and rolled over to take Blondie's pistol.

"The driver was completing a three-point turn. I stepped on the road and pointed the pistol at him. He stopped and put his hands in the air. I climbed into the passenger seat.

"Turns out," Sam continued, "The guy was nothing but a hired driver, and the vans were all rented. He wanted no part of the fight and just hoped to return the van undamaged and go home. I knew I had to hide, so I developed a plan. I took the driver's cell phone and slid it under the seat, hoping it was tracked, but then I acted like I threw it out the window so he wouldn't look for it. As we entered a nearby town, I jumped out. I told him to return the van and tell anyone who asked that I ran from the scene after killing the two security guys.

"And this is where Manning comes in?" I asked.

"I borrowed a car," Sam said, using his fingers for quotation marks around the word borrowed. "I drove about two hours and ended up in Odessa. I dumped the car and found an abandoned building to hide in. Late the next day, I found a hotel with a business center I could get into. I logged into a Hotmail account and drafted a message. The next day, I went back, and the draft had been edited to include a name and a location at the docks, along with a time, which was only about 40 minutes later. I headed out. As I approached the slip, a man waved me aboard and started casting off lines. Twenty-four hours later, I was in Istanbul. I cleared customs with the same passport I used to enter Ukraine, then I caught a ride to the airport and bought a ticket for Atlanta."

"That is a long answer to your original question, but Manning had arranged the transportation from Odessa in Ukraine to Istanbul in Turkey. I don't know how, but he knew someone who knew someone who had assets in the area. He always seems to work something out. I never spoke to the guy driving the boat, and when he dropped me off, we were at the fueling dock. I assume he turned around and went back to Odessa."

"One more question," I said. "Why me?"

"That is the most important question and the one I am going to struggle to answer," Sam said. He paused for a minute or two. If I had not known him, I would have assumed he was dreaming up a lie. But that's not Sam. I knew he was seeking the proper wording, the right approach.

"This job is dangerous, Joshua. Probably more so than I want to admit. I've always brushed that aside because I didn't want you, Lucy, or your mom before the cancer took her to worry. Many missions are no more dangerous than what a policeman or fireman faces regularly, but sometimes, things get complicated or go sideways.

"I have always told you this isn't like the Mission Impossible movies, or Vince Flynn, or Brad Thor novels. In real life, the good guy doesn't kill fifty or sixty people in five days and walk away. I am sure your unit took losses in Afghanistan. You know that no matter how good you are, someone will eventually get hit if the other team throws enough lead your way.

He paused again and continued, "I am getting old; I need out. I need to complete what I started in Argentina and then fully retire or just work as a consultant. Manning is probably 65; he will retire soon and mentioned wanting me to take over his role. I didn't tell him, but I don't see that happening. I can't deal with politicians."

"Everyone's a politician," I said. "It is just a question of motive."

"No argument from me," he replied. "Let me clarify by adding that I don't usually like the motives of the people in Washington. They don't always want what is best for America. They want what is best for themselves. A damn shame is what it is.

"Anyway, you can do this for six years or stay in the Marines for five more. While this job is dangerous, I argue it is far less dangerous than being in MARSOC. If you take this job, you can move back here, maybe build a house by the river, marry Lauren, make babies. Lucy seems interested in those last two items."

I started to interject, but he held up a hand.

"But the other fact is that I need a partner on this, and it has to be one I can trust. Manning now has several operatives. I have met two of them, and I am sure they are capable, but I have never trained with them. I have never seen them shoot, I don't know their story, and I don't know how any would operate under pressure. Potentially, heavy pressure.

"But I know you. I've likely seen you fire 75,000 rounds. I know your tactical mind and mentality. I know what you have faced in live fire situations, leading men in Afghanistan. I need someone I can fully trust, and you are my highly preferred option. Plus," he added, "you fit the profile for this plan I am bouncing around in my head."

"You really could have skipped the last hour and just told me you needed my help," I said. "If you need me, I'm in."

Sam just nodded. After several seconds, he said, "Thanks, Joshua. You are a good man, but that isn't a reason to do this."

"Tell me this," I said. "How much autonomy do you, do we, have on missions? Nothing increases risk as much as a suit sitting in an office making decisions."

"Manning and I typically talk about strategies before I embark on an assignment. Sometimes, they are well-planned; other times, we simply don't have enough intelligence or time to plan. Manning isn't an operator at this level, and thankfully he knows it. As long as any exposure can be managed if things go bad, he will sign off. I tell him to pound sand if he suggests something I don't like. I am a private citizen, so he can't throw me in Leavenworth. The thing is, it doesn't matter how much you plan. I have never had a mission go exactly as planned. Think of it as a rough outline that will change a hundred times before the story is complete. We adapt and overcome. Ever heard that motto before?"

"One final item," I said. " War is war, but people with little or no skin in the game dream up these missions. I am not going to kill innocents. I will walk away and disappear before that happens."

"So would I," Sam said.

That made me feel better.

"What exactly is the mission?" I asked.

"Let's wait for Manning before we talk through it," Sam said as he pulled his Blackberry from his pocket and held down a fast-dial key.

"Manning, Joshua is in. Let's get to work." Sam listened for a few seconds and said, "Okay. See you then."

Chapter 12

Manning's return to Rachael's Ridge was going to be delayed by "a developing problem that required his attention" or something like that, so with the rain letting up, Sam suggested we go for a ride. He wanted to show me something.

We went to the old tobacco barn, where he showed me a new addition: a John Deere Gator side-by-side all-terrain vehicle. It had a roof, windshield, and rolled-up doors held in place with Velcro.

We traveled down the drive and turned north on the county road. After about a mile, we reached the dead end at the Kentucky River. Sam took an old logging road back to the east before curving along the river. We were approaching the area where our running path met the water when Sam stopped and stepped out in the light mist.

"Just short of 1700 acres came on the market a couple of months ago—the land between our place, Dowsing Creek, and the river. We have been running on part of it for years. I bought it. Closed last week."

"Amazing," I said, looking out over the river. "This is such beautiful land. Congratulations."

We stood for about ten minutes, watching the river flow by. Despite the morning's rain, it was low this time of year and relatively shallow and wide.

Sam pointed to a log extending into the creek. Three snakes rested there. "Free rodent control," he said, smiling.

We got back into the Gator and continued riding along what remained of the old road to the portion of the running trail that ran along the river. The Gator handled the mud, roots, and ruts fine, but it was a bumpy ride. Eventually, we climbed probably four hundred feet above the river's level. High above, on the back side of Rachael's Ridge, we came to a clearing, and Sam stopped again.

The view was unbelievable. From this location, I could see about six miles of river and the green fields and forest across the river. The remaining mist obscured what I was sure was a fantastic view of the Appalachian foothills to the east.

"It's a little over a mile back to the road the way we came in," Sam said. "There is no other access road right now, and that is assuming we call the trail we just traveled a road. It would be a great place to build a house, settle down, make babies." He grinned again.

"You keep throwing that last part in. Lucy's putting you up to that?"

"Yep."

We continued to drive around on the land. With over forty-one hundred total acres, there was a lot of area to explore.

"When we get back from whatever we are about to do, I need to talk to Lauren," I said. "Lucy's plan sounds pretty good to me."

∞

Manning returned shortly after we got back to Rachael's Ridge. Sam and I were waiting in the office with the door open. The sun had burned off the remaining fog, leading to a scorching and humid day. It was cooler in the buried container but not much more so. Sam had installed a de-humidifier several years back to help protect the electronics. When the door was closed, the cool earth surrounding the container would cause condensation and problems. A steady stream of water flowed from the drain hose that extended below the barn.

Manning stood and stared.

"I had no idea this was here," he said, looking around inside the container but remaining outside the door.

"Need to know and all," Sam said. "Three people needed to know. You are now the fourth. Come on inside; it is a little cooler in here."

Manning hesitated as if the enclosed space might present a problem, but he moved inside. I grabbed an extra chair from over by the weight bench and pulled the door almost closed, leaving a small crack. Manning stared at the door. I had seen that look before.

"All you have to do is push the door, Manning, and you can access the wide-open spaces," I told him. He eventually nodded and placed the chair near the opening. Sam and I sat.

"So, you are in," Manning stated. It wasn't a question, but I nodded. "I will send the paperwork to the Navy office, and they will take care of everything from there. Consider yourself officially honorably discharged under the terms of the agreement we discussed. Your discharge papers will be sent..." he paused, "here?"

Again, I nodded.

"As a private citizen and discharged Marine, you are responsible for protecting the information you already know. You know what that means. However, I will treat you as if you were cleared for Top Secret/SCI. There is usually a months-long vetting and background check process. We can't vet you in this case and protect your cover. People would ask why a private citizen needs SCI clearance. In short, there is official, and there is unofficial. Things were more relaxed when Sam went through the process."

"What have you got?" Sam asked.

"What does Joshua know about Operation Hoplon?" Manning asked.

"I waited on you," was Sam's reply.

"Operation Hoplon?" I asked.

"Hoplon is ancient Greek meaning 'weapons of war'," Manning said. "You will understand the reference more after you know the story."

115

"I will have to take your word for that. My ancient Greek is rusty."

"Okay, from the beginning, but a condensed version. Sam can fill in the details. I have to catch a flight, so I only have an hour. Other things are breaking."

"About a year ago, someone discovered a connection between a gun runner in Argentina and weapons being used by the Taliban, Al Qaeda, and some of the tribal militias in Afghanistan and other areas – Pakistan, for example. Sam was tasked with finding this dealer in Argentina and eliminating him. We were provided with some good intelligence, so the search to locate him was pretty short. Sam had the opportunity and the smarts to ask the man some pointed questions before carrying out the termination request." Manning hesitated. "Sam, can you fill in that part?"

Sam took over.

"I was able to arrange a meeting with him. I explained that I wanted to place a large order that included enough hardware and ammunition for twelve hundred fighters in Chad. I had a list of items, some that I knew would be hard for anyone to get. The dealer, a guy named Vasques, told me he could get what I wanted, and we agreed on a price, but he hesitated on a delivery date. He said he would have to work some items out with his supplier. The hesitation told me he wasn't the big fish. He was a middleman. I told him I would arrange half the money when he gave me an acceptable delivery date, and I left.

"But I went back later that night. He only had one person working security, so it was easy to get to him. The bottom line is, in the end, I agreed not to kill him if he would help us. He wasn't a fan of my idea, but he was eventually persuaded to help."

"He is going to make an introduction?" I asked.

"Not exactly," Sam said. "He told me his supplier is in Venezuela. A German named Finn Weber, two "n's" and one 'b.' He will tell Weber he spoke to a white South African citizen named David Walker – the name I used – and that we reached an agreement on a $48 million deal, but then I went silent when I learned he would have to go outside to fill the order."

Sam looked at Manning, who just nodded before continuing.

"Someone provided Manning with the names of two suspected arms dealers operating in Venezuela, but neither is named Weber. We don't think they are major players. There is a rule I have always followed, and I think I have mentioned this before. Never go to your target; make your target come to you. I feel certain that if my partner and I," he looked me in the eye as he said that, "start asking around about the other dealers, the big fish will get the word, and he will come to us. Hopefully, by using the David Walker name again, he will remember the deal I left on the table. All of this assumes Mr. Vasquez informed him as I instructed."

"And then?" I asked.

"We do what we can to destroy his operation and come home."

"And what if Vasquez already sold you out?" I questioned.

"Then it is on to plan B, which I have yet to work out."

Manning spoke up. "There are still dozens of questions that must be answered. You also need to learn some things about how ACXN operates, our equipment, communication methods, etc. Sam will lead you through that. But we need you in-country in about two to three weeks."

"Can we use Montana to prep?" Sam asked.

"I think I can arrange that," Manning replied. "How long?"

"Book us for fourteen days starting four days from now. Maybe we can wrap up in ten, but I prefer the full fourteen."

"Let me go ahead and confirm; I will be right back," Manning said, swinging the heavy steel door open and letting the heat and humidity back in. He exited while dialing.

"What is in Montana?" I asked.

"It's a training facility for the most part, mainly used by security companies, rich people with private security details, and occasionally by mercenaries and some foreign governments. You and I need to train together before we take this on. You know how teams work. Everyone must think and react as one, without hesitation, without wondering what the others on the team will do. It has been years since I have been up there, but it is a good place to train and to plan. They have resources and huge databases of information. I don't know where they get it all."

I fully understood. The most dangerous time for any team in Afghanistan was when members rotated out and others replaced them. The required trust that the person beside you would respond as you expected during an engagement was not initially there. If that trust was not quickly developed, it got people killed.

Manning pulled the door open and stepped back inside. "I will book you a flight out of Lexington on Monday. When we have the arrival time, I will let Moni know, and someone will pick you up at baggage claim in Bozeman."

"Moni?" Sam asked.

"The last time you visited there, Phillip was still running things. He is no longer with us. His daughter Moni took over about three years ago."

"I remember a teen girl. Is that her?" Sam asked.

Manning replied. "Sam, it's been what, over 17 years since you were in Montana? That teen girl is in her thirties now. She grew up on that ranch and probably knows more about tactical operations than the three of us combined. I was there about six months ago with a couple of new operatives; you won't recognize the place."

"Anyway," he continued, "I need to go. Spend tonight coming up with three names to use as aliases, and I will start on some documentation. Joshua, I also need a first name that isn't yours. I am the only person who knows the real names of the operators in ACXN. Even accounting just knows you by a number and a bank account somewhere offshore. Sam, who is known as Jackson by everyone in the unit, will explain. Keep it short and simple."

"We will work that out and send you the info. I assume you will provide the addresses, dates of birth, etc.?" Sam asked.

"Can my employee number be double-oh-seven?" I asked. Manning ignored me.

"Just give me names you can remember. Common names. If someone searches for John Smith, they will get so many hits that it will take weeks to sort through them, which is a good thing. I'll take care of the rest. You will have a legend for each, and Internet searches will find exactly what we want them to find. Also, find three different places that can provide passport photos. We will use your military ID photo for one since it has short hair. Create a couple of different looks for the other three. Part your hair differently in one, and pull it back in a ponytail if you can in another. Do whatever you can to change your look. Overnight the photos to me. Sam has the address for a box at the FedEx store in Arlington. I'll get you passports and driver's licenses. I'll also arrange for credit cards, library cards, alumni association cards, whatever."

"Just send one set to Montana," Sam said. "Send the rest here."

"Will do," Manning replied. "Anything else?"

"Joshua and I are going shopping in New York. If we plan to present as big-time gun runners, we need to look the part. A new wardrobe and grooming are in order."

"Understood. Joshua, this is when I am thankful the Marines special forces are allowed modified grooming standards. It is easier to cut hair off than grow it out."

It had been months, maybe a year, since my last haircut. My beard was thick and probably two inches long. Operating in Afghanistan required a beard. Men without a beard were not trusted in the Muslim world.

"Sam, you know how to reach me," he said, walking toward the rental. "We will deliver a phone and some other equipment for Joshua to Montana. Beyond that, get me a list of what you need, and I will start working on it. Three weeks is cutting it close."

As Manning drove past the kitchen, Lucy stepped out and motioned for us to come to dinner. I noticed a familiar car parked in the drive. Lucy had called Lauren.

∞

Lauren greeted me with a kiss on the cheek and a hug. She still took my breath away. We chatted through dinner. She asked what brought me home unexpectedly, and I said I got a few days' leave before heading out on a special assignment for the Marines. I hated lying to her, but it was required and for the best. She never asked about Sam's pickup leaving the house as we came in.

After dinner, we walked and talked. She loved her job in Cincinnati. Again, she volunteered that she wasn't seeing anyone with regularity. After this assignment, I told her I expected to be home for a while and asked her to save up some vacation days.

"I can't explain," I began as we approached the area where Mom's grave was. Over the years, the dirt had settled, and the flora had returned. I could no longer identify the exact spot, "but I have reason to believe my situation will change after I return from this assignment. When that happens, I want to have a serious discussion about our future."

"I will be here," Lauren replied. "I love you. I always have. But I can't and won't wait forever. I was praying you would get out of the Marines after your initial enlistment was up. Then, with your move to special forces, it meant another six years. You will be thirty by then, and I will be thirty-one."

"Perhaps it will be sooner," I offered. "After this assignment, we will talk."

She kissed me long and hard. "Don't keep me waiting forever, Joshua Booker."

We strolled back to the house as the last of the sunlight faded. She got in her car and drove down the driveway and out of sight.

I wanted to be mad at Lucy for ambushing me, but I couldn't do it.

When I went back inside, Sam told me to pack for a couple of days in New York. I dug through my old clothes and found some jeans, one pair of khaki chinos, and a couple of decent shirts that fit. I felt like I needed to go shopping before I went shopping.

∞

The next morning, Sam and I drove to Lexington and bought the first available first-class tickets to New York. We chatted and batted around ideas in a quiet corner while waiting for our flight. We also discussed aliases for me. I liked Cody for my team name. I had a teammate named Cody in Afghanistan who was KIA. I wanted to use it to honor him. For possible aliases, we picked James Thames because it sounded European, even though the passport would be from the United States. William "Billy" Thomas and Jonathan "Jon" Ryan were added to the list. Sam used his Blackberry to send the names to Manning.

Beyond that, nothing was decided, but the planning had begun. Sam and I each took out a small notebook and pen. We took very general notes. I guess we didn't want plans for a foreign operation to end up in the wrong hands. It was a habit for both of us. I learned it just after basic training. Never trust your memory. It will fail you when you need it the most.

On arriving in New York, Sam told a cab driver to take us to the Marriott at Times Square. After checking into a two-bedroom suite, Sam asked the concierge to arrange visits to a couple of the higher-end men's clothing stores. Sam held a titanium American Express in his hand as he did so. She booked us into Barley Malt Haberdashery and Ralph Lauren Men's Store. Sam tipped her with a C-note. I had never heard of reserving a shopping slot before.

We walked down the street to a Times Square camera shop with a 'passport photos' sign hanging in the window and took care of the first set of photos, this one with my shaggy look—only two more to go.

On arriving at Barley Malt, I wondered what was going on. There was nothing in the store. There were no racks of suits and clothes to look through: only plush leather sofas, a bar, two dressing suites, and mirrors on the walls. Several seconds later, an older gentleman of undefined sexual orientation floated into the room.

"You must be Mr. Rutland," he said with a distinctly British accent, extending Sam a soft, well-manicured hand. "I am Max. How may I be of assistance."

Sam said, "I need a new suit or two, shirts, and maybe a tie, but I don't plan to wear it. Joshua is my nephew; he needs two suits, six or so shirts, and a couple of ties."

Sam handed over the AMEX and said, "Fix us up."

Max fixed us up. He disappeared into the back and returned with several suits. All sized as close to perfect as an off-the-rack suit could be given our unusually fit bodies. I, for example, needed a generously cut size 48-long jacket to allow for my shoulders and arms. My waist was only 33 inches, but we had to start with 36-waist trousers to get the thighs big enough. We each chose two suits from the six or so he brought out for each of us. I tried to imagine which ones an arms dealer would wear. All the clothing had to be significantly altered, but as Max measured, marked, and pinned, he promised it would all be ready for delivery the following afternoon. Sam told him to plan for a little extra room under the armpit, and when he asked, "Left or right hand draw?" it became apparent that Max had received that request before.

We repeated the same process at Ralph Lauren. Adding another two suits, some high-end jeans, and more casual shirts. Later, we visited a shoe store and wrapped up by hitting Nordstrom men's shop, where we added belts, socks, and a host of other items. In total, I calculated Sam had spent roughly $27 thousand.

As we waited for a taxi to stumble by, I asked, "So, how are expenses handled? I don't think my Marine El-Tee would sign off on that."

"In this case, I put it all on a Rolle Imports American Express card in the name of Jackson Jones. Rolle Imports will pay the bill. Other aliases have matching cards, and Rolle also pays those."

"And no one questions?" I asked.

"Only once. Manning wanted to know why I charged three nights in a hotel totaling over eighty grand. I just told him the truth. The suite was next door to the target, and I needed to be there. He never mentioned it again.

"With what we are doing, we have to play the part," Sam continued. "Would a gun runner willing to spend $60 million show up driving a Chevy and wearing tennis shoes? I don't think so."

When we finally caught a taxi, Sam pulled out his Blackberry and a card from the hotel concierge. When LaShern answered the call, he asked her to book a dinner reservation at the best restaurant within a block of the hotel for eight o'clock. Then he asked her to book a hair appointment for both of us at a place that could "make us look presentable." She said she would set everything up by seven o'clock and let us know.

She approached us as we walked into the hotel; everything was already set. Sam took a printed document from her that contained the time and locations for dinner and the salon the following day; then, he handed over another one-hundred-dollar bill. I decided that if this job with ACXN didn't work out, being a concierge in New York might be a good gig.

Sam went into the small gift shop at the Marriott and bought a set of black ponytail holders. He handed me one and said see how different you can look. I pulled my hair up into a bun like a sumo wrestler would wear, and we headed back across the street, where the man retook the passport photos. The term 'man bun' was still years away. Thankfully, that set of images was never used.

Dinner was at Trattoria Luchesca, and the next day, Bethany, a fifty-something woman with a shaved head and tattoos covering every ounce of exposed flesh except for her face and scalp, spent over an hour washing, conditioning, cutting, shaping, and shaving my hair and beard. I admit she did a good job. I looked like a new man. I wanted Lauren to see me.

Sam went through the same treatment with Genipher. She spelled it for us twice so we would know. On leaving, the total was sixteen hundred dollars. Maybe I could be a concierge, and Lauren could be a hairdresser. We could live modestly and be millionaires by forty.

After the makeover, we made one more trip to the camera store and retook the photos. Thankfully, it was a different employee this time. We walked down the street to a FedEx store and overnighted the three sets to Manning.

The afternoon was spent back at the hotel. Once again, we tossed around ideas for our assignment in Venezuela. I was ready to make a plan, but Sam insisted that we, for now, brainstorm and make notes regarding all of the questions we had about items like transportation, weapons availability, etc.

During the afternoon, Barley Malt Haberdashery and Ralph Lauren delivered the altered clothing to the suite. Later, we walked from Times Square toward Central Park and found a luggage dealer. We each bought a three piece set of Tumi luggage. Another five grand went on the AMEX.

On the walk back with the luggage, Sam decided we needed watches. I chose Tag Heuer; Sam picked an Omega. I put my Timex in my pocket. I couldn't part with it.

Dinner was room service. I got a burger and fries; Sam ordered a steak. We returned to Lexington and Rachael's Ridge mid-afternoon on Saturday.

"Manning sent a note saying details for Montana are on the shared server, and he needs a last name for Cody," Sam said. "Let me go check that. You see if Lucy needs help with anything."

"Clark," I shouted at Sam's back as he went toward the bank barn. "Cody Clark."

Lucy was sitting watching the Braves and Cardinals play baseball. She often fussed that she could watch the Braves and Cubs any time she wanted with the new cable television, but she couldn't watch the Reds very often. I didn't bother her. I took all the luggage to my old room, then returned and brought Sam's inside before I unpacked. I had no idea what to take to Montana and beyond.

A knock on the front door just below my room drew my attention. We rarely had a visitor other than Lauren, and she always came to the kitchen door. Lucy yelled she would get it, and thirty seconds later, she called me to come downstairs.

Just inside the front door were two mid-sized boxes, both addressed to me. It was everything I had left in my quarters at Pendleton that was not the property of the United States Marines. It suddenly hit me that while I would always be a Marine, I was no longer an active part of the Corps, ready to go anywhere, at any time. I would likely never see my teammates again, and they would never know what happened to me. Manning had mentioned that they would be told I had been selected for a special assignment. Some might call my cell and check in on me occasionally. All I could do was tell them I couldn't talk about it. I couldn't tell them where I was. I had to distance myself from my brothers and sisters in arms.

Sam helped me decide what to pack for Montana, and we both packed two suits and three shirts from the New York trip. A second bag held old jeans, hiking boots, tennis shoes, a light jacket, and some gym shorts and T-shirts. That evening, I went to Richmond to see a movie so Sam and Lucy could have time together. I saw Dark Knight, and I remember Heath Ledger being amazing. His death before the movie's release was a shame.

Chapter 13

We left Rachael's Ridge at 2 a.m. on Monday. I had managed about two hours of sleep. Lines at TSA checkpoints were still terrible seven years after the 9/11 attacks, and we barely made our 6 a.m. flight to Minneapolis-St. Paul, for the connection to Bozeman.

We each pulled three bags from the luggage carousel on arrival and started walking toward the exit. A tall and exceedingly wide man of obvious American Indian descent was standing near the exit with a sign that said "Jackson."

Sam approached and extended a hand, "I am Jackson; this is Cody." The man nodded and said, "Call me Thomas."

We exited and continued to a limo parking lot across from the pickup and drop-off area. Thomas pushed a button, and the back of a Cadillac Escalade opened. He helped put our bags inside. "We have a 45-minute ride," he said. "Moni will meet us and show you around. She remembers you, Jackson. From a few years back."

Sam looked surprised like he didn't believe she could remember.

We left Bozeman Yellowstone International and rode west on I-90 for about 30 minutes before turning north on a secondary highway. From there, Thomas exited the road on a gravel path that continued over a small berm running parallel to the highway. After cresting the ridge, the road was wide and paved, lined with spruce trees.

"We keep it rough out by the highway. No markings. It helps keep the tourists from accidentally visiting," Thomas answered my unasked question.

Sam chimed in. "The last time I was here, it was rough for five miles. When did it get paved?"

"We paved it ten or twelve years ago, but Moni widened it right after she inherited the ranch."

I was amazed. Some Marine buddies and I visited a ski resort in Utah one summer, where we hiked and relaxed, and this reminded me of that place. It was beautiful, irrigated, and well-manicured.

After about two miles, we approached a security gate. Huge hay bales formed a wall about twelve feet high on each side and extended all the way to the hills to the north and south. Thomas barely slowed as the gate opened, and he sailed through, waving to the two security guards with H&K MP5 submachine guns slung over their shoulders. Soon, we crested another hill, and before us was what appeared to be an enormous ranch. There were horses in corrals, cattle roamed, and there were several houses and some large barns. Again, everything was neat, orderly, and well-manicured. A wide canyon stretched beyond.

"Things have certainly changed since I was here," Sam said with awe.

Thomas pulled the Escalade in front of a huge log and stone house. He told us to leave our bags, and they would take care of them. He was going to find Moni.

Sam and I each turned a full circle, taking it all in. Beyond the houses and barns was another wall built of huge hay bales, all covered by silver tarps. Far beyond were the peaks of distant mountain ranges. I wondered what lay between the two.

"Jackson," a female voice called. "I never expected to see you again."

We turned to see an attractive, athletic, native-American woman coming down the steps.

"How are you, Monica?" Sam asked, extending his hand as she approached.

"Right as rain," she replied before eyeing me. "And what shall we call you?" she asked.

"Cody," I said. It wasn't lost on me that she didn't ask my name, just what I should be called.

"Jackson, you said, Monica. I haven't been called that in years."

"I remember a young girl named Monica running around here trying to be a grown-up. You have now succeeded in that endeavor."

I spent some time studying Monica. I had worked with some formidable women in the Marines. They were smart, strong, and fearless. Monica also appeared to be all three.

She wore black BDUs trousers with black boots and a tight-fitting tan T-shirt. Her waist was narrow but not too thin. At probably 5'10", her shoulders were broad, and her biceps marked someone who worked out to build strength, not just tone. She reminded me of an Olympic swimmer.

Thomas appeared around the corner, driving an extended four-seater golf cart. He parked beside us.

"Everyone calls me Moni now. Hop in; I'll show you 'round." She turned to Thomas. "Please put their bags in bunkhouse one. Give 'em privacy."

As we started rolling to the north, Sam said, "Sorry to hear about your dad. He was a good man."

"Thanks, Jackson." She replied. "He left quite a legacy. I am the third generation now. Do you know the story?"

"I know some, but I don't remember the details. Cody has no idea where we are or what you do."

She laughed. It was a nice, confident laugh, if there is such a thing.

"Well, let me start in 1933. My grandfather, Joseph Michel, left the poverty of the Flathead reservation about 200 miles north of here and joined the US Army. In 1940, he became a special forces operator. Most know them today as the Green Berets, but that wasn't their designation until the 1950s. He fought in the Pacific theater during World War II, earning several combat medals. Most importantly, he survived. Only twenty percent of his unit made it home. In 1946, he and three friends pooled their money and bought this ranch. It was only average size by Montana standards at about six thousand acres."

I thought about the twenty-four hundred acres Sam owned back home. Six thousand sounded big to me.

"They moved in and brought women from the reservation to be their wives. No dating, no ceremonies. The land came with about forty cows and a couple of bulls. Within three years, they were broke. But Joseph wouldn't give up. He managed to buy out the other three one by one until he owned it all. He named the ranch Qeyqeysi after one of our ancestors, a Flathead tribal leader. My uncle, Ben, was born in '50. Ray in '53, and my father Phillip came along in '58.

"Then, in '51, Joseph got lucky, at least in my opinion. He reportedly said the 'great spirits rewarded him.' A friend from the Army was working for the Pinkerton National Detective Agency, and he and Joseph ran into each other one day in Butte. The friend, I never knew his name, was traveling from San Fransisco to St. Louis and looking for a better way to train new agents to be bodyguards and security personnel. Hollywood was booming, and the stars needed to look important, so they all hired a security force. As the discussion dragged on, Joseph said he had the land and training to prepare these men for the job. He would only charge twenty dollars per person a day. That would include their training, room, board, and ammunition."

"The friend took the plan to his boss, and it was approved. Pinkerton would pay two hundred dollars daily for ten men to get trained. Each session would last two weeks, and then ten more men would come."

Moni had stopped at the north end of the canyon near a metal building, maybe thirty by fifty feet in size. It was tan, with a green roof, but we didn't get out or interrupt. I was fascinated by the story.

Moni continued. "Joseph called everyone he knew and begged them to come to the ranch on the promise of six dollars a week. Three agreed. Standing Bear, whom everyone called Gent, was a former Navy Master-at-Arms, so he had some knowledge to share. The others knew nothing about training people as security guards. Joseph and Gent put a plan together to do the training. The other two became the cook and handyman. In only three weeks, they built a bunkhouse for twelve men. It had a kitchen and classroom as well. It stood until two years ago when we tore it down to make room for this new armory." She pointed toward the building before us.

"Joseph ran that school only training Pinkerton agents for six years. The school was open from early May until the end of September, and the numbers grew, and the rates went up yearly. By the late 1950s, he profited almost $25 thousand a year, which was huge money. He bought more land and expanded his operation. The business continued to grow. Land in this part of Montana was cheap then. It's not so cheap today, but we have continued to expand. Qeyqeysi is now almost 87 square miles, over 55,000 acres. We use about 12,000 acres as a training ground. The rest is buffer land. We own from the road back through and over this canyon. No one can see what happens here without trespassing."

I looked around at the land and imagined what it would have looked like sixty-five years earlier. It was likely just a few rough shacks and some dirt roads. Today, it looked like a resort with paved roads and modern ranch—and farm-looking buildings.

"As I mentioned, this building set away from everything is the armory. Inside, we have over 400 different weapons and multiples of most. Ammo for all. It is staffed from 6 a.m. to 6 p.m. Check out what you need and return it, unloaded, each day. We will handle the cleaning and any repairs overnight. On the other side is a smaller building where you will find tech equipment. We have all the most common communications equipment for you to practice with, but not much current-generation government-issued stuff. They don't share that with us. Open six-to-six like the armory."

The cart began rolling to the east around the building. I could see the tech building; it was just a smaller version of the armory. We continued past two barns.

"These barns are simply for equipment," Moni said, pointing to the southeast. "Nothing to see here unless you decide you want to cut some alfalfa. We grow about two thousand acres of alfalfa and grass to feed a few horses and cows over the winter. We also use the extra bales to create blinds like these."

She pointed at the alfalfa wall. "We don't have many people on the property who are not employees or guests. For example, we typically handle our deliveries to the ranch. All food, ammunition, and other equipment we order goes to a warehouse in Butte, and we make a run once or twice a day to pick everything up. But during the late fall and early spring, we sometimes need to do construction, and for a lot of the work, like pouring concrete and erecting these steel structures, we bring in outside contractors. The hay-bale wall prevents them from seeing what is beyond. To these construction workers, it is just a Montana ranch, and the bales are waiting to be used. All the action takes place on the other side of the wall."

We continued south along the wall.

"By the mid-sixties, it was not unusual to have sixty people on property going through some type of training. The full-time staff was up to about 20, and prices had risen. The Treasury Department sent secret service agents to train here for a month. Arab sheiks were sending their bodyguards. Companies like IBM and Boeing were sending security personnel. Qeyqeysi Ranch and the services grew. The daily rate was up to about two-fifty per person a day. Joseph used the money to build more bunkhouses and expand the facilities.

"In 1968, Ben was drafted and sent to Vietnam; he never came home. Ray missed the draft and the war. Phillip, my father, served and came home. I was born in '77. Joseph died, and Ray took over here in seventy-three, but he was not the best businessman. He also had a serious drug problem. He died in '89, and the Qeyqeysi Ranch was pretty much out of business. Dad took over and started building it back. He did well. I hope I can continue the tradition."

She stopped behind the stone and log house where we met her.

"Ray built this building in the early eighties. It houses our offices, and I live here."

Sam asked, "How many do you employ these days?"

"At this location and this time of year, about sixty, but only thirty-five or so stick with us all year. Many companies bring their own training staff. Like you, they don't need us for instruction; they simply need the space and facilities."

"You have other locations?" I asked.

"We have other businesses and employ about two hundred and seventy total," Moni replied. "Over the last fifteen or so years, many companies stopped hiring internal security personnel. They preferred to lease the personnel because the liability can be so high. Some companies that once sent employees here for training started asking us to lease security teams to them, so we do. That was my first real job here, recruiting former military and law enforcement personnel to work on personal protection and building security teams. Nine-eleven increased the demand. We train them and assign them to companies and people in about a dozen countries. Sorry, I can't share which companies. I think you would be impressed."

I felt sure I would be.

We continued to another metal building. Again, with tan sides and a green roof. I guessed it to be at least two hundred feet long. If I were back in Kentucky, I would have assumed it was a chicken farm.

"This is the main dormitory," Moni continued with the tour, "but it isn't a typical ranch bunkhouse on the inside. We have a restaurant open from four a.m. to ten p.m. A small bar is open from four p.m. until ten. This is where you will eat, but room service to your bunkhouse is available if you want to eat there. This building has sixty sleeping quarters with private baths and a dozen meeting spaces that seat from six to thirty-six. There is also a reference library with maps, military strategy books, weapons manuals, and other similar items. We have a slightly smaller dorm without a restaurant and bar behind it. It has forty-two rooms and a gym. Of course, the gym is also available to you."

She continued south toward what appeared to be a barn, but it was in excellent shape.

"There's to be a lot of traffic here these days. Carts and side-by-side vehicles are everywhere." Sam stated.

"We are close to maxed out right now. I worked you in because Manning has been sending people to us since '91. You were one of the first he brought here," she said, nodding toward Sam. "As of this morning, we had ninety-three guests on the property."

As we arrived at the barn, Moni turned to Sam.

"Jackson, you should recognize this."

"This is where I stayed the last time I was here."

"It is now staff quarters. It's not as nice as the dorms, but far better than a hotel. They also have a restaurant and gym."

As we continued toward the canyon's south wall, three cabin-style structures, which Moni called bunkhouses, could be seen. Each had the same green metal roof, but one was tan, one was green, and one was dark brown on the sides. Moni pointed to the tan one.

"This will be your home for the next two weeks," Moni said as we stepped from the cart. "Inside, you have a small kitchen with a coffee maker, two bedrooms, a den with satellite television, and a meeting room stocked with a laptop, Internet, projector, whiteboards, notebooks, etc. The golf cart plugged in by the door is yours to use, number 23. Try not to jump in someone else's when you are out and about; they all look alike."

There were two additional smaller doors about the size of a window beside the door. Moni opened them. The space was about 18 inches deep.

"Housekeeping does not have a key and will not enter your bunkhouse. One of our senior staffers will let them in to clean after you are long gone. If you have dirty towels or sheets, put them in here. Same for your dishes if you get room service.

Someone will check this closet each day and replace whatever is dirty. If you need laundry service for your clothes, each bedroom has a couple of laundry bags with a bunkhouse label. Just put your clothes in a bag and put the bag here. Those clothes will come back clean and folded in about six hours or overnight."

"Cody, Jackson knows this, but I need to make it clear to you. We are your hosts, but we have no interest in knowing what you are doing here." She passed each of us a key. "Always lock up. The facilities and common areas are available for your use. You will meet others who are here for a variety of reasons. Please don't ask them probing questions. If they give you a name, it won't be their real name. It is just something to call them. No one on this property knows your real name, including me. We only have a problem when someone thinks another guest is getting too nosy. Do your thing, stay out of everyone else's way, and all will be good."

"Understood," I replied.

"Your bags are inside. Let me know if you need anything. There is a private phone system with phones in every building. Dial zero for the operator, and she will connect you. Each venue has radios set on the proper channel for emergencies. Jackson knows the drill."

"Is everything still in the same place?" Sam asked.

"Expanded since you were here, but yes, everything is still in the same place. We also have a road course now for defensive and evasive driving if you need it, but we have a school going on now, so availability is limited. We have a couple of armored and stock Suburbans, plus assorted Cadillac, Mercedes, and Lincoln limousines you can use, along with instructors. It is along the south side of the canyon, down in a depression. There are signs."

Jumping back in the cart, Moni waived as she turned toward the log and stone building.

I looked at Sam and asked, "Ninety-three guests at what rate? It has to cost a fortune to run this place."

Sam replied, "The last I heard, it was twenty-five hundred a day, all-inclusive, but that was several years ago."

I did some quick math. "So, an average of over a million a week in revenue and open thirty-five weeks a year?"

"Yep, sounds about right," Sam said. "Let's get settled and grab some dinner. We will start early tomorrow."

Chapter 14

Sam and I unpacked and settled into the bunkhouse, which, in today's terminology, would more accurately be described simply as a barndominium.

Later, Sam called and booked us into the pistol range at fifteen hundred hours each day for the next two weeks. He also arranged time in the Urban Warfare Tactical Training Center, a.k.a. the 'Shoot House' at sixteen hundred hours. Finally, he asked that breakfast be delivered at seven each morning.

That evening, after going to the restaurant for a steak dinner, we gathered the cryptic notes we had written over the past few days, and I created a checklist on the whiteboard. It was a long list, with major items and, in most cases, detailed sub-items that needed to be worked out. We added more items to the list as Sam explained his rough idea in more detail.

"We need to enter the country in a private jet," he said. "We should see about booking the Rolle-owned jet that flew you home from Pendleton. I told Vasquez that Rolle was my shell company, and he may have passed those details on to Weber. I also told him that by owning a semi-legit import-export company, I could more easily move products, be they legitimate or otherwise. We won't have to change the tail number if we can get that jet. If they check it, ownership will come back to Rolle."

"Will Manning go for that?" I asked.

"We will find out," Sam said, typing into the laptop. "Start sending him the items we may need. If there is something he can't get, we will plan around it as best we can. What else?"

"If we can't get that jet?" I asked. "What would our contingency plan be?"

"We'll have Rolle Imports book through NetJets. It's not a perfect solution, but that will allow the paperwork to back our cover."

I made a note.

We had no idea what we would face from customs when we landed in Venezuela. Would they simply see the small jet, assume we were big-shot businessmen, and stamp our passports? Or would they search everything and everyone? Again, I thought back to the novels I read growing up. No one ever seemed to have to face a customs or border control agent. As a Marine, it didn't matter. As a citizen, it was an obstacle we would have to overcome.

"Let's just assume we will have to source any weapons, radios, tactical clothing—everything but our everyday clothing—in-country," Sam said.

We had a short list, which I wrote on the board. We kept adding to it until Sam suggested we head to bed.

The following morning, there was a knock on the door, and a staffer delivered our breakfast right on time. As I placed the food on the table, another employee arrived, driving a Polaris side-by-side. Two plastic Pelican brand tactical boxes were in the back. The driver asked for Cody.

"That's me," I said.

"I was told to deliver this and to make sure it got inside," the driver said.

I grabbed one of the boxes, and the driver grabbed the other. I put mine in the meeting space. The driver stopped at the door and set the box just inside the threshold. I thanked him, and he went on his way.

After breakfast, we opened the containers. Inside the first were three three-ring binders, three envelopes with documents, and assorted books and other documents that didn't seem relevant. A note on top said. 'Cody, learn this; your life depends on it.' Well, that was motivational.

I opened the first three-ring binder and found my picture, the one after the haircut. It said that the person in the photo was James Thames, then in parenthesis, it added, 'pronounced Timms, as the British do.' My name in Venezuela would be James Thames.

Sam looked over my shoulder as I opened the second binder. There was my Marine ID photo from four or five years back, with my head almost shaved and the name William Thomas. The third binder was for Jonathan Ryan. That photo was the first we took in New York before the haircut and beard trim.

"There are about fifty pages – front and back – in each of those binders," Sam said. "You have to know James Thames front to back. You can learn the other two later. Those books tell you where you were born, when you were born, and three generations of your family tree. They have your banking information, where you went to high school, the first and subsequent girls you dated, when you lost your virginity, to whom, and where. Your actual blood type, the schools you attended, a fake but documented social security number, and your current and past address are all there. You must know everything inside and out. By next week, I will start quizzing you. Bring the binders and envelopes and come with me."

We walked to the meeting space, and Sam opened the laptop. It was connected to the Internet using Wi-Fi, which was high-tech in 2008.

Sam referred to one of the binders, then opened a Google screen and typed 'Jonathan Ryan, Knoxville Tennessee, class of 2000.'

There were several hits. Manning's resources were fast.

He clicked the first, a birth announcement regarding Jonathan Michael Ryan from the Knoxville Sentinel in 1984.

I began to read,

Jonathan Michael Ryan was born September 12, 1984, to Eric Edwards Ryan and Kana Lynn (Bevan) Ryan. Jonathan weighed in at seven pounds and ....

He closed the window and clicked another called 'yearbooks.com.'

He chose 1999, then junior class, and scrolled down to Jonathan "Jon" Ryan. Another click and a photo that wasn't me but looked a lot like me in 1999 appeared, along with a listing of clubs and other extracurricular activities in which I was involved.

Sam looked at me. "In today's world, there are no secrets, and there are no systems Manning's resources can't penetrate. If you are Jonathan Ryan or James Thames and you are asked a question that seems probing, know that it is, and know that it was asked for a reason. But also know that it will check out if you answer based on what is in those binders."

I shook my head. "Is there anything that we can believe anymore?"

Sam paused momentarily, then said, "You can believe in me, Lucy, and Lauren. You truly know all three of us. Beyond that, trust nothing. Never trust the news, never trust the government."

"But don't we work for the government?" I asked,

"We do, I suppose, but we take assignments that at least seem to fit our sense of duty. Plus, the government will be like Peter if we get caught. They will deny us." Sam said, then added, "One more story."

"Sometime early last year, I went on an assignment that sanctioned the assassination of an industrial magnate, a pharmaceutical company CEO. During the mission briefing, I was told that the company, on the instruction of this CEO, was developing biological weapons. Posing as an importer interested in expanding my operation into experimental pharmaceuticals, I got close to him. Before long, I learned, with high confidence, that he was working on vaccines for common viruses, like rhinoviruses, using a variation on a technology called MRNA. What our intelligence saw as a threat may help save lives one day. I aborted the mission and returned home."

"So basically, trust no one?" I said.

"What I am saying is 'trust yourself.' Many people with the best intentions are led down the wrong path by bad intelligence. That doesn't mean they are bad people and shouldn't be trusted. Just never blindly trust what you are told."

I nodded. Lesson learned.

∞

We spent the morning plotting and planning. Sam and I constantly sent messages to Manning regarding resources – use of the Rolle-owned jet was approved, by the way – and as Manning answered, we continued to tweak the plan outline.

Sam said several times, "We can't overthink this. If we try to cover every eventuality, we will get so bogged down in the details that we will never make any real progress."

I understood. In Afghanistan, the best plans rarely survived first contact. "We need an approach more than we need a plan," I said.

"Yep."

After lunch, Sam and I took the golf cart beyond the wall so he could show me around. To the north was another wall of hay; hidden behind it, down in a small valley, was what appeared to be a small town.

"The Shoot House," Sam said. I could hear rapid gunfire below.

"It's more elaborate than what we trained on in the Corps," I replied.

"Unless something has changed, the walls are thin plywood, and rounds go through them like paper. We will be the only ones there during our slot. We will start slowly and work out some signals for clearing a building in case it comes to that. I know you learned it from the same place I did. I imagine the tactics and signals are the same, but if there is something new, you can teach me that. I don't care whose tactics we use; I just want us both on the same page."

Sam continued, "There is a range master somewhere down there. He is likely following behind the team currently using the facility. He can set and trigger pop-up targets. Bad guys, hostages, and friendlies are mixed in. You know the drill."

I did know the drill.

We continued probably a mile down the road from there, driving almost due east into the canyon. Ahead, the road forked, and a sign directed us left to the 'Sniper Range.' To the right was 'SMall Arms Range and Training.' The capital letters spelled SMART. Clever. Sam turned left and continued the tour.

"How much experience do you have with a sniper rifle?" he asked.

"I qualified expert marksman," I replied, "but I haven't practiced, so I won't be sharp. I never shot long-range in Afghanistan. I've only shot over 50 yards once since I got back to the States. Let's just say I am probably rusty."

"We need to do two things. First, choose a rifle. It's much better to shoot with the same weapon and caliber every time. It would be best with the same rifle every time, but that is impossible in our line of work."

"I prefer the Barrett M82. That is the Marine choice and what I trained on. Plus, the .50 BMG ammo is relatively easy to find. Just expensive."

Sam laughed. "Yep, at four bucks a pop, it isn't for the everyday shooter."

When we arrived at the sniper range, it was empty except for a staffer sitting in a small shack. He greeted us.

"Hello sir, I am called Bundy, he said with an Aussie accent. What brings you to my little corner of Qeyqeysi today?"

"I'm Cody. Jackson and I will be here for a couple of weeks. How hard will it be to get some range time?"

"No problem this week," he said. "Almost everyone on site is working in the Shoot House. I was told last night they are destroying it faster than the carpenters can put up new walls."

I deferred to Sam.

"We have the pistol range and shoot house booked. Can you put us down for seventeen hundred hours for the next week?" he asked. "We will start there with the sun behind us. Maybe we will come early next week and shoot into the sunrise."

Bundy looked at a computer screen and typed.

"Cody and Jackson at the sniper range from seventeen hundred until we close her down. I have you in the system. Any particular weapon of choice? If the armory has it, I can secure the rifle and ammo for you."

I asked if he could have a Barrett M82 available.

"Murfreesboro, Tennessee's finest firearm," he said. "I keep two here on site. I won't even have to go to the armory for that. See you in about three hours."

From there, we continued to the SMART range. Honestly, it was set up much like the one Sam and I used back in Kentucky, but everything was nicer. They also had huge alfalfa bales, dividing the space into six safe shooting zones.

We continued south and to the top of a ridge. Before us, we could see what looked like a NASCAR road track. Two black Chevrolet Suburban SUVs were zipping around the track. The one in the lead couldn't shake the trail vehicle. I assume that was the goal. We were not here to learn to drive, so Sam turned and headed back to the bunkhouse.

"We have an hour. Let's get dressed, then shoot for a while. Tomorrow, we will resume running before breakfast. And maybe we can hit the gym after dinner each night."

Sam reminded me of my Parris Island DI. He was merciless.

∞

When we returned to the bunkhouse, we opened the second Pelican box. It contained radios with throat mics, night vision goggles, and many other toys like listening devices, trackers, and a pair of Iridium satellite phones. There was also an

143

encrypted Blackberry that could be used for secure communications. It matched Sam's and had two numbers preprogrammed. One was listed as "Manning," and the other said "Jackson."

I was familiar with most of the electronics, but some were new to me.

"These are representative of what Manning can usually line up for us, but I have been thinking that we might be able to smuggle this in. The military and most government agencies have equipment caches spread all over the world. Local resources keep them fresh and update them as items are smuggled in," Sam told me.

Sam picked up the Blackberry phone, found its number, and entered it into his phone as a shortcut under the name Cody.

Also in the case was information about two suspected arms traffickers in Venezuela.

The first was named Victor Perez Pancheo, a local. The second was Artura Simonyan, an Armenian.

Pancheo was last thought to live somewhere near Maracaibo. His age was estimated at 80, and he didn't seem to be active.

Simonyan was thought to be younger, maybe 55, and living in Caracas, which was convenient. Manning's source reported that he commonly jetted from Caracas to Miami, where he would party, snort cocaine, and hire local escorts to spend the evening in his suite on Miami Beach. He also seemed to make regular trips to Moscow. No one was sure what he did there, but dealers have to buy from somewhere.

I tacked the information sheets to the bulletin board.

We changed and took the cart to the armory, where we checked out two H&K VP9 handguns and a couple of shoulder holsters. From there, it was to the range where we familiarized ourselves with the feel of the weapon.

At four, we moved to the Shoot House. We discovered that tactics, terminology, and signals had changed little between Sam's initial and my recent Marine training.

We took turns, day to day, at the sniper range. Each day, one person would act as a sniper and the other as a spotter. The .50-caliber Barrett was amazingly accurate to a thousand yards. That was far enough. We were not Chris Kyle.

On our sixth day in Montana, we received word from Manning that he had a source for handguns and a sniper rifle if needed. The H&K pistols were available, but the Barrett was not. He said he could arrange an Arctic Warfare Magnum (AWM) from Accuracy International chambered for the .300 Winchester Magnum cartridge. Neither of us had ever shot that particular rifle, which was surprising given its popularity in Europe. Luckily, the Qeyqeysi armory had one.

Manning also filled us in on other equipment that could be made available, including radios, hand-held GPS units, and most of the same electronics he had already supplied us with.

The second week, Sam started calling me James and asking me questions. "So, James, where are you from?" he would say. "Where did you go to school? Tell me about that Ellen-Ann chick from high school." On and on he would go, every waking hour. I answered right most of the time. By the end, I was tired of learning about James, but I knew the importance of the exercise.

Each day was a replica of the last for the final ten or so days. We continued to develop our operational outline. We continued to exercise each day. We also shot thousands of rounds at SMART and the Shoot House. After 14 days, we were very comfortable with each other.

Since Venezuela was in my future, I found an online Spanish refresher course. I had the opportunity to practice my Spanish in the Corps with some fellow Marines, but it had been a long time since I studied the language. Thankfully, what Lucy and I learned came back to me quickly. I wasn't proficient, but I was functional.

In the end, we knew how we wanted everything to go, and we had some contingencies. Still, as we started to get two or more degrees of separation from the original operational outline, we would write "JWI" on the whiteboard. That was our code for "just wing it."

We were headed to Venezuela but had to make two stops along the way.

Chapter 15

The air was crisp and cool, and the sky was a cloudless blue on the morning of October 12, 2008, when we loaded up in a Suburban. This is why they call Montana "Big Sky Country." Moni had offered to drive us to the airport. We had not seen her since our arrival. We removed all documents from the bunkhouse and placed them in the two Pelican cases, along with the equipment Manning had provided us. One case held things, like paperwork, that we could not take to Venezuela. The other contained some electronics we believed we could get into the country. We had a plan for that.

We erased and used alcohol on the whiteboard to remove any trace of what had been documented there. We scoured the building for any other trace of our presence, and Sam and I even wiped down the smooth surfaces that would hold fingerprints. No one knew why we were there or what we were doing, and those on the property didn't even know who we were. But we did it anyway.

With our luggage loaded and Moni behind the wheel, Sam jumped into the back seat, and I slid into the shotgun position. I remember looking around. At a little over 4,000 feet above sea level, with rocky soil and little rain, the area was primarily a desert, but plant and animal life still thrived. It was beautiful.

Moni spoke for the first time when we exited the ranch and turned south.

"Cody, I hope your visit was productive."

"Very," I replied. "You have an incredible facility."

"Thanks. The staff works hard to make sure our guests find it worthwhile."

"May I ask a question?" I said.

"Ask anything you want. But I may not answer."

"There are many signs around the facility reminding people not to talk about the ranch, what goes on, who was there, or what facilities are available. I even searched the Internet trying to find you. The only reference I found was on Wikipedia, which listed Qeyqeysi Ranch as a working cattle farm. So, my question is this: If no one can talk about it, how do people know it is available to them?"

"That, Cody, is the second most asked question I hear. The answer is simple. When Ben was in charge, he hired a sales team. He wanted to see four or five hundred people running around the canyon. Dad and others told him it was a bad idea, but he sent them out anyway. We ended up with mafia gunmen, radical militia groups, and likely foreign terrorists, though I can't confirm that. Let's just say the quality of our guests went down, and they were not very good about paying their tab at the end."

"Today, we are very selective. That was part of the restoration Martin brought to the table. People sometimes share what we do with people they know, but we don't want that. Since I don't know our guests' names, I can't ask them to sign a non-disclosure agreement. We do have two people, people we trust, who meet with Fortune 100 corporations, government agencies, and security companies, and they share what we do. If there is interest, we will show them photographs of the facilities and talk about pricing and things like that. But we never tell them where we are until we have a deal."

"There was a time," she continued. "That we picked people up at the airport or met them at a parking lot in Bozeman or Butte in a panel van so they couldn't see where we took them. We stopped that practice under Ben in the mid-80s. Now, anyone can go to Google Earth and search a one-hour radius around Bozeman and find the ranch if they know what to look for, so trying to hide the exact location from guests is pointless. It looked like any other ranch from the air until we put in the driving course."

"Any more expansion plans?" Sam asked. "You seem to be doing well."

"We have two things we may do. There was one week that we had over 100 guests. That is enough. Too many, really, unless we increase staff size, so I am not interested in expanding the tactical part of the facility."

"Last year, we got a couple of proposals to build a 7,500-foot runway and six hangers about five miles down the road. This is past the entrance to Qeyqeysi. We would have to buy the land, but it is for sale. The total project would be about 16 million dollars. I am struggling to see a return on that investment."

"The other item I am considering is buying land closer to Bozeman and building a training facility for women executives. High-paid women are targets. They need to know how to defend themselves, escape, and evade. It would be a small facility, probably a two-to-three-million-dollar investment. That may happen soon. Let me know if you ever want a job doing training or security work. I am always looking for good people."

We continued to chat, and occasionally, Moni would point out a landmark and share her knowledge. She was an impressive woman and leader. I wanted to ask more questions but felt I would be probing. One question, however, had to be asked.

"Moni, you said that my question was the second most asked. May I ask what the most asked question is?"

She grinned. "The most asked question is, 'Are you single?'"

I didn't say anything, but it was a good question, and I imagined she heard it often.

∞

We unloaded at the Jet Aviation FBO, said our goodbyes, and took a cart with our suitcases and Pelican cases to the G150 I had first flown on three weeks before. The captain helped us load our bags and equipment and then ushered us aboard.

We had a different pilot this time. He was a very fit black man with a shaved head. He introduced himself as Captain Cecil Abercrombie but said everyone called him Crumby, just Crumby. No 'captain' needed. He didn't fit my mental image of someone named Cecil, or Abercrombie, or Crumby, for that matter.

"Our flight to Arlington is normally a little over four hours," the captain said. "But we should have a sixty-knot tailwind most of the way, so let's guess twenty minutes under that. We fought the headwind all the way here. Mr. Manning said he would have a ride waiting for you at Reagan National."

A woman of about 40, only five feet two inches tall at most, with a dark complexion and closely cropped dark black hair, stepped through the boarding door and bounded down the five steps.

"Lieutenant Colonel Candice Cruz," she said with a slight accent that I couldn't exactly place. "United States Air Force retired. Nice to meet you."

"I also understand," the pilot added, "that Cruz and I are with you for the next three days to three months. Whatever you need. She is your co-captain and is fully trained and certified to pilot the G150. We will be ready whenever you need us. May I add our cell numbers to your Blackberry?"

Sam handed his phone over and nodded for me to do the same.

"Just call and give one of us a location and a time. Every time we land, we refuel immediately. You won't have to wait on us."

"Thanks, Crumby. We will try not to surprise you."

∞

The surprise was waiting for us when we landed. As the Gulfstream pulled into its designated parking area, a Ford Crown Victoria with government plates and two Cadillac Escalade SUVs pulled up beside the boarding door. Crumby, the pilot, spoke over the PA system.

"Gentlemen, I have been told that you are to remain aboard, and the copilot and I are to exit the aircraft." They completed the shutdown procedures and appeared from the cockpit.

While lowering the boarding door, Cruz said, "Let me know when you wrap up, and we will come back, lock everything down, and prepare for the next leg."

It quickly began to get stuffy on the plane. It was still warm in Washington. Sam and I lowered the window shades on the west side to keep the sun out.

When the pilots disappeared into a nearby hanger, both back doors on the Ford opened. Manning emerged from the passenger side, and Senator Parker Landry of Indiana, the chairman of the Senate Intelligence Committee, climbed from the driver side.

I was very familiar with Landry. He was one of those senators who would run over his mother to get in front of a camera, so it was impossible to watch the news and not know him.

Over the years, Landry's slight stature and ill-fitting suits had earned the nickname Laundry. It was fitting. Landry's suit coat was at least two sizes too big to accommodate his belly, and his pant cuffs dragged the ground. It was hard to believe he was one of the more powerful men in Washington. He was also considered one of the most intelligent people in Washington. Having grown up in Montgomery, Alabama, his heavy southern drawl caused many not to take him seriously, but armed with a law degree from The University of Virginia, he moved to Indianapolis and became a rising legal star. After one term in the state legislature, Landry set his sites on Washington and was elected to Congress. Then, after twelve years, he ran for senate. He had just been re-elected for his fourth term and had served as the chair of the Senate Intelligence Committee for nine years. Many wanted to see him on the ticket for President, but he was neither conservative enough for the Republican Party nor liberal enough for the Democrat Party. He caucused with the Republicans because they were more suited to his strong border and military stance. Where he disagreed with them was on the social side. He was, to some degree, a man without a party.

The two of them climbed the stairs. Sam and I took the sofa seats and motioned the two guests to the plush chairs across the way.

Sam extended his hand, "Senator, it is a surprise to see you here. I am Jackson; this is Cody." Sam gestured my way.

The senator shook both offered hands and settled into a seat. He wasted no time.

"Gentlemen, I want to share some information with you before you leave." His southern accent seemed even stronger in person. "I have some knowledge that is important to your mission. An overview of your operation made its way to my office – don't ask where I got it – and it became apparent that you are somewhat in the dark about some things on which I can shine a little light. I contacted Manning and asked for a face-to-face conversation with him. As chair of the intelligence committee, I have tried to avoid that. When he told me you would be in D.C. today for a final briefing, I thought it would be best to share this with you directly."

Neither Sam nor I said anything.

"Yes, thank you for that, senator," Manning said. He seemed nervous.

"Another official agency sent three operatives into Venezuela about 18 months ago. Their goal was to infiltrate the operations of a couple of arms dealers. It seems you know of those two men, but neither is your target. We didn't know about Finn Weber until someone's report from Argentina brought him to our attention."

He looked at Sam when he said this.

"Are we stepping on an ongoing operation?" I asked, knowing that could cause problems for both parties.

"I am afraid not. One of the three men was trying to work his way into the Pancheo operation. Another was trying to get in with the Armenian cartel, Simonyan, I think it is. The last was digging into arms traffic in and out of Venezuela in general. All were American citizens, but each was only one generation removed from Venezuela. They were all experienced, they all looked and spoke like natives when they needed to, and they all stopped reporting to their handler during the same week."

He paused. "It gets even stranger. None knew the other two were even in the country or that another person was on a similar mission. In total, only two people at the head of the agency knew the big picture. Different teams were handling each operative, each unaware of the other."

"So, how do three separate operations get blown at once?" Sam asked. "The odds seem impossibly low to me."

"I would have a better chance hitting the lottery," Landry said. "Again, these were experienced professionals with professional handlers. If it had not happened, I would have said impossible."

"And no one knows what happened to any of them?" I asked.

"Nothing. There have been no communications, sightings, bodies, ransom requests, or acknowledgments from the two camps."

I looked at Sam. He looked at me.

"What does this mean for our mission," Sam asked.

"Jackson," Landry said. "I don't like sending people out without all available information. I was on the intelligence committee for several years before I took over as chair. My predecessor would have said, 'screw 'em; they don't need to know.' I don't work that way. You are being entrusted with an off-the-books mission. If we can trust you with that, we can trust you with the truth."

Sam spoke immediately. "I appreciate that, Senator. I really do. If you know what we are about to undertake, you know we are taking a different approach. There will be no covert infiltration. We are going to go into the country as big-dollar buyers. We are going to be loud; we are going to be visible. We aren't going to Finn Weber; we will make Finn Weber come to us. So, while that knowledge is a big help, I ask you this. Does it change our mission or approach in any way?"

"It might be important because you may learn of their fate along the way. I would like to know what happened to these men. I am certain their families would like to know. If I had not told you, you might have learned what happened to them, but without a point of reference, the information wouldn't have meant anything."

Sam and I both nodded.

"Jackson, I have followed your work over the years. I appreciate everything you have done."

"I am starting to feel like ACXN may not be as independent as we were led to believe," Sam said while looking at Manning. His voice was accusatory.

Manning never said anything, but Landry did.

"When I became chair, I knew there was a shadow asset, very black, very secret, that could get things done, but I knew nothing other than a phone number I could call.

"After nine-eleven, I made it a point to find out more, and I pushed Manning, and only Manning, to step at least one foot into the light. One of my predecessors worked to create ACXN. The team is an asset to the country we all try to protect. I needed to know more and use the team more effectively. So that is what I have done."

With that, he stood and walked to the door.

"Best of luck, gentlemen. We had seventeen soldiers die in Afghanistan last week. I watched the transport bring them home to Andrews AFB early this morning—seventeen grieving families. About half the arms that get into Afghanistan are being trafficked through Venezuela. Help us stop it."

With that, he was gone.

Manning keyed his phone and ordered his driver to pick us up.

Sam and I needed to talk.

∞

Nothing was said in the car. We reached a strip mall near Potomac Yard in Virginia fifteen minutes later. Continuing through the parking lot, we passed a dry cleaner, a pizza and beer joint, a cosmetics store, two clothing stores, a travel agency, and a tobacco and smoke shop.

Circling to the rear, we stopped at a door labeled "Truly's Travels." The three of us exited, and Manning used a four-digit combination, then a key, then two more digits, to open the door. Inside was a single room. A sink, a small refrigerator, and a coffee pot were in one corner. In the opposite corner, there was a small half bath. A table and eight chairs rounded out the furnishings of the sixteen-by-twenty-foot space. Nothing was on the walls, but three heavy-duty Pelican shipping cases were lined up beside the small kitchenette. One door provided access to the front of the building.

"A few years ago, another federal agency arranged this space for us. Truly Mae Winkler wanted a place to put in her travel agency but couldn't afford the rent, so we helped her out. Rolle Imports rents the entire space. She has the front half, and we use the back half. All Truly Mae knows is that if she ever comes through that door," Manning said, pointing at the lone door in the wall leading to the front half of the store, "It had better be life or death. Building codes required us to put it in just in case of fire. She doesn't know or care who pays the rent. She doesn't know who pays the water or power bills. She never knows when we enter or leave, and she doesn't have the key or the code to the back door. Except for the insulated door, the wall between the front and back is made of concrete block and filled with sand. She will not hear what we say."

"That is probably a good thing," Sam said. "I feel that I... that we have been misled."

"I understand your concern," Manning said while staring at the floor.

"And I feel like we were ambushed," Sam added.

"We were all ambushed!" Manning replied with a passion I had never heard in his voice. "I got a call from the Senator this morning. He said we needed a face-to-face meeting, our first, by the way. I was concerned that our funding had been cut or, even worse, that we had somehow been outed. He just told me the same story he told you. I mentioned that you were coming through town for a final briefing today, and I would pass the information along to you. He insisted that he wanted to tell you personally. Part of ACXN's success has been predicated on separation, on anonymity. I pointed that out and said I would brief you, but he insisted. The separation has been shrinking slowly but surely since nine-eleven. The anonymity broke down today. I apologize; I should never have mentioned you coming to town."

Again, Sam responded before I could. "True, Manning, you should never have allowed that meeting to happen. What kind of deniability, what kind of separation do we have left?"

The room was silent for a few seconds.

"None," I said.

After about thirty seconds, Manning looked up. "If you choose to leave, choose to drop this operation," he paused again, "Hell, if you choose to drop ACXN, I will understand. We are no longer in the position we started in, but I am more exposed than you are."

"Joshua and I are going to take a walk around the block and discuss this development. We will be back."

"You stay here," Manning said. "I am hungry. Do you want me to pick you up anything?

"No." We both replied in unison.

"You go get some food," Sam said. "But we are going for a walk. We will be here when you get back."

With that, Manning turned and left.

I mouthed 'Bugs?' to Sam, and he nodded. We heard the Suburban start and then drive off. Sam and I exited the room and started walking away.

"I don't like this," Sam said.

I agreed and offered, "However, I'm not sure it affects the mission as long as the senator doesn't try to become involved."

We were both quiet for a while, circling the outside of the strip mall parking lot in a clockwise direction. I pointed at Manning and the driver walking into the pizza and beer joint. Sam just nodded.

As we neared completion of the parking lot circuit, Sam spoke again.

"It seems that Senator Landry has been very aware of us for a while, but I can't think of one time that I felt anyone was trying to direct a mission."

I thought about that as we stood by the back door to Truly's Travels.

"I will defer to you on this. If you want to go ahead, I am with you. If you want to return home and tell Manning to kiss your ass, I will be right behind you."

The Suburban rounded the corner and parked beside the door. Manning got out with four pizzas, two six-packs of beer, and a sack of sodas and bottled water.

I said, "I thought we told you we weren't hungry, and neither of us drinks beer."

"You will be hungry before we leave here, assuming you are sticking around. And who said I was sharing the beer with you?"

Manning once again unlocked the room, and the four of us entered. The driver placed the drinks in the refrigerator while Manning spread the pizza on the table. It smelled wonderful, so I grabbed a piece and walked to the fridge for a Diet Coke. Manning asked me to bring him a beer. Eventually, the three of us, minus the driver, settled around the table.

Manning wasted no time.

"Gentlemen, where do we stand?"

This time, I spoke up first.

"Confused is where I stand. I understand how things might have changed slowly over the past eighteen years, and maybe there were never any changes that seemed to warrant a conversation with Sam, kind of like the frog in a pot of water on the stove. Eventually, the frog is cooked, and he never knew the water was getting hotter."

"But when you spoke to me three weeks ago, you acted like you knew nothing about who oversees ACXN. I don't believe that was accurate."

"Remember," Manning replied, "That I told you this whole thing started with a proposal to the Senate Intelligence Committee. I can honestly tell you that until today, that meeting twenty years ago was the only time I had knowingly spoken to any committee member. Now, I guess I know where our missions come from. When I recruited you, Joshua, I swear I did not know for sure."

"But you suspected," I said.

He nodded. "Yes, I suspected."

I again looked at Sam, who had also taken a slice of the pizza.

"One more question," I said, still irritated but calming. "If someone put a gun to the senator's head and asked who Jackson and Cody really are. What would he say?"

"He would say that he does not know. I can't imagine how he would know."

"Let's move forward," Sam said. "We need to be in Miami tonight. But Manning, you better let me know the next time someone turns on the stove and starts boiling water. Am I clear?"

The look on Sam's face was one I had rarely seen.

Manning took a deep breath and again lost the color in his face. It reminded me of the night in the barn.

"Message received, loud and clear," Manning said before draining his second beer.

"Mr. Thames," Sam said, using the alias I would use during the assignment, "Please fill Manning in on our plans."

"I will be happy to, Mr. Walker," I replied, using his fake identity as well.

Part 2

"It is not the critic who counts; not the man who points out how the strong man stumbles or where the doer of deeds could have done them better. The credit belongs to the man who is actually in the arena, whose face is marred by dust and sweat and blood, who strives valiantly... who at best knows in the end the triumph of high achievement, and who at worst, if he fails, at least fails while daring greatly."

~Theodore Roosevelt

Theodore Roosevelt, Jr., the 26th President of the United States, is a hero of mine. I read this quote when I was about fifteen, and it stuck with me.

I will tell you that I have a very low opinion of "Monday Morning Quarterbacks." Those who sit back in the safety of their recliner or office chair and critique the actions of others, others who put their life on the line, and those who face the oncoming bullets and bombs with fear born of the knowledge that each breath may be their last, and courage born of honor and duty to a greater cause.

By contrast, I honor those who join in the real fight, the fight on the front lines, and those who offer true support without judgment of action. Those who know that the past is much easier to see than the future and know that operators often work with limited knowledge, doing their best with only a partial picture of the playing field in their heads.

Sam and I were simply betting, and possibly betting our lives, that Senator Landry was of the latter group. Obviously, he would not be found on the front lines. Still, if he offered his support, protected our relative independence and anonymity, and otherwise stayed out of the way, perhaps we could do some good.

We would see.

Chapter 16

We discussed our outline with Manning for nearly an hour before going to the Suburban to bring in the Pelican cases we had packed in Montana. The driver was sitting inside with the air conditioner running. He didn't get out.

We asked Manning to ship one case – the one with the documents inside – to Kentucky, but he refused.

"We will fly that down later. Shipping isn't secure enough, and I now have a new paranoia."

"Yep, a healthy paranoia keeps people like Joshua and me alive," Sam said. "Embrace it."

Manning placed that Pelican case by the door while Sam and I moved the cases stacked near the kitchenette to the table. One was larger and heavier, much heavier. Manning opened it first. Inside, protected by custom molded foam, was a McIntosh MC1.2kw audio amplifier. My knowledge of high-end audio equipment was limited. Still, I remembered the name and model from the Rolle Imports brochures Manning gave me when traveling from Pendleton to Kentucky.

"This is a perfectly functioning McIntosh unit made here in the States," Manning said. "Rolle imports these to the Bahamas, then distributes them worldwide. It's low volume. They are single-channel amplifiers and are usually sold in pairs. Two of them run about thirty-seven grand. There are not many buyers."

Manning retrieved a toolkit from another case and removed the amp's cover, but he never stopped talking.

"Because of the heat generated by the tubes and power supply, there is some room inside these cases. Room that you can use to hide similar-looking items."

Inside the Pelican case, with the electronic equipment we had used in Montana, was a smaller cardboard box containing the items we wanted to smuggle into Venezuela without raising any red flags. We felt sure that other than getting past a search by the customs authorities, we would be fine, barring arrest. In that case, we would have difficulty explaining what we were doing with items like satellite tracking devices and encrypted tactical radios.

"I don't think anyone will go through the aircraft, luggage, or the cargo hold," Manning said. "But to be safe, let's hide your toys inside these samples. You are exporters looking for wholesalers in Venezuela, and you have samples. No one searching will know what the inside of this equipment is supposed to look like."

It was an idea that Sam and I had floated to Manning while we were in Montana. He embraced it and promised to have some assorted equipment for us. He had come through.

I pulled two small tactical radios from the cardboard box and placed them inside the amplifier case. They wouldn't be hidden, but they looked like they belonged. Two-sided tape held them in place.

Another shipping case contained a pair of Naim Audio reference speakers with a "non-functional model" sticker on them. Each had been modified to allow the back panel to be moved aside. Manning straightened a paperclip and inserted it into a very tiny hole on top. The back popped loose.

"The speaker magnet has been removed, so we don't destroy the electronics."

Sam placed radio earbuds and some other items inside the first speaker. I placed several listening and tracking devices inside the other. We packed it tight with insulation so that it would not rattle if an inspector picked it up.

The final case was the smallest. It looked like it was filled by a pissed-off roadie for a rock band. There were cables, microphones, assorted balanced and unbalanced audio plugs, and other accessories. We threw other items in, and they blended well.

Manning handed us an envelope as we loaded the shipping cases into the Suburban. "You will need to spread some cash. Here are twenty thousand American dollars and three million Venezuelan bolivars for each of you. That's worth about a hundred thousand American dollars. Use it judiciously.

"I also have your visas for Venezuela inside. Each matches the passport information for James Thames and David Walker.

"One final question," I said, facing Manning. I still didn't fully trust him, so I wanted to see his face when he answered. "The pilot and copilot, Abercrombie and Cruz, said they could fly us anywhere at any time. This isn't the same crew that flew the two of us to Kentucky three weeks ago. Are they simply pilots, or might they have another role, like supporting or reporting our activities?"

"They are not the regular pilots; no, they are not in place to spy or report on you. All they are to do is fly. But I requested them because they both have extensive experience flying in combat zones. Crumby – I was told he prefers Crumby – was Air Force, then Air National Guard. He spent the first Gulf War in a fighter jet and the second Gulf War, flying military brass all over Iraq, Kuwait, and the rest of the Middle East. Candice was a Navy pilot before retiring, but I don't know her details. Today, they are part of a pool of pilots who are certified in several aircraft types that the government keeps on retainer. They are not operators; they just hire help. Venezuela is a dangerous place, so I wanted pilots that I knew could handle any pressure that might come along on the ground or in the air."

In my mind, I determined that he was telling the truth before I remembered that deception is a requirement in his role. In short, I still didn't fully trust him.

∞

It was almost midnight before we landed at Miami International. Sam and I had changed into our suits during the flight since we had to look the part of two successful importers-slash-arms dealers. The information said that Simonyan spent much of his time in Miami, but we also knew that the odds of catching him there were minuscule. Still, if word got back to him that we were looking for him, it would put us on his radar, which was the goal.

When Sam and I checked into the Ritz Carlton on Miami Beach as David Walker and James Thames, Sam suddenly went into character.

Just so everyone will understand, Sam can be quite loquacious when he has something to say. The thing is, he doesn't believe in or participate in idle chatter, and he is never loud or over the top. Growing up, and even today, if I ask him a question, he will take all the time needed to answer it fully. But don't expect him to talk just to be talking.

"Hey, I got a buddy, Artura Simonyan; he is supposed to meet us here. Can you ring his room and let him know David and James finally made it? Tell him I said to get his ass down here. We are going out."

The clerk and everyone else in the lobby looked at Sam.

"I am sorry, sir. Can you spell that name for me?"

I spoke up and spelled it.

"I don't show a guest under that name. Could you call his cell?" the clerk, a short and wide woman of probably sixty, said.

"I tried, but he never has the damn ringer on," Sam said. "What good is a phone if you can't hear it ring?"

Sam was using a bit of an accent. Having never been to South Africa, I had no idea if it was accurate, but he had spent a couple of evenings in Montana practicing it. He said it was the same accent he used as David Walker in Argentina. There was a slight Brit or Aussie sound to it—nothing drastic, though.

"Well," I said. "Maybe we beat him in. Can we leave a message for him?"

"We usually make a note on the reservation," the clerk told me. "So that it pops up when the person checks in. The thing is, I don't have a reservation for anyone under that name."

Sam and I looked at each other as if we couldn't figure it out.

"If he isn't here, he must be at another hotel. Maybe he will answer tomorrow." He looked my way. "Let's go get changed and hit some bars. Maybe we'll see the SOB."

As we approached the elevator bank, a concierge introduced himself as Hector. "I will take care of your needs. May I make a reservation for you?"

Sam continued in character. "Probably a little late for a reservation tonight. Might look you up tomorrow," Sam said.

Hector leaned in. "I know Mr. Simonyan but haven't seen him in months. I used to work at Fontainebleau, and he stayed there under that name. About a year ago, the same man started staying here but always reserved his room under a different name. It is the same with the NBA players who come to Miami."

"I never know what Artura is doing," Sam said conspiratorially. "If that is the case, I imagine it is to keep his girlfriends back home in the dark about his girlfriends in Miami."

"Maybe, sir," Hector said a bit more warily. He was beginning to grow suspicious.

Sam pulled a hundred-dollar bill from his pocket and handed it to Hector. The next time you see Mr. Simonyan, tell him that David Walker and his associate James Thames were looking for him."

Hector took the bill and nodded.

Sam and I continued to the elevators and ascended to our connecting suites on the ninth floor. We each opened the connecting door, and Sam waved me into his suite.

"Thoughts?"

"I don't think he is here right now. We knew it was a long shot."

"I agree. I think Hector was fishing for a tip, and he got one. But I also believe he knows him. Hotel personnel at places like this know their guests demand privacy. I guarantee you there are sports figures and movie stars in the bar right now, not that I would recognize any of them, and they often want privacy."

"Next step?" I asked.

"As planned. We make noise for two or three days and kick a few rocks. See if anything emerges."

It was late, and we were both tired, but South Beach was just getting cranked up at 1 a.m.

∞

We hailed a taxi and asked the driver, an older Hispanic man, to take us to the most popular bar on the strip.

He looked us over carefully before responding in heavily accented English. "Sir, do you want to go to the most popular bar on the strip, or shall I take you to one that will let you in?"

I was hurt.

He continued. "The most popular will have a line. Only the famous, or regular big spenders, can get in tonight."

"Take us to the best place a couple of rich but unknown white dudes can get in," Sam said.

"We will go straight there," he replied before hitting the gas and pulling away from the curb.

Sam asked the driver how much it would take to hire him for three hours. The driver explained that it was against company policy not to continue taking radio dispatches. Sam passed a wad of cash, I have no idea how much, over the seat, and we had a driver for the night.

We went from club to club, four total, always flashing cash, buying drinks, tipping doormen, and asking if anyone had seen our friend Artura Simonyan. We learned nothing, but that didn't mean we were not progressing.

When we returned to the Ritz, I walked over to Hector, who was sitting at his desk. He quickly rose, remembering the hundred-dollar tip he had received earlier in the evening, and asked how he could help. Sam and I had discussed that I should be the one to approach him. My age better fits the profile of a South Beach clubgoer than Sam's.

"Hector," I said. "I am disappointed in South Beach."

He looked shocked.

"Why, sir?" he asked. "This is a beautiful and fun place."

"It is no fun if I can't get into the clubs. The best places have two hundred people waiting to get in. Looks like a food line at the Salvation Army. I do not stand in line. How do Mr. Walker and I get in tomorrow?"

"Yes, sir, getting into most clubs is hard unless you arrive early."

"What time is early?"

"No later than eleven p.m. on a weeknight, ten o'clock on weekends. But you will just sit and drink until the music starts around midnight." Hector paused, then continued, "Look, I have friends. Maybe I can help you out. Where do you want to go?"

"You tell me. What is the biggest, hottest club in South Beach? Where might we find our friend if he ever shows up in town?"

"I know where Mr. Simonyan likes to go, but I will have to call in a favor to get you and your friend on the list."

That was my cue. I pulled a wad of $100 bills from my pocket and peeled off five.

Hector's eyes grew big, but he hesitated. I knew the play he was making, so I started to withdraw the money. Suddenly, he reached out and took it.

"I will be here tomorrow starting at 10 p.m. Come see me, and I will set you up."

Sam and I returned to the room and slept. Tomorrow night, we would repeat the show.

∞

I slept until ten a.m., then showered and shaved my itchy neck. I dressed in another suit and walked out into the heat and humidity of southern Florida. I needed different clothes and another haircut.

Just across Highway A1A, I spotted a men's clothing store. I purchased off-white linen slacks, a light coral-colored shirt, and a pair of loafers. My knowledge about what a wealthy international importer would wear in South Beach was non-existent, so I looked around at others in the store and bought what they were wearing.

The store clerk was kind enough to call a salon inside the Lowes Hotel, about two blocks away. They could work me in. I wore the new clothes out of the store and had the clerk place the suit in a zippered bag. From there, I walked to the salon. An hour later, my shorter hair and beard were back to the clean look I first experienced in New York three weeks before.

Sam and I met for lunch at three that afternoon. When I entered the restaurant in the hotel lobby, I realized it had been almost twenty hours since my last meal. I ordered a steak sandwich with fries; Sam chose halibut with grilled vegetables.

Sam mentioned the haircut and said he should "get cleaned up" as well. "Maybe tomorrow if we stay another day." He added.

We looked out over the Atlantic while we waited for our food.

"Go ahead and check in with Manning," Sam instructed.

I used my Blackberry to call the preprogrammed number. When the answering machine picked up, I entered a passcode to listen to messages. There were none. I hung up and dialed back, letting the message play this time. The recording said I had reached Rolle Imports in Savannah. Please leave a message.

"This is James," I said. "It has been hard to get appointments with buyers in Miami, but we'll keep trying. Just call if you need anything."

Manning would understand the message.

After lunch, we agreed to rest during the afternoon and then meet for a late dinner. Hector wasn't working, but the desk clerk recommended a nearby steakhouse. Sam has never turned down a steak, so we made a reservation for 8:30 that night, the first available reservation.

After a nap and dinner, Sam and I changed back into our suits and went down to the lobby and Hector's desk. He stood and grabbed another business card.

"Mr. Thames," he said while shaking my hand. I've got everything worked out. Mr. Walker, you will be pleased." He also shook Sam's hand.

"I have arranged to get you into Mansion, and – he paused as if to build anticipation – Opium Garden. You are on the list for both tonight and tomorrow night." He was literally bouncing, rocking on the balls of his feet. "Your friend typically goes to Opium Garden but sometimes visits Mansion. These are the hottest places in town, but you will get in. Just give your name and my card to the doorman. He will let you in."

I thanked him and passed him another C-note. "One more question. Our friend said he likes strip clubs. Where might we find him?"

By this point, enough cash had changed hands that he didn't care if he violated confidence.

Hector leaned in and whispered. "Mr. Simonyan usually orders a couple of the girls to his room. But if he goes out to a gentlemen's club, he goes to Victoria's Cocktail Lounge, up in Little Haiti. It is small, not the best girls, but that is where he goes. I don't know why."

I peeled off one more bill. "Can you call and get us a Town Car for the evening? Someone who will wait while we party."

"Certainly," he said. "I will have one here in fifteen minutes. It is $75 per hour. Cash."

I again thanked Hector.

Walking to the foyer lobby, Sam and I agreed that Opium Garden was the place we had passed the previous night, where the line was well over one hundred people. Where better to make a splash?... but that would come later. First, we were off to northeast 79th Street in Little Haiti with a single thought in mind. Why would Simonyan go there?

∞

Victoria's Cocktail Lounge simply didn't fit the profile. This was a small, seedy joint. The clubs near Miami Beach were all lit with purple and pink neon. Lights flashed, and the signs danced more than the girls. Often, techno music could be heard as one drove past.

This was different. The lone security light in the parking lot was not working. The globe was broken. It had been shot out. Maybe fifteen cars were in the lot, and unlike South Beach, these were beat-up Chevys and Toyotas. Not the Mercedes, Lamborghini, and Ferrari makes we had seen the previous night.

We asked the driver to wait. He agreed but asked if he could go across the street and park under the lights at a bank. He handed me a card with his number and promised to return as soon as we called. I doubted he would show if things went south.

As we approached the door, three men exited the club. All spoke with a strong dialect, I assumed, Haitian.

As we walked through the single door, the smell of marijuana was overwhelming. It was very dark inside, and the reggae music was loud. The stage was behind the bar, and two girls were dancing, if you could call it dancing, on separate poles. Another one was dancing atop the bar. A man reached up with a bill, and she used her breasts to pull it from his hand.

A mountain of a man met us. He stood at least six-foot-eight and must have weighed three-fifty. Did he have the stamina for a fight? I doubted it, but I also knew it would be a short fight if he got his hands on you. He wore a black suit with a black shirt and no tie and had a metal detector in his hand. A white wire ran from his collar to an earpiece.

"You sure you guys want to come in?" he asked, again with a heavy accent that sounded somewhat French. "Not exactly the place for a couple of white dudes in suits."

Sam nodded. "Hoping to meet a friend."

The Mountain looked skeptical, but he stepped forward. "Arms up, I got to wand you. No guns or knives inside."

Sam and I had already discussed this. We assumed most high-end clubs would have magnetometers for patrons to pass through, so we left our handguns in the room. However, I wouldn't have expected it here.

We raised our arms, and after a cursory search, we were allowed to go forward.

"Three drinks minimum," the Mountain said. "And no touching the girls."

Sam and I sat near the back in a booth. Other than the Mountain, we were the only white faces in the place.

Within seconds, a young Haitian girl, I assume she was of legal age, but she looked about fourteen, approached the table.

"I am Pinky with a Y. What can I get you two pretty boys?" She didn't have the strong accent we had heard from others.

"Looking for a friend, Pinky," Sam replied.

"Well, for ten dollars, I will be your friend for a dance. For twenty-five I will be your friend for three dances. For fifty, we will go in the back, and I will be your friend for as long as it takes." She smiled at Sam and then at me. "How about a hundred, and we can all go to the back."

"Sorry, but not tonight. I am looking to meet a friend I already have," I said, flashing her my biggest and brightest smile. "He isn't as pretty as you, but I still need to talk to him. His name is Artura Simonyan. Do you know him?"

"Until you buy three drinks each, I don't know anything," she said as her smile disappeared.

"Bring us six beers," Sam said, placing three twenties on her tray. She stood, looking at the money, but didn't move.

"That will get you three," she said.

Sam just grinned and pulled another three twenties from his wallet.

She took the money and headed away.

"How many people in here do you think can pay twenty bucks for a beer?" I asked.

"Two," Sam said. "Just two."

About five minutes later, Pinky returned with six warm beers. The bottles weren't even sweating.

"Who did you say your friend is?" Pinky asked.

"Artura Simonyan," I told her.

She turned and headed toward the bar, where she leaned over and whispered to the bartender. He looked at us and then walked to a door beside the stage.

He knocked, and when the door opened, he spoke to someone and then glared at us as he returned behind the bar. I remember noticing that there were now two girls wiggling around on the bar, dancing and dodging beer. I wondered how sanitary that could be, but I don't think anyone else cared.

"We've made contact," Sam said without moving his mouth. "Someone here knows him."

We sat for twenty minutes. Three other girls rotated off the stage and offered various services in return for cash. When they were not on stage, they wore an assortment of bikinis and lingerie. One pulled small bags of heroin from her tiny bikini bottom and offered it to us.

Later, the Mountain came over. "If you gentlemen don't want dances and don't want to tip the girls, we will ask you to move on."

"We're drinking your twenty-dollar beers," I told him. "I could drink faster if they were cold, but hey, what can you expect for twenty dollars, right?" I joked, reaching out and slapping him lightly on the shoulder.

As I expected, he was wearing a holster under the jacket. Good to know.

"Anyway, we're just hoping our friend will show up. You know Artura, don't you?"

The Mountain didn't say anything.

I saw the door beside the stage open about that time, and a woman emerged. She was likely in her early thirties, tall and exotic, and wearing a black cocktail dress. She walked over to the table.

She was stunningly beautiful—certainly not one of the dancers. Her skin was lighter, more Mediterranean. Her hair was dyed a dark auburn, and her eyes were a brilliant blue. The dress and shoes she wore were expensive.

"I am the owner," she said. "You don't seem interested in the girls, and you aren't drinking your beer. Perhaps I can point you to another club just down the street. Maybe you will find those dancers to your taste. They don't like girls either."

I could tell that Sam was watching something behind me. I guessed the Mountain had called in help.

"What I like," I said, "is helpful people. I need to speak with Artura Simonyan; I think you know him. If you will be helpful, we will move along."

She didn't move. She didn't say anything for fifteen seconds.

"Take them out, Jean. I don't want to see them again."

Before 'Jean' could move, Sam's right leg shot out and connected with his left knee, hyperextending it. He howled in pain and rage. As he moved forward, Sam connected a second time with a knuckle punch to his Adam's apple. The Mountain stumbled backward and fell over a table, clutching his throat and trying to protest. No sound emerged.

I turned in the booth and caught a Glock pistol just as it came around the corner. I pushed it higher. Sam was already out of his seat and headed toward the Mountain. As the gun arm rose higher, I delivered three blows to the ribs before bringing the arm down over the back of the booth. I didn't land it perfectly, so I didn't destroy the elbow as I intended. He did, however, drop the weapon. I punched him twice more. The first broke his nose, and the second rendered him unconscious.

I grabbed the Glock from the floor and turned, ready for more. Sam stood over the Mountain, holding a pistol he had taken from the giant. Jean was still clutching his throat, still trying to draw a breath.

Through it all, the woman in the black dress had not moved.

She stared at me. "I don't think you are Artura's friends. I think you want to harm him."

I responded. "We just want to do some business with him. We were hoping to find him in Miami. If he isn't here, we'll make our way to Venezuela. We have a jet waiting."

Again, she was silent for a while. The man I put down began to stir.

"Artura is not in town. I will get a message to him if you like. If you go to Venezuela, he might meet with you. Or, he might kill you. Is this a risk you want to take?"

"You tell him that David Walker and James Thames need to do a business deal with him. I am guessing he doubles his cost, so let's round off and estimate that he will make twenty-five, maybe thirty million dollars from the deal."

"I will tell him."

"How do we find him," I asked.

"You won't. But he will find you if it suits him. Maybe you will even live long enough to pitch your business deal."

With that, she turned and looked at her two men, both still lying on the floor. Then she looked at me.

"It seems my driver and bodyguard are incapacitated. Take me to Miami Beach; I want to dance."

When I looked past her to Sam, he just shrugged.

We told the driver to take us to Mansion, but she told him to go to Opium Garden. I nodded my consent, and that is where we went.

I remember wondering if we would all be able to get in. Hector had only set us up for two. But as we passed those lined up and approached the head of the line, the doorman unhooked the velvet rope and stepped aside.

"Welcome, Ms. Simonyan. Randall will escort you to your table."

Sam and I followed like puppies, wondering what the hell just happened. Was this Artura Simonyan's wife or daughter?

A young man in a tuxedo escorted Ms. Simonyan to "her" table. She thanked him, and we all sat.

"I assume you have questions," she screamed over the pulsing music. "I encourage you not to ask them. Yes, I am Victoria, Artura Simonyan's daughter. I own Victoria's Cocktail Lounge. That is all you get to know. Stay here. Order drinks. They know what I like. I am going to dance."

She looked at me. "Care to join me?"

"I don't dance," I said.

She looked toward Sam, who shook his head.

"Figures," she said as she walked off.

Victoria danced until they closed the Opium Garden at 4 a.m. We had the Town Car driver take her to an address she provided. We hopped in a cab and headed back to the Ritz Carlton.

Sam called the answering machine and left a message.

"Making progress. Headed to V tomorrow. Comms limited going forward. We will check in when we can."

We decided to fly out at noon the next day. Takeoff to landing would take about four hours, and because Venezuela does not recognize daylight savings, the time zone would line up with the Eastern time zone until the States returned to Standard Time.

We slept until nine, then met for a quick breakfast. I called Crumby and told him we wanted to be wheels up for Caracas at noon. He said he would file the flight plan.

We quickly packed and took a taxi to the airport.

As we threw our bags into the luggage closet, Crumby approached. "May I assume you have weapons?" he asked.

"You may assume," Sam replied.

"Please unpack them. I have a place."

We were to pick up most of our hardware in-country. Manning had made arrangements for us. But we each still had small concealable handguns in our luggage.

In the back, near the on-board head – sorry, toilet for you non-military types – the captain removed the cover on a maintenance hatch and held out his hand. I handed him my Glock 43 and a spare mag. Sam handed over a Ruger LCP. Captain Crumby reached deep into the opening and wedged the guns in a corner.

"They will be there when you need them. I have had customs open the hatch before, but they don't want to reach into the workings of the toilet."

I believed him. We lifted off precisely at noon.

Chapter 17

After stumbling across Victoria Simonyan, I knew we must modify our approach. Our original plan didn't even survive our leaving the United States.

We were convinced she would tell her father we were looking for him. We were also confident he could find us anytime and anywhere in Venezuela if he looked for us. Arms dealers typically have extensive networks and a long reach. But would he reach out? The lure of millions of dollars would likely sway him, but one never knows.

We planned to fly to Caracas and land at Simón Bolívar International Airport. After clearing customs, we would rent a van, load our 'product samples,' and proceed to Marina Deportiva, only three kilometers away. Over the past two weeks, Manning had worked with his contact to arrange a large motor yacht or fishing boat; he wasn't sure which, but it would serve as our base of operations and accommodations. Plus, it would give us mobility and transport between Caracas and Maracaibo. We were told pier three, slip seventeen. The rental agency representative would meet us with the keys and instructions. Manning had already paid for thirty days; if we needed it longer, we would have to work that out. I didn't expect to be in Venezuela longer than two to three weeks, but as we have discussed, plans rarely work out. After securing the vessel, we were to offload our luggage and then visit a storage unit less than one kilometer away. If all went as planned, the guns, ammunition, equipment, and explosives we had requested would be found inside.

According to our original plan, we would start hitting bars and restaurants in three places. First was the high-end El Rosal neighborhood. We assumed this would be the area where Simonyan might live, or at least where he might eat and party.

Our second planned area was the neighborhood around Saint Gregory the Illuminator Armenian Church. We had been told that ninety percent of the approximately 4,000 Armenians living in Caracas lived in that area, and humans tend to navigate to those who share their culture.

The third area we would visit was the Petare and Carapita neighborhoods. Petare is considered one of the biggest slums and one of the most dangerous places in the world. The odds of two white Americans asking questions and walking away unscathed were slim, so that was to be our last option.

But because we were confident that Artura Simonyan was already aware of us, we modified our plans and moved on to step two. We would take the boat, be it a yacht or fishing vessel, to Maracaibo, Venezuela's second-largest city. The journey would take us northwest along the coast, between Venezuela and the islands of Bonaire, Curacao, and Aruba. Beyond Aruba, we would turn south into the Gulf of Venezuela and continue to Maracaibo City, which lies between the Gulf and Lake Maracaibo to the South. It would be a journey of just over 1,000 kilometers, or about 630 miles. We hoped the boat was up to it.

From there, we would do what we had skipped in Caracas, but this time, we would ask for Mr. Pancheo. Maracaibo is half the size of Caracas, but that still meant we were seeking one person in a sea of over five million. We had our work cut out for us.

∞

We landed in Caracas just before four o'clock and taxied to a hangar as instructed. The pilot broadcasted the ground controller's instructions over the PA so we would know what was happening. It took almost an hour for customs to arrive. Captain Crumby collected our passports and started down the stairs, hoping the agents would just check our visas, stamp our passports, and send us on our way. It wasn't to be.

The pilot was told to return to the cockpit. One agent boarded and positioned himself in the cockpit doorway. I could hear him asking for our passports and visas. Another agent continued to the back of the plane and opened the closet. Inside were our luggage and the black shipping cases with our samples. He began removing items until he got to the last one. He couldn't lift the 180 pounds from the closet. I was watching him while Sam watched the cockpit area. He waived me forward.

"Take out," he said.

After watching him struggle to lift the box, I wanted to make it look easy. I took a little extra time to ensure I was balanced in the cramped space at the rear of the jet, then grabbed the handles and lifted.

"Where do you want it?" I asked.

He motioned to the small table on the port side, and I placed the container on it. He motioned for me to open it.

"What is it?" he asked.

"Audio equipment. For concerts," I said, realizing I knew no Venezuelan singers. "Rolling Stones. U2. Garth Brooks."

He smiled. "The Stones are coming to Caracas?"

"Maybe. They are coming if we can make the arrangements for the equipment. That is why we are here." I made that up on the fly.

"I want to meet Mick Jagger," he said. "Jumpin' Jack Flash."

"Well, it will be several months," I told him in a whisper. "But if this visit goes well, maybe we can talk again the next time I come. You can meet Mick Jagger."

He never looked at anything else.

The other agent was very professional but stalled without stamping our passports. Sam pulled a one hundred Bolivar note from his pocket and laid it on his seat.

"My associate and I need to change clothes; just let us know if you have any questions."

183

With that, Sam joined me at the back of the jet. Fifteen seconds later, the money and the agents were gone. Our passports and visas were in order and lying on the seat.

"You seem to like sharing Manning's money," I goaded him.

"Yep. That was about three bucks. Manning can afford it."

∞

Clear of customs, I went into the private jet aviation hanger to rent a van while Sam and the crew moved our luggage and equipment to the tarmac beside the jet.

I called all six rental agencies listed on the wall, but none had anything suitable for rent. One of the airport employees overheard my calls and said he owned a van. He would rent it to us. "One hundred dollars a week, American."

I dug out two hundred dollars.

"I will have it back to you tomorrow." I thought he was going to cry.

"Come, come, I will show you."

Parked beside the hanger was the saddest looking Chevy Astro van one has ever laid eyes on. It was brown and tan, except for the right front fender, which was likely green at one time. One side had plastic woodgrain panels on the doors; the other didn't. The tires were bald, but it started quickly when he turned the key. The rear seats had been removed, which would be helpful for us. I thanked him and asked for directions to the tarmac.

When I pulled up beside Sam, he looked at me and shook his head.

"Really?" he said as I climbed out of the driver's seat.

"Really," I replied. "Best rental in town."

Twenty minutes later, we were parked at Marina Deportiva. Looking at the vessels docked there, one would never know Venezuela wasn't the French Riviera.

We strolled down the main walkway about 120 meters before turning right and finding slip 17 on our left. Floating there was a stunning yacht. The name on the stern was *"Guppy Love."* A small non-Hispanic man wearing all white was relaxing on a lounger on the fantail.

I looked at Sam. "This isn't a yacht, it's a ship."

"Yep," Sam said.

"Are you Walker and Thames?" he asked, with no trace of an accent.

We confirmed that we were.

"I am Fletcher. Born in Wellesley, Vermont, I came here to work as an oil production engineer in the eighties. Everything went to shit here, but I had found a wife, had some kids, and they let me stay, so I never went home."

We both said it was nice to meet him.

"Well, I understand you have rented the *Guppy* for a month. Everything is paid for; I just need to see your license."

Sam and I pulled our fake driver's licenses from our wallets and passed them to him.

"No, I am sorry. I need to see a captain's license. It is required for any vessel over 20 meters sailing in Venezuelan waters."

Sam and I just looked at each other.

"We were not expecting this. We expected something in the 10-to-12-meter range. Plenty big for the two of us," Sam said.

"The gentleman who called said he wanted big, flashy, and fast. That is what I have. This is a Vosper-Thornycroft from the United

Kingdom. One just like her set the record for the fastest crossing of the Atlantic a few years back. She is almost 36 meters stem to stern and will do over 65 knots, though I don't recommend it unless there is an emergency. You are burning almost sixteen gallons of diesel fuel every minute at that speed. Cruise at 40 knots and cut fuel consumption by sixty percent. Drop to 22 knots and cut fuel consumption by eighty-five percent."

I did some mental math and turned to Sam. "At 35 knots, we are in Maracaibo tomorrow afternoon. It beats the hell out of the four days we expected."

Sam just nodded. I expected another 'Yep,' but it never came.

"Where might we find someone with a captain's license?" I asked.

He hesitated. "What exactly are your plans? Pleasure? Fishing? Chasing tail?"

Fletcher was being nosy.

"We are in the audio equipment business. Hoping to make some contacts," I said. "Here and in Maracaibo."

"Who in this cesspool of a country would want high-end audio equipment?" Fletcher asked.

"Look around you," I answered. "People who buy ten-million-dollar yachts are the people who spend a quarter million on a sound system. Plus, our distributors sell to concert halls and music venues."

"Well, I am a licensed captain. I could help you out for twenty-five hundred dollars a day."

Sam interjected, "How about two grand a day if we are on open water and a grand a day for sitting your ass on the fantail drinking beer and scratching your balls when we are docked."

Fletcher seemed to think about it for a moment before agreeing.

"Stay here," Sam said. "We don't have a deal yet. James and I need to talk this over."

Sam and I turned in unison and started back toward the van. "Thoughts?" he said.

"CIA, no doubt, we have been screwed again."

"Yep," was Sam's reply. He was back in form.

"Why is it that after working without prying eyes for fifteen years, you, we actually, suddenly have the CIA watching us?"

"I imagine the CIA wants to know what happened to their men, and I guess they believe they are alive and well and working for the cartels. But that is only a guess."

"Sam, you have more experience with this than I do. I am not one to walk away, but I wonder if that is what we should do."

We were almost back to the van when Sam answered. "Not yet," he said. "Assuming this Fletcher guy is CIA, he isn't new to this game. Maybe we can use him and his expertise. We just need to know what we are dealing with. Let's go ahead and hire him to drive the boat. We can switch out watches on the open water and make it to Maracaibo faster than we expected. After we get him away from land, I say we hang him over the side and see if we can get some answers."

I looked at Sam. "Do you mean that metaphorically?"

"Yep. Well, maybe."

We grabbed a rolling bin used by fishing charters to take their catch to the cleaning stations near the docks' entrance. It smelled of fish but appeared to be relatively clean. We loaded the heavier containers, and Sam pushed the cart back to the yacht while I carried two suitcases and slung a backpack over my shoulder.

When we arrived at the boat, Fletcher was still seated with a beer in hand.

"Okay, we have a deal," I told him. "You are hired, but we want to leave tonight."

"We can leave whenever you are ready, but I want my money upfront."

"Five thousand now, balance when we wrap up."

Fletcher just nodded. I pulled the cash from a hidden pouch attached to my belt and tucked it inside my slacks.

"We have to go get some more equipment, then we have to return the van," Sam said.

"Just take the van back. Your other equipment is already on board and stashed in various hidey-holes." Fletcher grinned at us. "Figured it out yet?"

"We figured it out a long time ago," Sam replied. "But you are smarter than I thought because you just saved yourself a very long swim."

"I don't know who you are," Fletcher said. "I have worked for the 'Company' down here for almost twenty years," he said, invoking the name most everyone called the Central Intelligence Agency. "Everything else I told you is the truth, except my wife is long gone, and I don't see the kids much. I have watched Chavez come into power twice and seen him booted once. I think a second expulsion from the president's office is coming soon, but who knows? The bastard is slippery. I have kept an eye on things from my little charter service here. I report interesting observations to some unknown bureaucrats in Washington. I occasionally go out into the Caribbean and pick up some items that I distribute to secure locations across the country for future use by people like you. The Company puts money in my bank account, but the *Guppy* here charters about 40 days a year for twelve to twenty grand a day, depending on the number of people and the time of year. I don't need their money."

"What do you know about us and what we are doing?" I asked.

"I was told that two men, David Walker and James Thames, would be onboard and on a mission. I was later told to make sure I was aboard as captain. I was provided a list of equipment you would need and told to put it in a locker. Then something changed, and I was told, 'Just put it aboard.' That is about it."

"And you were told to report our activities to your contact," I said.

He shrugged, "I was told to keep an eye on you."

Sam spoke up again. "I don't expect any heat to find us onboard, but if things turn ugly, can we count on you?"

"Never been much of a fighter. Remember, I am an engineer. But I haven't run yet except when I was told to. I don't expect to start now."

"Who owns the *Guppy Love*?" I asked, reading the name off the stern again.

Fletcher paused. "I guess that is a matter of debate. Until about twelve years ago, it was owned by a Russian oligarch. One of Putin's men. He and his beautiful new yacht disappeared one night in a storm. Everyone assumed it went down with him and his mistress aboard. In truth, she was boarded by Navy Seals while she sat at anchor off the Azores. The Seals moved the yacht, the Russian, his girlfriend, and his crew to an unknown location. Eventually, the boat was in a covered drydock in Mobile, Alabama. There, it was painted white instead of the original gaudy gold, and the electronics were upgraded. They also extended the salon aft of the wheelhouse so that the profile was different. She doesn't look like the same vessel, but she moves like it. The company offered it to me as cover if I would stay and work for them in Venezuela. Everything is in my name, and she is registered in Venezuela. In my mind, that makes her mine. I doubt the Russian has a claim. The Company might, though."

∞

I left to take the van back. Fletcher decided he needed more beer if we were cruising non-stop to Maracaibo. Sam loaded the luggage into the salon and chose to go shopping with Fletcher.

There seemed to be insufficient protein aboard to suit Sam's taste.

I got back before them to find *Guppy Love* locked and unattended, so I took a seat on the fantail. It had been a long day already.

As I took in my surroundings, I noticed someone, likely a man, on top of the protective jetty to the northeast. I guessed he was at least a hundred meters away. He seemed to be watching the marina. After a few minutes, I climbed the external stairway to the salon deck and found the door unlocked. Inside, I made my way forward to the bridge, where I found Zeiss binoculars. From behind the tinted glass, I looked back to the seawall and watched the man walk along the top. The rocks made his footing perilous. He occasionally stopped, lifted a camera with a long lens, and scanned the marina. Was he just enjoying the view? Taking photos? Or was he watching us? I didn't want to take a chance.

I pulled my Blackberry out and called Sam.

"Problem?"

"Not sure, but someone is watching the marina from the seawall. I am going to get off the boat and leave. I will meet you back outside the gate. Work out another place that Fletcher can pick us up."

I heard Sam and Fletcher talking for about thirty seconds before he came back on.

"You stay there. Fletcher will come to you. You help him cast off his lines and then walk back out. He said he often gets someone from the marina office to help him cast off, and maybe the watcher will assume that is who you are. I will be outside the gate, and we will catch a ride to another marina about a mile down the road."

I acknowledged.

"Fletcher is about five minutes out. He will have groceries in the cart; help him unload, then bring the cart back out with you."

I hung up and lifted the binoculars again. Yes, he was looking right at me, but I was confident he couldn't penetrate the tinted, reflective glass.

I felt the slightest movement in the boat and returned to the fantail to help Fletcher unload.

Three minutes later, he had the engines warming up. The Textron Lycoming diesel engines created over eleven thousand horsepower and made a deep, throaty sound at idle.

Fletcher told me to leave the fenders in place on the port side. I helped him cast off the lines and headed quickly down the dock. I glanced over my shoulder several times, peaking between other large yachts, but I never saw the man again. Was I paranoid? Maybe. But in Afghanistan, I found paranoia to be my friend. I embraced paranoia.

Sam had already managed to secure a taxi. The ride was only five minutes. We watched behind us to see if we were being tailed, but the dense traffic cut both ways. It would have been hard to follow us, but it was also hard for us to identify any pursuers.

Guppy Love was rounding a seawall protecting this smaller marina when we arrived. At the end of the second dock, Fletcher expertly turned the stern toward the T and began backing the yacht toward it. Sam and I jumped to the elevated dive platform when the gap closed to three feet. Fletcher headed out of the marina below wake speed as we pulled and stowed the fenders.

Moving into open water, Fletcher entered a waypoint 300 kilometers to the northwest into the autopilot. "How fast do you want to get there?"

"Let's plan to sleep at a marina in Maracaibo tomorrow night," Sam said. "We will take shifts on the watch on the way and then get a good night's rest."

Fletcher nodded. "I will continue at twelve knots for about 90 minutes. That will get us into international waters. After that, we will push her to thirty knots when the traffic clears. When we reach the waypoint at about sunrise, we will recalculate and lay in another course."

Fletcher asked questions about our experience with thirty-meter watercraft. Since our cover was blown with him anyway, we told him that most of our experience was riding on boats in the Marines, but we each had some basic knowledge, experience, and training.

"Truth is, all you have to do is stay somewhat awake," Fletcher explained. "I will set an alarm on the radar for two miles. If anything gets closer than that, just avoid it. Autopilot will get you back on course afterward. Note these gauges. Green is good. Yellow, come get me. Red shut down the engines. The kill switch is here."

We worked it out so that 'Fletcher' would take the first four-hour watch to clear the traffic nearer shore, 'David' would take the second, and I would take the third.

"We should get to the waypoint about two hours into your watch, James," Fletcher said. "Just wake me when we reach the end of the line plotted on the autopilot. I put you two in the larger berths in the bow. I am in the captain's quarters down the stairs from the galley."

Sam and I went down to the main deck, found our suites, and changed clothes. *Guppy Love* was simply an incredible vessel—exactly what one would expect of a custom yacht built for a Russian oligarch. The décor was over-the-top flashy visually but also very functional and luxurious. It's not my style, but I could easily adapt.

We also spent some time taking inventory. The weapons and equipment that Fletcher had secured appeared to be well-maintained. We separated our equipment, like radios, trackers, satellite phones, and other items, from the audio equipment we had flown in. With everything in order, we fixed sandwiches, including one for Fletcher, and returned to the pilothouse. The sun was setting almost due west of us.

Just as we sat down, a pod of dolphins began surfing along our bow.

"Legend says it is good luck for dolphins to see you off on a journey," Fletcher said.

Sam and I had no opinion about that, so we said nothing.

Chapter 18

I watched the sun come up behind me. It had been an easy journey so far. Sam said he never touched the wheel and only saw a few smaller vessels at the edge of the radar. About an hour into my watch, I adjusted the course once to move north of and around an oil tanker moving at about 15 knots. It only took about half an hour to overtake him and continue on my way.

Guppy Love handled exceptionally well at 30 knots, sitting high in the water and easily splitting the waves with almost no rocking or side-to-side movement.

Fletcher climbed the stairs just before I was going to wake him.

"I felt a slight course change a couple of hours ago. What'd you see?" he asked.

I pointed astern. "Oil tanker doing about half our speed. I just went around him at about two kilometers away. We are almost to the waypoint."

Fletcher turned his attention to the GPS, radar, and autopilot. I noticed Sam standing just behind the pilothouse with the satellite phone to his ear. I decided to distract Fletcher by asking questions. We reviewed every control, light, and gauge until Sam entered the wheelhouse.

"No sleep?" I asked Sam.

I got a "yep." I wasn't sure what that meant.

"We're south of Curacao. I'll turn her a little more to the west so that we pass just south of Aruba. The autopilot is off, so just stay on the line on the chart plotter and back off to about 25 knots. There will be traffic ahead—commercial and a lot of dive boats. I'm going to cook breakfast. I'll take over again after we eat."

After Fletcher was off the deck, I turned to Sam.

"The call?"

"I got in touch with Manning. He wasn't aware the CIA would be involved. He will talk to Landry and try to find out what the hell is going on. He didn't want to involve the senator, but I told him that if he didn't talk to him, I would. I don't think he liked that."

I had nothing to ask or add, so I changed the subject. "We should clear between Aruba and the Paraguana peninsula and turn southwest in about four hours, just before noon. Then we have about 250 more kilometers to Maracaibo. I imagine we will arrive around six o'clock if we continue to average 30 knots.

We spent the morning loading magazines and firing over the rail. Just a few rounds from each gun to make sure they were all in working order. One should never trust a firearm without testing it. We also assembled radios and tested them. Again, all seemed to be in working order.

We did have one problem. We found that Fletcher had brought a two-kilo block of Semtex plastic explosive on board. It was a nice addition, but there were no detonators. Oh well.

As we approached Aruba, Fletcher slowed us to fifteen knots and cruised about 500 meters from shore before increasing speed and heading for the Gulf of Venezuela. Ten miles offshore, he idled the engines.

"Let's catch our supper," Fletcher said. "There is a deep trench just off our starboard side. In thirty minutes, we will have enough Wahoo and Mahi to feed us for a week."

Fletcher grabbed the gear and cast one line over the port side and another off the stern. I took one, and Sam took the other. Fletcher used an auxiliary cockpit to control the *Guppy*, and we began trolling at about two knots. Within fifteen minutes, we had hooked and landed two 30-inch Wahoo. We continued fishing until Sam's reel screamed again; whatever he caught was taking line fast. Fletcher stopped the boat and began giving instructions. After ten minutes, I gaffed the fish, about four feet long.

"Holy Bonito," Fletcher exclaimed. "Nice fish."

"What is it?" I asked.

"Atlantic Bonito. I don't see many of them. They like shallow water away from shorelines, and most of my charters want to catch billfish. Bonito is good to eat, though. We will get a dozen meals out of that one."

Fletcher led me to the pilothouse and laid in a new course. "Just keep your eyes open. There's a lot of traffic around us. Watch the radar as well. We'll make up for lost time after I get these fish cleaned and put away."

An hour later, we were in the Gulf of Venezuela. Fletcher returned to the pilothouse with Sam.

"Let me show you what the *Guppy* can do," he said with a huge smile.

He increased our speed to forty-six knots, and the ride was surprisingly smooth. Then, suddenly, he yelled, "Hang on," over the engine noise as he pushed the throttles to the stop.

If a boat could fly, we would have gone airborne. Soon, the knot meter read 61.3, then 61.5. Fletcher turned left and right a few times. Gently at first, then sharper turns. The boat bit into the water each time and executed a smooth turn. Watching the ocean go by at 70 miles per hour was surreal. After about 30 minutes, Sam slowed us down to 30 knots again.

"Enough of that. Let's get to Maracaibo. I need to reserve a place to park the *Guppy*. Any preferences?"

"The most visible slip available," I told him. "We want to be found."

"Los Andes Yacht Club is the best bet if you want a slip. Let me see what they have available."

Fletcher pulled a satellite phone from a charger in a cabinet, then pulled a worn paperback book that looked like a road atlas from another cabinet. Seconds later, he was dialing, and while my Spanish isn't great, I understood that we would be paying seven thousand Bolivar per day for a berth. Fletcher had talked them down from ten thousand.

"Not my money, but he is robbing us. Last time, it was only four thousand," Fletcher said, then added. "Get out your card, James, because it isn't going on mine."

Maracaibo is located on the banks of Lake Maracaibo, about 40 kilometers from the lake's northern end. Technically, a bay and not a lake, water from a dozen or more rivers provide nutrients, but pollution, pesticides, and sewage runoff mean that the fish are no longer safe to eat. The water near the marina had a sheen of oil floating on the top, and it smelled like death.

We refueled and tied *Guppy Love* up at the T on the end of the longest pier. Her 110' length extended slightly beyond the space we were allocated. At six o'clock, we stepped onto the dock. Even though the *Guppy* was stable at sea, it took a while to regain solid footing.

We were not flying a quarantine flag, only a Venezuelan flag, per her registration. Still, a police officer stopped us almost immediately and demanded to see our passports and visas. Fletcher stepped forward and had a word. We handed over our passports with the visas inside, and the officer flipped through them before handing them back. Thankfully, he did not search the *Guppy*.

After a short walk around the marina and a visit to the Los Andes yacht club building - it wasn't what one would expect for a yacht club - we returned to a dinner of grilled Wahoo and mixed vegetables aboard the *Guppy*. The fish was excellent.

As yacht clubs go, this wasn't much. Fewer than a dozen boats were docked on site. Most were 18 to 40-foot sailing vessels. I have seen nicer facilities and nicer boats on the Kentucky River. I imagine it was quite grand before Chavez and the communists destroyed the country with socialism.

So where does one begin when looking for an arms merchant in one of the most dangerous countries in the world? Sam and I had extended discussions about that. We had some information: a name, Victor Perez Pancheo, and a primarily blank bio sheet; that was it.

It was our shared belief that we would be better off just asking for a meeting with Pancheo than randomly asking people if they happened to know any arms dealers from whom we could place a large order. That may sound like an easy decision, but it wasn't. In a metropolitan area of over five million people in South America, where almost every name is rooted in its Spanish past, asking to meet with Victor Pancheo will typically result in one of two outcomes. The first outcome is that, yes, the person you are speaking with knows Victor Pancheo. They even tell you where to find him, but it turns out he is a twenty-year-old college student. The second outcome is that they know five men named Victor Pancheo.

In contrast, flat-out asking shady people in shady places if they know an arms dealer will likely get you shot, arrested, or passed from person to person until you get to someone with enough power to acquire and sell millions of dollars of illegal weapons. That would be our second option if we made no progress.

At nine the next morning, Sam and I went to eat breakfast at the marina restaurant. Being the better Spanish speaker, I ordered us both pork chops with eggs, coffee, and juice.

I told the waiter we were looking for Victor Perez Pancheo. He said he didn't know him. Oh well, it was a long shot.

After a light lunch onboard the *Guppy* in the early afternoon, Sam and I dressed in suits, nice shoes, and expensive watches. I tucked a Glock 19 into a small holster clipped inside my pants at the small of my back, and I am sure Sam did the same. We walked to a nearby store. It had a little bit of everything, including prepaid cell phones. We each bought a Motorola flip phone, activated it, and programmed each other as a speed dial number.

The clerk provided us with a phone book, and I arranged for a limo and driver to pick us up. We had no idea where we were going.

While we were waiting for the driver, I questioned Sam.

"Did you ever hear back from Manning?"

"Nope."

"One thing is bothering me," I said, planning to continue with a question. But Sam interrupted my thought.

"Just one thing?" he quipped.

"If the CIA, or whomever, had three operatives in Venezuela for a year before they all went off the grid, don't you think they would have collected some basic information about their targets? How could they be infiltrating an organization but not even know where to find them?"

"I had the same thought," Sam replied. "I can guess at the answer if you want."

"Let's hear it."

"In November 2002, the government launched the Department of Homeland Security. One goal was to bring all the intelligence from all the different agencies into a single area—no more silos. But here we are, six years later, and the bureaucrats are not playing by the rules. In Washington, information is power. They all want power, or they want to maintain power, so they don't share information."

"And someone like Landry, or the DHS director, can't fix that?"

"All bureaucrats," he said, shaking his head.

I had told the limousine service that we needed the car and driver until midnight. The limo was a Ford Explorer. It had seen better days, but it was clean. Sam and I climbed in. The driver, a young guy about my age, said his name was Bart, but I doubted it. Thankfully, his English was far better than my Spanish. That was a positive.

"Bart," I said. We are looking for someone. We have no idea where to find him, and we have no idea where to begin. What do you suggest?"

"Do you know this person's name?" he asked.

"Victor Perez Pancheo."

"Give me ten minutes," he said before leaving the vehicle and walking to the back, where he put a foot on the bumper.

Sam and I just looked at each other and shrugged. At least he left it running and the air conditioner on. It wasn't that hot outside, but the suit and the humidity made it less than comfortable.

After about five minutes, he tapped on my window and made the international sign for roll down a window, a twirling finger.

For the first time in my life, I rolled down a window with a crank instead of hitting a switch. The Ford had manual windows.

"Old guy?" Bart asked.

"Yes, that is my understanding," I told him.

Bart turned and put the phone to his ear, walking off again. I cranked the window back up.

Shortly, he knocked again.

"I have a contact who has access to tax records. Illegal, but," he didn't continue.

"He wants money," I said.

"She wants money. A thousand bolivar."

So, the price to break the law and risk prison in this hell hole of a country is about thirty American dollars.

"Tell her we will pay. No problem."

"She is off work at eight. Can we meet her tonight? At a bar or restaurant? She wants to meet somewhere public."

"Work it out for us, and there will be some additional tip money for you," I told him. Bart walked away again with the phone to his ear.

"We will meet her at eight," Bart said when he returned to the car. "There is a restaurant near her work. They serve steaks and fish and have a bar. We will meet her there, and we will all have dinner together. She wants it to look like we are all friends."

I thanked him and told him that was great.

"It is about an hour from here, in the north of the city," Bart said. "We have about five hours. Where do you want to go?"

"Show us the city," Sam said.

It turns out that Bart was an architect by training, but he had little work because the economy was so bad that nothing was being built. He took us to Basilica de Nuestra Señora de Chiquinquirá, then to the Governor's Palace and Teatro Baralt. At each, he spoke about the architecture and history of the building. He was an excellent tour guide. Later, he took us into what he called "the real" Maracaibo, where poverty and hopelessness hung in the air, along with the smell of open sewers and rotting garbage. The traffic picked up at six when we began moving north. Bart skipped the major highways and drove through the neighborhoods. At one point, the scenery changed from absolute poverty to beautiful mansions with high fences and gates just by crossing a single intersection.

"People in Maracaibo call this road 'línea divisoria,'" he said. It is the dividing line. On the west side live the poorest of the poor. On the east are the government officials—the communist and socialist leaders who talk about equality for all before they retire to their mansions to hide from the people."

It was clear that Bart was not a fan of socialism.

"I visited los Estados Unidos when I was young. Even your poorest can eat. Can work. Can go to school. Here, there is no hope. I am lucky. My family held on to some wealth when the socialists took over in '99. I was able to finish university. My family has little remaining, but we get by."

Sam asked if we could get to the restaurant a little early. He didn't say it out loud, but he wanted to scout the location.

When we arrived, I asked for a table in the back corner near the kitchen. Habit. Most people don't want to sit by the kitchen, but I always do. There is always an exit through the kitchen.

There, dear reader, a free lesson for you.

Sam and I sat in the corner, another habit, and Bart sat with his back to the door. Bart used his cell phone to call his contact and let her know we had arrived and where to find us.

"She is off in twenty minutes, but she works only minutes away," he said as the waitress placed menus before us. "She will be here just after eight."

The restaurant was nice. A waiter walked by with a steak sizzling on a plate. It had mashed potatoes and grilled peppers with it. Sam closed the menu and said, "I need to find out what that is." When the waiter returned to take our drink order, Sam told me to ask what the dish was across the aisle. The waiter said it was a ribeye of beef cooked on the grill with a Venezuelan marinade. I told the waiter to remember that. We would wait for our guest before we ordered, but the old man wanted that. Sam knew enough Spanish that he understood, but he just stared at me. Bart laughed.

Just after eight o'clock, Bart's contact arrived. She was a cute but plain woman with long dark hair and a caramel complexion. Bart stood and kissed her before sitting back down and introducing her.

"This is Elaina. My fiancé." He was smiling from ear to ear.

Elaina extended her hand, and we each shook it. She had a firm grip. She was very polished. She, too, spoke English very well.

"Elaina is finishing law school," he said. "We have a great need for lawyers in this country. After her classes, she works for the state of Zulia. Maracaibo is the capital.

Elaina wanted wine, and we asked her to choose it. She decided on a Malbec from Argentina. Sam and I drank bottled water, but I tasted the wine, and it was delicious.

The steak was also excellent. Bart ordered a burger, and Elaina chose a dinner salad with seared tuna.

Eventually, we finished, and the waiter brought a check. It was just a number written on a scrap of paper. Twenty-eight hundred bolivars. Bart said the bill would include the service charge, but a small additional tip was appreciated. I pulled three one-thousand bolivar notes from my roll and placed them on the table. A quick calculation told me that it equaled about $85. What a bargain.

As we stood to leave, Elaina hugged Sam and discreetly slipped a folded piece of paper in his pocket. "You can pay Bart. He will get it to me. Thank you for the wonderful dinner."

And with that, she was gone. We returned to the Explorer and headed toward the same store where we had met Bart earlier in the day.

Sam unfolded the paper and reached up to turn on the map light, but it didn't work. He passed it to me in the front seat. I read it as we passed a working streetlight—a rarity in Maracaibo.

Two people named Victor Perez Pancheo were in the state of Zulia's tax records. We had two addresses.

"What are you doing the next three days?" I asked Bart.

"I am available if you need me. If I work directly for you, I will cut the price because the service only pays me a small amount. I own the vehicle."

"Where is Campo Mara?"

"It is about 40 kilometers to the north and west. About an hour, maybe less on the toll road."

"And Paraguaipoa?" I asked.

"Further north along the coastline. It is on the north end of the lake, not far from Columbia. It is a three-hour drive."

"Meet us back here at noon tomorrow. Bring a change of clothes, just in case," I told him. "We will pay you the same rate, maybe more."

I put Bart's cell number in the Motorola and paid him for the day, plus Elaina's money, before he headed off. Walking from the hardware store to the marina at the yacht club, we were followed by two teen boys dressed in black hoodies and jeans. Sam stopped and turned around. They scattered.

"What is the plan?" Sam asked as we watched them cross the main road to the west.

"Two possibilities. It sounds like one is slightly inland, the other near the coast. I think our guy is the one on the coast. I would want to be near the water if I were dealing guns. But I am not a dealer, so I don't know how they think. Let's start in Campo Mara since it is closer. If we don't find him there, we will move the *Guppy* up the coast and check Paraguiapoa."

When we returned to the *Guppy*, Fletcher sat on the fantail, drinking a beer and watching the stars.

"How are you, Fletcher," I asked.

"Just drinking beer, scratching my balls, and making a grand a day." That Fletcher was a clown.

Chapter 19

Bart was late. After 15 minutes, I called, and he said he was close; a wreck had blocked the road. When we climbed into the Explorer, I told Bart to take the toll road. Maybe it was faster, maybe it wasn't. We averaged about thirty miles an hour, dodging potholes and washed-out sections. What were the tolls paying for? It certainly wasn't maintenance.

The landscape was primarily flat and agricultural, with mountains off to the west. Everything was an amazing shade of green, lush and tropical, with expanses of grassy fields.

When we arrived in Campo Mara, I told Bart to ask for directions to the street, not the exact address Elaina provided. He was told it was to the north, just out of town. With no signs to indicate road names, it took a while to find the right road and another fifteen minutes of winding around to find the correct address. There, we found a small home, maybe eight hundred square feet. On my instruction, Bart continued past the house about a mile before stopping.

"David, what do you think?" I asked.

"Not the right place, but let's see if anyone is home."

I told Bart to go back and stop in front of the house. I would knock. Bart offered to translate, but I didn't want him involved more than necessary.

When we arrived, Sam and I both exited the car, but Sam just leaned on the back while I approached the house. I knocked. Then again. I heard Sam cough, and when I glanced his way, he tilted his head to the south side of the house. A moment later, an older man came around the corner.

He shuffled along slowly. He saw me but continued walking until he was right before me. His right eye was cloudy with cataracts, and the other was beginning to show signs. He put his face right up to mine.

"I am looking for Señor Pancheo," I said in my best Spanish.

"Que deseas," he replied. I thought it was 'What are you looking for?' or something similar. Maybe 'what do you want?'

Again, I asked for Señor Pancheo.

"Soy yo," he said. I knew that one. 'Is me.' But he didn't stop talking. He began to get mad and talk faster. I only got a few words, it sounded like a strange Spanish dialect, but he generally said that he didn't understand why gringos came to him wanting to do business. He had nothing to sell and no money to buy.

When he quieted, I thanked him and apologized, "Gracias, lo siento."

I returned to the vehicle and climbed in. The best news was that we would not spend days in Campo Mara trying to make contact with Victor Pancheo.

"Back to Maracaibo," I told Bart.

When Bart dropped us off, I pulled five 10,000 bolivar notes from my wallet and handed them to him. It was equivalent to about $1,400, the average annual income in the country. He thanked me over and over. Elaina would be thrilled. I explained that his help and contact with Elaina had saved us days, possibly weeks, of guessing. He even invited us to his wedding the following spring.

It was growing dark when we walked back down the pier to the *Guppy*. This time, six youths stepped out from behind a small building, holding knives and bats. The two from the previous night had found some helpers. They were about 30 feet ahead of us.

We stopped and looked around; it was a quick battlefield assessment. Something we both had drilled into us in the Marines.

Sam said in a low voice, "How do you want to handle this?"

"Well," I replied, "They are between us and the *Guppy*, so if we draw guns and they run, they have nowhere to go but in the water. However, I feel a little saucy after bouncing around in the car all day. Let's see what they've got."

"Yep," was the only reply I got.

Instructors say that with any non-military group, whether in the States, Venezuela, or Afghanistan, only a few are dedicated to the fight. Usually, a few will enter a fray half-heartedly, and others will flee when challenged. I hoped at least two would just jump in the water and swim away. It turned out that there were no cowards in this group.

Sam and I resumed walking down the pier. When we reached them, the biggest one, maybe twenty years old, held his knife up and said, "Tu dinero." 'Your money.'

"What did he say," Sam asked, but I knew he knew what was said.

"He said he wants to fight," I told him.

"Can you tell him his boyfriends are cute?"

"Tus novios son lindos," I said. I think that was close.

The big guy lunged at me with the knife. I was ready, catching his hand and throwing a punch into the inside of his arm just under his shoulder, striking the nerve. Guess what. When properly delivered, that move will render an arm numb and almost inoperable for several minutes. He dropped the knife and turned to regroup. I felt a blow from a bat to the back of my thigh. It hurt and would leave a bruise. If he had been smart, he would have aimed lower at my knee, but he wasn't smart. His momentum moved him close enough that I could punch him in the nose. He staggered back, bloodied but not out of the game.

I heard a splash and looked at Sam long enough to ensure it wasn't him. He twisted the arm of one smaller guy and then delivered a kick to the face. He went down.

The first attacker, now without a weapon, came back at me, but without the use of his right side, his punch was weak, slow, and telegraphed. I stepped aside and buried a knee in his ribs. I feel confident that at least one or two were broken. He stumbled off again, trying to catch his breath.

Another knife slashed and caught my suit jacket. I felt the sting of a cut but knew it wasn't bad. I stepped into the attacker and head-butted him on the nose, then pushed him into the water. At least two of them were out of the fight. The one with the bat had blood pouring from his nose. He ran at me and swung wildly. Again, he wasn't a smart fighter. When the swing passed me, I spun and caught him from behind. I could have broken his neck in about a half second, but I chose to show him some mercy and sling him off the pier and into the nasty water. Only one remained in front of me, one with a broken and bleeding nose, which meant Sam had two to deal with. I didn't wait for him to attack this time. I moved straight toward him and hit him in the jaw. He was out cold before he hit the boards.

I looked at Sam; he held one of the bats. The final two of the gang were in a sitting position, leaning on the small building, bloodied but conscious.

I checked my wrist to see where the knife cut me. It was barely bleeding, but the cut and the blood of the attackers ruined the suit. Sam's suit, however, was still pristine.

"Did you know," Sam said. "That they have Louisville Sluggers in Venezuela?"

I laughed. "Nope, News to me. You okay?"

"Yep," he said. Have I mentioned that he rarely elaborates?

"What do we do with these two?"

I heard splashing behind me and saw two of the teens climb from the water on a ladder and head off down the pier. A couple of people were standing on their boats watching.

"Let them go. We are out of here as soon as we can cast off."

"Tell them," he said.

"Toma a tu amigo y vete," I yelled at them. They stood and ran down the pier. They must not have heard the 'take your amigo' part.

I walked over to the one I knocked out. His jaw was swelling. That meant blood was circulating, and he was alive. We headed on to the *Guppy*.

Fletcher was in his usual place with a beer in hand.

"Let's get out of here," Sam told him.

"Woohoo," Fletcher exclaimed. "I thought it was just going to be another thousand-dollar day, drinking beer and scratching my balls."

The joke was getting old.

∞

Sam and I had cast off the lines and stowed the fenders within minutes. Fletcher was moving us slowly out of the marina. It was only forty kilometers north along the lake to San Rafael. He suggested we continue past San Rafael and enter the gulf. We could anchor in shallow, clear blue water and then motor back into the marina tomorrow morning.

It sounded good to us. The temperature had risen since our arrival, and the stench from the water had gotten worse throughout the day. I was ready for some crisp, clean sea air.

We sailed past the San Carlos de la Barra Fortress and around the point at San Bernardo. Fletcher found us a place to anchor. I released the safety chain, and he let out 40 meters of nylon anchor rode before setting the anchor in the sandy bottom.

Sam cooked blackened Bonita filets on the grill while Fletcher prepared garlic and butter pasta. The combination was fabulous.

Late that evening, Sam walked out to the fantail with the satellite phone. I was sitting with Fletcher; he told me about his twin daughters, Heather and Hanna, who were now 23 years old and living somewhere in Caracas. His former wife had worked hard to erase Fletcher from their minds, and she had been mostly successful. It had been four years since Fletcher had seen them. I could tell it hurt.

Sam motioned me forward, and we walked as far from Fletcher as possible. He plugged earbuds into the satellite phone, and we each took one bud.

"Go ahead, Manning. We are both here."

"I got in touch with Landry," Manning said. "My contact apparently asked the CIA to make arrangements for your boat. The head of the CIA heard about it, put two and two together, and got four. Landry said that more than anything, the CIA just wants to know if those assets that disappeared last year are dead or if they joined a cartel. Neither really makes sense to them. Beyond that, they are curious about who you two are. That secret is safe."

Sam spoke. "Regarding the second item, our true identity, you had better protect that with your life. Are we clear?"

"Crystal clear, Sam."

"Regarding the first item, that isn't a part of our mission. If we learn something in the process, we will pass it along. We will not, however, look for them or ask any questions about them. That would blow any cover we have. Are we clear again?"

"That has been explained to the Senator."

"Anything else?" I asked.

"Sam filled me in on your progress. Keep pressing forward, and guys, stay safe."

The connection was broken.

"Well, your hunch about why the Company is so interested seems accurate," I told Sam. I got another "Yep" in response.

I slept on the sun deck that night. I am always amazed at how ambient light on land blocks our view of the stars. I had not seen a sky like this since my time in Afghanistan.

The following morning, we slowly motored to San Rafael de El Mohan. We had learned that there was another city called San Rafael, without the 'de El Mojan,' to the east. We chose to drop the 'de El Mojan' from our conversations because we would not get them confused, and it was a mouthful for someone from the Commonwealth of Kentucky. Fletcher had arranged for us to pull the *Guppy* alongside an abandoned cargo pier because the fishing marinas could not handle our 36-meter length. The concrete pier was over 150 meters long, and the *Guppy* was the only vessel there.

In truth, there wasn't much at all there. Fletcher had an old atlas from 1998 that said the population was 25,000 and change. We saw very little activity.

It was a hot day, but Sam and I put on suits and used the jackets to cover the pistols stashed in the small of our back. I filled an empty Crown Royal bag I found in the galley with several adhesive-backed tracking beacons and two small listening devices. The bugs were a newer model that records only when voices are detected. The recording is stored on a chip and retrieved by getting within about 100 meters and sending a signal that triggers a very short burst broadcast. This prevents broadcast detection unless someone gets lucky and picks up the quick burst.

We walked northwest along the main road toward the city center. There, at Saint Rafael's Church, we located a taxi. The driver was a woman named Liza. She was maybe five feet tall but weighed more than me. Her hair was pulled straight back into a tight ponytail.

This time, my Spanish was better than her English.

I asked her if she knew where Paraguiapoa was, and she said, "Yes, it is a small town." I showed her the full address that Elaina had provided. She told me it was a post office box.

I wasn't sure what else to do, so I asked her to take us to the post office. The forty-three-kilometer trip along the coast road took us about an hour. There was little traffic.

Sam paid her when we arrived, assuming we would poke around a while and then catch a cab back to the *Guppy*.

We started by walking the block around the post office. The area was almost exclusively empty, with buildings in various states of disrepair. I expected two large white men in suits to attract some attention, which is what we wanted, but it didn't happen. The town seemed abandoned.

The next circle was wider, and we came across an open store. It was small, but it had everything from tools to housewares to guns. We paid special attention to the guns. When the lone employee strolled over and asked what we were looking for, I replied, "Armas, muchos armas." 'Guns, many guns.'

He just pointed and said, "Eso es todo lo que tengo." 'That is all I have.'

I then asked if he had "Grande armas." 'Big guns.'

Again, he pointed and said, "Eso es todo lo que tengo."

I asked where I could get a lot of guns.

He just said. "Aqui no. Esto es todo lo que tengo." 'Not here, this is all I have.'

I was beginning to think that was all he had.

Sam and I moved on to our next circuit of the post office. Three blocks wide by three blocks long now. I spotted what appeared to be a bar or restaurant down a side street. Upon entering, I knew it was more than a bar and restaurant. The place was about 16 feet wide by maybe 40 feet deep, and the bar took up about half that down the left side. The ceiling was low, and the place smelled like Bourbon Street in New Orleans on a hot summer day: stale air, stale beer, and stale urine. Two older men were sitting on stools near the far end of the bar. We saw no one else. They looked at us, and we looked at them. We pulled up stools closer to the open door.

At last, a young woman dressed in a thong and bikini top came down a set of stairs I had not noticed before. She didn't go behind the bar, however. She came and stood between Sam and me.

She was probably in her early twenties, but she looked older. I imagined her to be very pretty at one time, but life had not been good to her.

She placed one hand on my back and her other on Sam's. Her hand traveled south until she felt the Glock in the small of my back. It stopped her hand, but if she was surprised, she didn't show it. Over the next five minutes, she offered us everything from sex to drugs, one at a time or together, or she could get another girl to join us. The offers went on and on. What she never offered us was a drink.

I finally said we were in town looking to make a purchase, but we just wanted a drink for now. She went behind the bar and grabbed two Polar beers from a cooler. She placed them on the bar top and told me it would be 400 bolivars. I pulled the entire roll of currency from my jacket pocket and passed her five 1,000 bolivar notes. I told her to keep the change but didn't return the money roll to my pocket.

She stared at me for a few seconds, then eyed the money. I just kept looking at her. She asked if I wanted sex now. I told her no, but I started fanning through the bills, drawing her attention to the money again.

"Entonces qué quieres?" she asked. 'So, what do you want?' or something close to that.

"We want to buy guns, many guns, big guns," I told her.

I had been paying attention to her, but I noticed that Sam slid off his stool and passed behind me toward the men at the other end of the bar.

She told me she didn't know where to get guns, but I felt she was lying. I learned it in Afghanistan: Just follow the eyes and listen carefully. But because I am not as familiar with inflection in Spanish, it was harder to know for sure. Still, I felt confident.

I heard Sam asking for the baño to distract the men from my conversation with the woman. I told her to come around the bar again.

She did, and I said in a low voice. "Can we go to your room?"

She took my hand and led me to the far end of the bar, past Sam and the two men, and up the stairs.

The room was very small, with a twin-size bed and several boxes I assume she used to store her belongings. She sat on the bed and removed the bikini top before I could stop her.

I tried to tell her to put it back on, but apparently, I wasn't saying it right, or she was just confused by the request, or maybe she thought her odds of getting more of the money were better with the top off.

She patted the bed beside her, urging me to sit, but I remained standing and told her I would pay her if she knew where we might get guns. She started to respond, then said no. Again, I thought she was lying.

I asked her name.

"Diamante," she answered. No surprise there.

"Piénsalo," I told her. Think about it. "Volveré mañana a las 2 p.m." 'I will be back at 2 p.m. tomorrow.'

I dropped another 5,000 bolivars on the bed and left the room. We would see if it provided motivation.

I filled Sam in as we walked an even wider block. We finally hit an area where it looked like people lived, but still, there were not enough people to justify the town's size. It was strange.

As it grew dark, we realized we had made a mistake. While we were walking around, we had not see even one taxi.

Eventually, we returned to the bar-slash-restaurant-slash-brothel and asked where we could catch a taxi back to San Rafael.

"No taxi," a new face behind the bar told us in English. "Too dangerous after dark."

"How do we get back?" I asked.

"Walk or sleep upstairs," she winked as she answered.

"Is there a motel?" I asked.

"It is closed. The people left town, and the businesses closed."

I looked at Sam, who tilted his head toward the door. "Let's talk this out," he said.

Outside, neither of us said anything for a minute until Sam offered, "I say we find someone with a car. We have cash, and people need money. See if you can find your friend, Diamante."

Diamante had just gone upstairs with a client, but the girl at the bar said she would let her know I wanted to see her as soon as she was free. Five minutes later, Diamante came back down the stairs, following a teenage boy. She saw me and came over.

"Regresaste," she said. ¿Quieres ir de fiesta ahora?" 'You're back. You want to party now?'

I told her I needed someone to drive us back to San Rafael. She said something like, "How disappointing; the boy was too fast."

"¿Cuánto dinero?"

I told her I would pay 5,000 bolivars.

She walked to the end of the bar and spoke to an old man. He returned with her. He was so drunk that he could barely stand.

Sam and I again looked at each other. Venezuela. What a country.

We paid the man cash and followed him to an eighties model Chevrolet pickup. He paused beside it and urinated on the front tire.

I was kind and took the middle seat. I remember measuring to see if I could reach the brake if needed. We never said a word to the man. He drove us back and never even swerved. He dropped us in the middle of town, and we headed back to the *Guppy* on foot. Before he drove off, he climbed out and whizzed on the front tire again.

When we arrived at the *Guppy*, Fletcher was in his usual spot. Sam and I both had our jackets slung over our shoulders, and we were sweating through our clothes. Thankfully, the *Guppy* had a washer and dryer.

"Fletcher, do you know anything about Paraguiapoa? It seems almost like a ghost town." I asked him.

"Not a lot," he said. "At one time, there were copper mines just south of there and along the border with Columbia. Many of the workers lived along that coast. It was an affluent area by local standards. Then, when Chavez nationalized all oil and mineral production, this area was pretty much abandoned. Oil is plentiful in the middle of the country and more profitable for the socialists, so that is where the work is. Many people moved there. Others headed west into Columbia to work in the poppy fields."

After we ate more of the bonito that evening, we called Lucy and talked to her.

Then I called Lauren. I was very vague and unable to answer some of her questions. I think she understood. She mentioned Lucy several times, and I felt they had been talking. I guess that

Lucy was keeping her on the hook for me just a bit longer. I didn't mind.

Sam called Crumby and Cruz to see how things were at the airport. They were just hanging out, being bored. Sam told them he would love to let them head out somewhere for a while, but he didn't know when they might be needed on short notice.

We also talked to Fletcher about the transportation problem. He said he would make a call or two and see if anyone he knew had a solution. It had been a long day. Sam and I went below and threw our shirts and other dirty clothes into the washer. I climbed into bed and was asleep in seconds.

Chapter 20

I was making coffee aboard the *Guppy* when Fletcher climbed the stairs from the captain's quarters. He was dressed in his usual white linen pants and shirt.

"Spoke to a friend back in Caracas last night," Fletcher said. "He has a cousin in Maracaibo who will rent you a car, but he can't bring it to us here. It will be a long commute from Maracaibo to Paraguiapoa, but at least you will have your own ride. Want to return and get the rental?"

"That sounds good, but let me run it by Jackson when he gets up here."

"Just let me know," Fletcher said. "I will fire up the grill and cook some sausage and eggs. Bring me a coffee when it is ready."

When Sam came out, Fletcher and I were sitting on the fantail near the grill. I passed him some sausage and now-cold eggs, and we filled him in on the car rental option.

He thought it over.

"I would prefer Bart," he said, "if we are going back to Maracaibo anyway. But I don't want to endanger him, and I feel like we are getting closer."

He thought some more. "Cody, your thoughts?"

"Same thoughts," I said. "If we have our own transportation, we can take more hardware with us."

"Good point," Sam replied. "Fletcher, call your contact and see when he can have the car at the yacht club. Let's shoot for about eleven this morning. You told Diamond we would return at around two this afternoon, correct?"

"Correct."

Fletcher got up to make a call. Sam and I took the dishes to the galley and washed and stored them.

Sam whispered. "Describe the man you saw in Caracas the day we met Fletcher."

"Not young, not old. Likely Hispanic. Neither tall nor short. He held the camera to his face much of the time I watched him. He had on a big cowboy hat. I do know he had a big mustache. Why?"

"Your back was to him, but someone was at the end of the pier while we ate. Can't say if it is the same guy."

"Just one more reason to leave. Let him chase us back to Maracaibo."

"Yep," Sam whispered.

∞

We returned to the Los Andes Yacht Club, but another boat, a small twelve-foot john boat, was blocking the T, so we had nowhere to park the *Guppy*. Fletcher radioed the clubhouse, and eventually, someone came out and moved the boat around to the long leg of the pier. It took 45 minutes that we didn't have. We used a duffel bag Fletcher had on board to gather additional supplies, like a pair of H&K MP5s with a half dozen extra magazines. We also threw in binoculars. We each strapped the full-size H&K VP9 handguns under our suit jackets. This was in addition to the compact Glock 43s tucked into the small of our backs.

At 10:45, we headed out toward the clubhouse. I was carrying the duffel. We had been told to look for a black Toyota Camry, and sure enough, one pulled up right at eleven o'clock.

Amazingly, it was almost new. Sam passed the driver an envelope containing 60,000 bolivars, and he simply walked off. It was a three-day rental, but it would make his payment for the next couple of months. I put the duffel in the trunk. Sam took the keys and climbed into the driver's seat.

As requested, a paper map was sitting on the passenger seat.

"You navigate," Sam told me.

We drove along the coast road for almost two and a half hours, passing small communities on our left and extensive tidal plains on our right before reaching Paraguiapoa. Since we had a car and a little extra time, we drove an ever-expanding circle and mentally noted escape routes, places to hide, and places for potential meetings.

If we had possessed a physical address for Pancheo, we would likely have just knocked on his door like we did with the first Mr. Pancheo. But given the circumstances, we were willing to play this game for several more days if needed.

At two, we returned to the bar-slash-restaurant-slash-brothel and found Diamante behind the bar. She set two cold Polar beers before us and said, "Esperar." 'Wait.'

An hour later, we were still sitting there. A few others came and went, always staring at the two gringos as they entered and exited. The same two men we had seen the day before came in and sat in the same place at the far end of the bar. At about three, the other girl from the previous day came in and spoke to Diamante, who came out from behind the bar and took my hand. We were headed back up the stairs.

When we entered her room – she left her top on this time – she held out her hand and said in good but accented English, "Do you have American dollars?"

"You could have saved me some trouble if I had known you speak English," I replied.

"I learn a lot when people don't know. English speakers come in occasionally and say all kinds of things while sitting on a bar stool, thinking I don't understand. They talk about my body—sometimes good, sometimes bad. They talk about what they will do to me when their turn comes. I find funny. But you and other man are different."

"We are just in town trying to conduct some business."

"You like men?" she asked.

"I have a girlfriend back home."

"You love her very much?"

"Yes."

She turned and sat on the bed.

"Most men don't say no to me. You say no but still leave money," she said, seemingly stunned.

"I simply need your help, and your help is valuable to me."

"I know someone. He isn't man who sells guns, but he works for him. I will tell you for five thousand American dollars."

"That's big money," I said.

"It is cost of freedom. Coyotes will take me to the border of America for five thousand dollars. Then I will cross and be free like you."

I couldn't argue with her mission.

I told her that my partner downstairs had American money, while I only had bolivars. It wasn't true, but I wanted to get Sam involved.

"I go get him," she said. "Stay here."

I stayed. I soon heard two sets of feet climbing the stairs.

"Tell him," Diamante said.

I skipped the whole going to America part, but I told Sam about her knowing someone who works for the man who sells guns. Then I told him the price. He looked at me with a questioning gaze.

After a moment, he turned to Diamante. "Do you know the dealer's name?" he questioned.

"I think is Pancheo," she said. "Victor Pancheo."

Bingo.

Sam reached into his coat pocket and withdrew a stack of dollars. He counted out fifty of the one-hundred-dollar bills but didn't hand them over.

"Half now, half when we meet the man."

She nodded. "Pay half and come back tomorrow at six. He is regular. He visits me on Wednesday nights when his wife goes to church. Find a place at the bar. I let you know if he talk to you."

She took the half-stack Sam offered and headed out. "I must go back downstairs. Tomorrow, six o'clock."

∞

Sam and I made our way back to Maracaibo. There were still variables, but unless this was a setup, we had taken a big step toward at least contacting a dealer. It wasn't the one we ultimately sought, but it was progress.

On Wednesday, we repeated the trip but arrived in town at four. We parked on the main road, with the Camry pointed toward Maracaibo. From there, we walked to an abandoned gas station we had noticed before. It was built of a combination of block and stone. The roof would soon collapse, but for now, it held. The windows were broken, but the inside was dark, and from there, we had a view down the alley. We could not see to the other end, but we could see the door of the bar-slash-brothel. I had not seen any food inside, so I dropped the restaurant part and shortened the name.

At about 5:30, the two men we had seen at the bar the previous two days exited and went down the alley away from us. Then, just before six, and just before we walked across the street, a policeman walking by stepped into the building - to get out of the sun, I assumed.

He was just inside the door, between Sam's position and mine, and he did not notice us at first as his eyes adjusted to the darkness. After taking a drag on the cigarette, he suddenly saw Sam and reached for his revolver, but I caught his gun hand from behind and wrapped my other hand over his mouth.

"Tranquilo," I told him.

He nodded.

"Por favor no dispares a mi amigo," I said. 'Please don't shoot my friend.'

He nodded again. I took my left hand from his mouth and used the other to guide his revolver back into its holster.

I explained that we had just sought shelter from the sun while we waited for the girls in the alley bar to finish with their customers. At least, that is what I think I said.

He smiled. "Ah, Diamante!"

"Si, si," I said, nodding my head.

He picked up the cigarette he had dropped on the nasty floor and stuck it back in his mouth before slapping me on the shoulder and rattling off a string of Spanish that left me wondering. It was something disparaging about Diamante's line of work and, if I wasn't mistaken, the slim chance I had of urinating pain-free in about a week. He finally resumed his walk, and Sam and I crossed the street and walked down the alley. We were about ten minutes later than we had hoped.

Inside, four other men were seated along the bar, along with Diamante and the other girl I had seen the day before. Diamante placed two beers in front of us but said nothing. I glanced at my watch; it was 6:15, and I wondered why she wasn't upstairs. Five minutes later, a man came in. He said hello to "Maizy," I guess that was the other girl's name before continuing to the back and up the stairs. I noted that he spoke English with only a light accent. He was maybe five foot eight with an average build and thinning hair that created a widow's peak, which I thought was unusual for a Hispanic. Diamante headed up the stairs after him.

Sam and I sat, occasionally talking about nothing, for over an hour before Diamante came down the stairs. She stood between us with her hands rubbing our backs again, this time wearing a see-through teddy.

"You have money?" she whispered.

Sam replied in the affirmative. "Make the introduction."

"Step out in alley. He will meet you in a minute. You pay me rest?" she asked, looking at me.

"I promise."

Sam and I stepped outside and, as always, evaluated our surroundings. I paid special attention to the abandoned gas station across the street. I knew it was a good hiding place, so we moved several yards further down the alley where we couldn't be seen. We had only been outside for about ninety seconds when the man we had seen earlier stepped out. He looked at each of us, seemingly frustrated, then pointed toward the door and said, "Pay her."

I watched the man as Sam entered the building once again. He was back out in fifteen seconds.

"Come with me," the man said, and we took off walking down the alley and into another smaller one.

After two blocks, he stopped and turned. He was holding a small handgun, which was pointed at my midsection.

"Who are you?" he demanded. "Why are you looking for Señor Pancheo?"

Sam immediately launched into our story and fell into using the slight accent I had heard before.

"We need a new supplier. I have been supplying the guerilla fighters in western Africa for many years. My friend here has been doing the same with anti-government militias in the United States. For the last five years, we have used the same supplier, Docic Josovic, in Yugoslavia. He is out of the game."

We used Docic Josovic because we knew he had been arrested six months ago and was awaiting trial at the International Criminal Court in the Netherlands. We hoped it added credence to the story.

"We decided to work together to find another supplier to meet our needs. We heard through the network that Mr. Pancheo could help us."

"Your name?" he asked. "Your real name."

Sam continued, "I am David Walker; this," he said, pointing at me, "is James Thames. What is your name?"

The man ignored the question but lowered his weapon.

"Where can I find you?" he asked.

"Los Altos in Maracaibo," I replied.

"On a boat?" He seemed perplexed asking the question.

"On the boat," I said, emphasizing the word 'the.' "You will know it."

"I am not saying Mr. Pancheo can help you," he said. "But if he were in this business, what would you be looking for?"

Sam slowly reached into his front pocket, pulled out a thumb drive, and held it in the air. "It is all on here. I know what I would have paid Josovic for this. Don't try to rip me off."

"Ah," he replied, "but Mr. Josovic sits in a cell awaiting trial. Mr. Pancheo does not. Assuming he is in this business and willing to do business, he will set the price. Not you."

This guy was familiar with Josovic and his plight. I doubted the average citizen of Campo Mara had that information.

He pocketed the thumb drive. "If you have not heard from me in three days, sail away and do not return."

With that, he turned and walked away.

More progress.

Chapter 21

The next two days were miserable. The heat continued to build, and a hurricane in the Atlantic drew energy from the west, greatly reducing the normally easterly winds. The winds were never cool, but at least they helped. We were in no danger of the hurricane, as it would turn north long before it arrived in our area, but it did increase the heat.

Thankfully, Sam and I dropped the suits while waiting aboard the *Guppy*. I wore some shorts I had thrown into the bag and a Pink Floyd T-shirt. I never saw Pink Floyd, but I love their music. Sam chose jeans and a long-sleeved shirt. Why? I don't know.

Neither Sam nor I are good at sitting and waiting, but that is all we could do. We spent much of our time behind the tinted glass in the air-conditioned salon, with the binoculars to our eyes. Fletcher rotated a 24-hour watch with us – four hours on, eight hours off – just so we could hopefully have some advanced warning if our contact headed our way. That assumed someone would show up.

We had spotted some people near the clubhouse who seemed to be looking our way, but it was understandable that a yacht the size of *Guppy Love* would draw attention. Were they watching us or the boat?

Near sunset on the second day, a young boy started walking down the pier. Sam was on watch, and he used the onboard intercom to call me to the salon. When I arrived, he passed me the field glasses.

"What do you think? Is he coming to us?"

"He's too young," I said. "Maybe twelve. Perhaps one of the other boats?"

The boy stopped about thirty yards away and looked back over his shoulder for a second before continuing. I couldn't see what he was looking at...or for.

The nearer he got to us, the more certain I was that he was coming our way. When he passed the last yacht along the T's long leg, I was certain of it. Did he just want to see the *Guppy*, or was there more to it?

"Why don't you go down and meet him?" Sam said. "I will look on from up here."

I knew 'look on from up here' was code for 'cover you.' Sam swung an MP5 over his shoulder and picked up a Remington 870 TAC-14 pump-action shotgun before stepping out the starboard side of the salon, away from the pier. I exited near the stern, paused momentarily to let Sam get into position, and then started down the stairs as if I didn't know the boy was approaching.

When I reached the fantail, the boy was still 10 yards away.

"Hola," the boy said when he reached the end of the pier. Once again, he looked back toward the clubhouse before continuing.

"Hola, ¿Puedo ayudarle con algo?" I asked. 'Hello. Can I help you with something?'

He reached into his pocket and pulled out a small piece of folded paper. It looked like an index card.

"De Panchco el mayor," the boy said, extending the paper toward me. It was from Pancheo.

With the fenders in place, I could not reach the paper, but the boy reached into his other pocket and pulled out a rock about the size of a lime. He placed the paper on the dock and carefully placed the rock on top before turning and running away down the pier. I waited several minutes. I didn't want to step out into something – like a sniper – that I wasn't prepared for. Just call it another lesson learned in Afghanistan.

After a couple of minutes, I heard Sam say, "Go ahead. Everything looks clear."

I opened the door on the port side of the fantail and placed a small aluminum gangplank between the *Guppy* and the pier. Then, I quickly stepped out and retrieved the paper and the rock before reversing the process and closing the small door.

"It is a set of coordinates," I shouted up to Sam.

Fletcher stepped out of the galley door and held out his hand. He looked them over, then motioned for me to follow him up to the salon and into the pilothouse. Sam joined us.

"I think I know where this is," Fletcher said while keying the numbers into his navigation system, "or at least close."

After entering the coordinates, Fletcher asked. "You guys do any diving? For fun, I mean."

"I try to avoid it, but I did a lot of 'not for fun' diving in the Marines," I told him.

"Well, it looks like you may need to do some more diving to maintain cover. We are headed to Bonaire. It is about 260 nautical miles from here. The coordinates are just north of the cruise terminal. There is no anchoring in Bonaire, only mooring buoys. The whole damn island is a marine park; they don't want to damage the coral. The limited spaces in the marinas aren't big enough for us."

"Why Bonaire?" I asked the obvious question.

"Not a clue," Sam said. "Fletcher, any thoughts?"

"Bonaire is primarily a diving and snorkeling destination. That is about it. Coral reefs surround it. Only about ten thousand people live on the island, and most of them support the diving industry. I doubt that your target is a diver. So no, I have no clue."

"It says five o'clock tomorrow afternoon. I assume we can get there early?"

Fletcher once again pulled the worn-out book from the cabinet and flipped the pages. Next came the satellite phone and a short conversation. He described *Guppy Love* and stated that he had rented a mooring before. He requested the southernmost location.

"It is just after six. I say we eat dinner, then book it over to Bonaire overnight." Fletcher said as he put the book and the phone away. "We can be there by sunrise without taxing the engines or burning too much fuel. I have reserved a mooring, but the busy season is starting, and they may run out of space. Reservations mean little. Will that timing work?"

"Yep," Sam replied.

∞

Dinner was grilled wahoo and rice pilaf from a box. It wasn't our best effort, but it was quick and filling. After cleaning and stowing the dishes, we cast off and headed north with a beautiful sunset on our port side. I sent a short message to Manning: "Contact made, heading to Bonaire." That should leave him scratching his head.

Fletcher loaded our course into the autopilot, and we set a watch schedule. Fletcher took us out of the lake and into the Gulf of Venezuela, where I took over. Four hours at 25 knots took us to just south of Aruba. Fletcher returned to the wheelhouse and moved us around Aruba, then set a new course that took us about 25 miles north of Curacao before turning southeast toward Kralendijk, the capital of Bonaire. Sam was at the helm for that run.

The sun was just coming up as we approached Bonaire. I had set my alarm, and Fletcher was brewing yet another pot of go-juice as I came through the galley.

"Here, take this up to Sam," he said, handing me a Stanley thermos full of coffee. "Tell him to turn off the autopilot and slow to about six knots. I will be up shortly."

Arriving in the wheelhouse, I relayed the message, filled Sam's mug and sat in the port side pilot's chair.

"Thoughts?" I asked. "I know you have been analyzing this."

"I have been thinking. There's not much else to do staring into the blackness."

The sun had just peeked over the horizon. Sam switched off the red lights and turned on the standard white lights before continuing.

"I don't think they are setting us up. I don't know anything about Bonaire other than that it is Netherlands territory. I highly doubt it is as lawless as Venezuela, so if they wanted to attack or kill us, this isn't the place. Venezuela would have been better."

I, too, had been thinking and had reached the same conclusion.

We sat in silence, something we were both good at, for almost 45 minutes. Fletcher joined us and passed out ham, egg, and cheese sandwiches.

"This island," Fletcher told us, "is only 22 miles from north to south and six miles at its widest point east to west. The northern third is a national park called Washington Slagbaai, but don't trust that pronunciation. The south end is the salt flats. They are really the only reason anyone ever cared about this exposed piece of coral until recreational SCUBA diving became a thing. An American Company called Cargill controls the salt flats now. They took it over about ten years ago. Last I heard, they produce 400,000 metric tons of salt annually."

"Finally, donkeys," Fletcher added after a second.

Sam and I both looked at Fletcher with raised eyebrows.

"The salt flats have been around for centuries," Fletcher said. "Initially, the salt was collected by slaves and moved to the shore by donkeys. Slavery was abolished in the 1860s, just like in the States, but the donkeys continued to move the salt. They were enslaved, too, but I guess abolition didn't apply to them. In the mid-twentieth century, the owners of the salt flats brought in Caterpillar equipment and turned all the donkeys loose to fend for themselves. I was told there are about 2,000 on the island. Maybe 20 percent are in a donkey sanctuary. The rest are feral but friendly."

"Does this have anything to do with why we are here?" Sam asked.

"Nope. I just thought you might find it interesting, and who knows, that information might come in handy one day."

"Anyway, I suggest we travel down the west coast; there is nothing on the east coast to see but rocks and cactus. That is the windward side, and it is quite rough. After we reach the southern end, we will return and pick up the mooring."

We cruised at nine knots down the west coast, between the town of Kralendijk and the smaller island of Klien Bonaire. As we approached the southern tip, we saw the mountains of salt piled high across a highway from the salt pier, where huge cargo ships moved the salt to facilities around the world. It was amazing to see.

It was just after ten when we tied off on the buoy. Once again, the *Guppy* was the largest vessel to be found, except for a small container ship that was likely used for inter-island distribution. It was perhaps a 70 meters long and docked at the cruise pier, which obviously served dual purposes.

"I am going to drop the tender over the side," Fletcher said. "Can someone help me?"

I told Fletcher I would help.

We walked out to the bow, and it occurred to me that I had not seen a tender on board. Fletcher walked to a control panel and began pushing buttons, which caused part of the deck to open on double doors. Afterward, another set of buttons raised a 16-foot Zodiac with a 75-horsepower Yamaha outboard mounted on the back up to just above deck level. I had seen the crane folded neatly against the deck but paid it no attention. At the touch of another button, it lifted and moved into place over the Zodiac.

Fletcher moved to a box at the crane's base and removed a loop with four heavy ropes attached.

"Climb in and hook the ring over the hoist," Fletcher instructed. "Hook the four ropes to the eye hooks in the corners; then I will move it to the water. You can ride it down. Just unhook the corners when you are in the water, then crank it up and ride around for a few minutes. I will put the hoist away and meet you at the stern to tie it off."

I did as he instructed and spent several minutes driving the Zodiac around slowly. After getting used to the feel, I opened it up toward open water for about a mile before returning to the *Guppy*. I had spent hundreds of hours in - and hundreds of repetitions getting into and out of - Zodiacs. I felt comfortable there.

Fletcher noted that we needed food, and he knew of a grocery store on the island. He climbed into the Zodiac at about two o'clock and promised to return by four.

"Get steaks," Sam yelled. "I need red meat!"

Fletcher waved an acknowledgment.

Chapter 22

Sam and I were both in the Salon, trying to escape the heat, and five o'clock was approaching. We had both changed into suits, but Fletcher hadn't returned from the store.

"Any guesses?" I asked, breaking a long silence.

"Nope," was Sam's eloquent reply. Due to the wind flowing around the hills on the island's northern half, the *Guppy* was pointed northeast toward the marina. Sam watched that direction while I kept an eye out into the Caribbean.

Just after five, Sam told me he had a contact headed our way—a Zodiac. Then he reported that there were three people on board, none of whom were Fletcher.

I joined Sam; the Zodiac was about 100 meters away. I lifted my binoculars and studied the approaching boat.

"They are not divers, and I am almost certain that is the *Guppy*'s tender," I said. "I am going to the fantail to meet them. You cover."

I kept an eye on the approaching boat as I descended the stairs. They came in at a higher speed than one would expect in a daylight tactical situation. There was no element of surprise, and Sam and I controlled the high ground. We had the advantage. That told me they were unconcerned about us.

The driver stopped the boat about a dozen yards from the *Guppy*'s dive platform, which Fletcher had lowered earlier to provide easy access to the tender. The three men were all dressed in lightweight golf shirts of various colors and khaki shorts. None were very big men. All were dark-complected with short hair.

One rose off the bench seat and stood at the bow.

"Ahoy," he said. English, I thought, but then I wondered if that was a universal word when greeting another boat. "May we approach?" He looked up to where Sam was standing. I imagined he looked a little intimidating with the shotgun in hand and the MP5 slung over his shoulder. I didn't look back, however.

"Where is our captain, Fletcher?" I asked.

"He is fine," the man said. "He just loaned us the tender so we could come talk to you."

I doubted that.

"Are you armed?" I asked.

"No. Gun possession is illegal on the island."

"Raise your shirts and turn around slowly so I can see."

They all did as I asked. I saw nothing, but that didn't mean they were unarmed.

"Pull up to the platform and throw me your bow line, but stay on board," I told him.

The *Guppy* barely moved in the still waters, so when he threw the line, I pulled about two feet of the Zodiac's hull onto the dive platform before tying him off.

"What can I do for you?" I asked without inviting him aboard.

"Mr. Pancheo would like to speak with you."

"We are here; he is welcome to join us."

The man laughed.

"Señor Pancheo does not come to you."

"Does he not want my money?" I asked.

"Do you not want his goods?" came the reply.

I paused before responding. "My partner, Mr. Walker, and I will speak with Señor Pancheo."

"Only one. Those were my instructions."

I put my hands in my pocket and stood for several seconds before turning around. I looked at Sam and lifted the purple Crown Royal bag from my pocket. He nodded.

Pancheo's men had, to some degree, outsmarted us. By taking Fletcher and using the tender – I was still assuming he was taken and not dead or working for the enemy – they had removed our ability to get to shore easily. They had also eliminated our captain. While Sam or I could handle the *Guppy* in the open water, docking required practice, and finesse with the thrusters. A skill that neither of us possessed.

"While Mr. Walker and I are partners in this, we each have our own deals to make. I may not be able to negotiate on his behalf," I told the men.

"Let's get through this first meeting," he said. "Then, perhaps, Señor Pancheo will agree to meet with both of you."

The hand in my pocket pulled the small tracking device from the bag. It was slightly larger than a quarter and twice as thick, and once activated, it would send a radio signal every fifteen seconds for about two weeks. I felt for and slid the small switch along the edge into the transmit position, then dropped the device to the bottom of my pocket.

"Let me untie the tender, and I will go with you," I told the men.

As I moved behind the short wall at the stern, I acted as if the line was tangled. Going to one knee to fix the imaginary problem, I placed the Crown Royal bag against the wall, in full view of Sam but hidden from the view of the three men. After a second, I stood again and released the tender before stepping onto the dive platform and over the bow of the Zodiac.

The man to whom I had been speaking held out his hand. "I am Manuel. Please remove your jacket; it is hot."

241

I shook his hand, squeezing perhaps a bit too hard, and did as he asked. He ran his hands around my waist and pant legs, searching for a weapon, but found nothing.

The driver motored away, and I looked back at Sam. He was headed down the stairs toward the Crown bag. I wasn't sure how he would get to shore to follow me, but I guessed he would find a way.

∞

The driver took us straight east toward shore before turning north for perhaps half a mile. We entered a protected marina with various sailing and motor vessels ranging from five to twelve meters in length. We pulled alongside a ladder in the back corner of the marina. A high fence secured the people and boats. A uniformed guard waited at the top of the ladder. Manuel went up first, and the remaining two men indicated I should follow.

When I reached the top of the stairs, Manuel said, "Come with me. Señor Pancheo is expecting us."

I was led through the gate and to a small pickup parked across the street. Manuel climbed into the driver's seat, and we headed north along the shoreline before turning northeast into the hills. The roads made Venezuela's roads look good, and the suspension on the Chinese-made pickup was non-existent.

"I apologize for the ride," Manuel said as we passed three donkeys standing on the edge of the road. "They spend nothing on the roads, and it is silly to buy a nice vehicle because they won't last. The salt air is damaging."

I said nothing. I was concentrating on where I was being taken and making mental notes of landmarks and turns. I was somewhat surprised they were letting me see. Eventually, we pulled up to a gate in front of a large but not extravagant house near the top of the hill. Manuel motioned for me to get out. He did the same, and we walked toward the house while I reached into my pocket and again checked to ensure the tracker was switched on.

The house was built like many I had noticed along the shoreline, with open-air spaces that used the breeze for cooling. In this case, an open kitchen and living area in the center overlooked a deck, pool, and the Caribbean off in the distance. I could also see Klien Bonaire and, perhaps, with some binoculars, the *Guppy*. I imagined Sam pacing the fantail, awaiting a ride to shore. Down each side of the open area were doors that likely led to bed and bathrooms.

The breeze through the open area was nice, but the afternoon sun shone almost directly into the space, creating a searing heat.

"Have a seat," Manuel instructed. "He will be out in a moment." With that said Manuel walked out to the edge of the deck and sat, staring out over the water perhaps a kilometer away.

I moved the nearest chair slightly to get my back closer to the wall and into the thin shaded area. The experience was nothing like I had expected. While I received a cursory search upon climbing into the Zodiac, had the tables been turned, Manuel would have been forced to endure a full body and cavity search. Something else I learned in the Marines and had driven home in Afghanistan. Manuel had a pleasant demeanor, even though he held all the cards. I had not seen a gun, and there was little security around the house. The scene simply didn't fit my idea of an international arms dealer.

After just a few minutes, a door on the south side opened, and a small woman of some Asian descent walked to the kitchen without acknowledging me. She began to pull pans from the shelves below the counter and place them on the stove. Next, she took assorted items from the refrigerator and began cutting and seasoning fish and vegetables. I just watched her. She never looked up.

After a wait of twenty minutes, according to the Tag Heuer watch I was wearing, another door opened to my right, just feet from where I was sitting. I stood.

The man who emerged also wore a golf shirt, white, and I noticed the polo pony logo stitched into the left breast. His slacks were dark navy but of a very lightweight material. He wore woven loafers. He was in his fifties, close to my height, and obviously fit. He extended his hand.

"Victor Pancheo, Mr. Thames. So nice to meet you."

I shook his hand. "Nice to meet you as well."

"Let's take a walk," he said in clear but accented English before turning to the woman and speaking in a language I didn't understand. Perhaps it was Chinese, Maybe Korean or Vietnamese. "I asked her to prepare for two. Will you join me for dinner?"

"Considering I have no ride out of here, it would seem like my best option."

"Yes," Pancheo laughed. "It does seem that way."

He led me back to where the truck was parked and then into the shade on the east side of the house. It was more comfortable on the hill where the winds were stronger.

"Let's discuss business before we eat. Then we can sit together and enjoy the view. It will be comfortable on the deck as the sun sets. May I ask how you found me?"

"We live in a small world, Mr. Pancheo. There are only so many dealers who operate on a global scale. You probably know, or know of, most of them. There are also only a few people, like me and Walker, who have contacts within the militias, the guerillas, and the countries no government wants to supply. We're your sales force, so to speak. When our primary supplier, Mr. Josovic, was arrested, we began asking around. Walker and I had worked together before to fill several large orders. He owns an import business in the Bahamas called Rolle Imports. The business is legitimate, importing and exporting high-end audio equipment. But he also uses the business as cover to import and export less legitimate items."

"You are working with your competition?"

"There is enough for everyone. I can make five to ten million a year just selling within the United States. He works mostly in Africa and occasionally in Europe. Like I said, it is a big pie. I can't eat it all."

Pancheo nodded. "Assuming I can supply you, how will you receive the goods? Not the easiest thing to import to the United States."

"We have a tried and successful method that I won't discuss in detail. Call it a trade secret."

"We both operate in a world of secrets, do we not?" Pancheo asked rhetorically. "The items requested add up fast. I have most of it in my inventory. I assume you have access to seventy million."

"I do," I said. But we are not paying seventy million. The list is worth forty to forty-five million at most."

"Perhaps that is the price when dealing with Josovic. He did not have the overhead I do. Staying out of prison is expensive."

I laughed. He had me there.

"Walker and I will want to see the deliverables and get details on what you are selling. The list simply stated items like 'automatic rifles chambered in 7.62 x39' or 'chambered in 5.56 NATO,' for example. There is a big difference in the value of a Colt versus a Chinese-made weapon. My American buyers want American-made weapons."

"Here is my offer to you. Send me five million dollars. Call it a down payment. I will provide wiring instructions to a bank in the Cayman Islands. When I get that, we will return to Caracas and perhaps reach a deal. At that time, you can see one of my warehouses, a sample of the goods, and a complete manifest. But know before we continue, it will be closer to seventy million than forty-five."

"I will need to speak to Walker, but I believe that is acceptable. I have other questions, though."

"I imagine the first is, 'Where is your captain?' I think he said his name is Fletcher," Pancheo offered.

"That is the first question, yes."

"Let me ask, how did you come to find your captain?"

I didn't like where this was going.

"Walker did an Internet search for a yacht we could lease to move between Caracas and Maracaibo. The leasing agency told us to go to a certain slip at the marina in Caracas. We didn't expect something that big, and we had no captain's license or expertise in piloting large boats. We agreed to hire Fletcher to serve as the captain."

"Your 'Fletcher' is actually Roman Thompson, and he is with American intelligence," Pancheo stated matter-of-factly. "I wonder if you are American intelligence as well, but so far, you check out. A friend of mine in Argentina knows Walker. He said he had dealt with him in the past."

"We are what we say we are. As for Fletcher, all I know is the dude can drive the boat, but he is harmless. Why would the CIA have a man on a yacht in Venezuela."

"We have known about him for about a year. We keep an eye on him, but he seems to be looking toward the President's office more than at us."

"And why do you think that is?" I asked.

"America is obsessed with communism and socialism, so they pay attention to the government and not to us. They see it as a huge threat to your way of life. Also, we keep a low profile. You will notice that I don't have a dozen guards around me. I don't ride around in armored vehicles. I don't travel on a twenty-million-dollar yacht."

He delivered the last line while looking me in the eye.

"This is how I stay out of prison. I, too, have legitimate businesses—auto parts stores here, in Curacao, and all over Venezuela. I live like a small business owner, moving between Maracaibo, Caracas, and the islands. No one bothers me."

"This news concerns me," I said. "I wonder if he is watching us or watching you? Perhaps both."

"He appears to do a few charters each year, primarily diving, around the south Caribbean islands. Perhaps he sees you as a legitimate charter client and has no clue about your intentions. But I doubt he doesn't suspect something since you have weapons. Let it play out. Ultimately, he may need to be eliminated, but I see that as a last resort. Again, I like to remain low profile, and killing people who are no threat draws attention."

"So, he is alive?"

"Last I heard, he is alive, well, and very drunk at La Cantina Restaurant in downtown Kralendijk. He will be in the Zodiac with you on the way back to your yacht, but I suggest you take the wheel. One of my girls is filling him with tequila, promises, and expectations that will never be fulfilled. Let's go eat dinner and end this business talk."

When we sat at a small table beside the pool, the sun was just dropping below the horizon. A bottle of white wine was chilling on a stand, and the Asian woman delivered a small plate of fish with one thick stalk of asparagus on the side.

"It is tuna local to the waters of Bonaire. It lives primarily in the brine waters of the mangroves. It is good, but a different texture than the tuna of the oceans."

I couldn't argue with that assessment.

The next course was tenderloin of beef. Again, a small portion by American standards. Sam would have scoffed. It was cooked perfectly with spices I didn't recognize. "What is the seasoning?" I asked.

"I do not know. Lu Chan is from China, and she is an amazing cook. But I don't know what seasonings she uses."

"So, you were speaking Chinese to her?"

"Yes, Mandarin. My background is in the military, and thirty years ago, long before Chavez, I moved to China for training." I wanted to ask what kind of training as it could have been valuable intel, but I didn't. "I spent four years in that country before returning home to Venezuela. I learned Mandarin Chinese while I was there. I also have Chinese nationals running my stores and performing some other tasks for me, like cooking and cleaning. They are very loyal."

No dessert was offered, but Pancheo suggested a nightcap before my return. I had gone light on the wine, so I felt safe having one more drink.

He returned to the kitchen and reached into a high cabinet, where he withdrew a bottle. Then he picked up two glasses and returned to the table. When he placed the bottle on the table, I saw the label. It was Pappy Van Winkle bourbon, 23 years old. I have stated before that I have never been much of a drinker, but being from Kentucky, I knew what I was looking at.

"Amazing," I said to Pancheo. "I can't find this in America, but here it is on a tiny island in the middle of the Caribbean."

"I do have a weak spot for American bourbon," Pancheo said. "And I have a source for a bottle or two of the Pappy Van Winkle each year. That is enough. I like Elijah Craig and Elmer T. Lee. They are not nearly as expensive and just as good to my taste. But on special occasions, I offer the Van Winkle."

He poured two fingers into each glass and lifted his. "To business," he said. "To business," I repeated.

∞

Manuel drove me back to the marina, led me past the guard, and entered the combination to get me through the gate beside the Zodiac. "Your captain will be along," he said, lifting his cell phone to his ear. A moment later, he handed me an envelope. "Wire instructions. Make the transfer and then return to Caracas. We will be in touch." With those final words, he turned and was gone.

Within ten minutes, two men dragged a very drunk Fletcher to the ladder. It was only three steps down into the Zodiac. Fletcher descended one step before falling into the boat. I nodded to the men, started the motor, and slowly made my way through the marina. I was concerned about finding the *Guppy* in the dark, but as soon as we left the narrow protective entrance, I could see her profile in the moonlight from a half mile away.

I had no idea where Sam was, so when we reached *Guppy Love*, I swung around to the stern and ran the Zodiac a couple of feet up on the dive platform. Then I climbed out and tied off.

Should I leave Fletcher where he lay or carry him inside? Neither option was appealing. As I was thinking, Fletcher stood and said, "What? Were you going to leave me out here?"

He bounded over the side of the Zodiac and onto the dive platform. I turned and buried my fist into his jaw. It was a good connection. Fletcher was out before he hit the water. My hand hurt, but I didn't care.

"Why?" I heard from above me. Now I knew where Sam was.

"They know he is CIA," I explained. The water had revived Fletcher, but he seemed unsure about what had happened or why it happened. I let him splash around for a few seconds before offering him a hand. He didn't want to take it.

"Fine," I said to him. "Sam, raise the platform for me."

"Okay, give me your hand," Fletcher said.

He wasn't going to drown. With a little effort, he could have pulled himself into the Zodiac, but without a ladder and the diving platform raised four feet above the surface, getting back on the *Guppy* would have been harder.

"Dry off and get changed, then meet us in the salon when I call you," I said before turning and climbing to the fantail. "Sam, we need to talk."

I relayed every detail to Sam, which took well over an hour. We then spent another thirty minutes discussing how to handle the Fletcher situation.

"Before we discuss this with Fletcher, maybe we need to make him disappear," Sam said. "I'm not talking about killing him, but he is exposed and apparently has been for years. Just work it out so that when we get to Caracas, Fletcher is no longer with us. Maybe we drop him in Curacao or Grenada, and he can fly to the States and start fresh somewhere else if the Company will keep him on the payroll."

I considered it and did some math. "It would be a long and fast run, but we could make the round trip to Grenada in a day doing fifty knots, or we could reach Curacao in an hour. Let's see what his side of the story is. I called him over the intercom, and he was in the salon two minutes later.

We started with the easy questions.

"Where are the groceries?" Sam asked. "I requested steaks."

Fletcher sat and looked at us. He was way more clear-headed than I would have expected two hours ago. His face was swollen, and the orbital around his left eye was turning black.

"Fuck you!" he yelled. "What the hell was that about?"

Sam continued the questioning.

"You went for groceries. You didn't return. Pancheo's men delivered you, shitfaced, I might add, to the tender. What happened?"

"A small boat followed me in and tied up next to me," Fletcher said, having blown off some steam. "I called for a taxi to take me to the store, but while I waited by the road, the men from the boat walked up to me. There were three of them. One stood on each side, and the other stuck a needle in my ass. The next thing I knew, I was locked in a room in the dark. It took a bit to clear the cobwebs. After some time, I had no clue how long, the door opened, and two of the men returned. I pretended to be semi-conscious, and they walked me to a small car. Two minutes later, we were at the marina. I continued the charade, fell into the boat, and rode back to you. I wasn't sure if they were watching, so I just laid there until we were back here. Then I got up, and you slugged me."

"Any idea why they did that?"

"None. What all happened while I was out?"

"We will get to that later. Fletcher, does anyone here or in Venezuela know you are CIA?"

"I have a couple of contacts at Langley, plus you two. That is all as far as I know."

I took over. "Pancheo knows you are CIA, Roman." There was no mistaking the look on his face.

"Why did you tell them?" he asked.

I just stared at him. Was he really that stupid?

Finally, he tried again. "How do they know?"

"I have no idea. Pancheo didn't share that tidbit with me. He just said they have known and kept an eye on you for years."

The reality sank in. "Then I am finished here."

"You are likely finished, period, as far as the Company is concerned," Sam said. "And you are a liability to us."

"What is your financial situation?" I asked.

"I have money stashed away—enough to start over. And I have *Guppy Love*. I can continue to make money by chartering somewhere else. Maybe I will take her to Greece."

"You don't have *Guppy Love*," Sam said. "We have *Guppy Love*, then the CIA has her."

"Truth, do you have any family?" I asked.

"Two daughters in Venezuela. All of that was true."

"Will they miss you?"

"They haven't so far."

"Ever been to Grenada?"

"Once," he replied. "Several years ago."

"The purpose of your visit?" Sam asked this time.

"I had a charter here in Bonaire. Two men, attorneys, were diving. I don't know what happened, but suddenly they had to go home. There are very limited flights from the islands during the off-season. Their quickest option was a fast run to Grenada and a flight to Miami the next morning. They paid me an extra five thousand dollars to cover the fuel burn on the high-speed run."

"So, you were not working for the CIA on that trip?"

"No."

"And you have never worked for the CIA in or near Grenada?"

"No."

"Pack your bags," Sam said, "then teach us everything there is to know about this boat in the next ten hours. We are making a high-speed run to Grenada."

"I am a little hungover from the drugs, and my face hurts. Can I rest for a few minutes?"

"No. You have thirty minutes to pack. Sam and I need to discuss some other items. Meet me at the bow," I looked at my watch, "at ten-thirty. Your first lesson will be teaching me how to stow the Zodiac."

Fletcher nodded and headed down the stairs.

"The right thing?" I asked, looking at Sam.

"Yep," he said. Then he added, "I think so."

Chapter 23

I will give Fletcher –a.k.a. Roman Thompson – credit. He was very helpful. He explained stowing and removing the tender boat. Then, he spent time explaining the gauges and the electrical system. We were unable to spend any time in the engine room. The gas turbines were so loud when traveling 50 knots that it was painful inside. He promised to show us everything there before he departed.

I took over at the helm, and Fletcher toured Sam around every nook, cranny, and hidey-hole, as Fletcher termed them, on the *Guppy*. We were low on fuel when we arrived in Grenada after nine hours of running hard.

Fletcher allowed us to practice with the thrusters at the fueling dock. We took on almost 8,000 gallons of marine diesel fuel during the next hour. With just three of us on board, the water maker was keeping up, and the freshwater tanks were full.

Fletcher took us below. The engines were popping as they cooled following the trip to Grenada. Sam and I helped check and clean the pumps and filters that provided cooling seawater to the twin Textron Lycoming TF-40 engines. We checked the oil and hydraulic fluid levels.

We were also introduced to a chart on the wall showing all the items that required regular maintenance and the hours between checks. A digital readout for the number of hours on each engine was displayed nearby. "Keep this up to date. Do the maintenance. The chart says to check the filters every 20 hours, but if you run at over 40 knots like we did coming to Grenada, divide that and everything else in half. Honestly, considering our speed, we should have stopped halfway here. The engines are supposed to shut down automatically if they get too hot, but I never trust the fail safes. Costs about a half-million each to replace."

I charged a little over $29,000 to my James Thames American Express Card to pay for the fuel. We still had not picked up any groceries, so we negotiated a place to dock for a few hours. After the fuel purchase, the harbormaster didn't charge us for the space.

Sam volunteered to go to the store while Fletcher and I did another walk-through. Truthfully, the *Guppy* probably should have had an experienced crew of three or four at a minimum. I wondered how Fletcher did it alone, so I asked.

"I know a few people in each town who will help me when needed for a charter. I used to have a regular crew, but as they moved on, I never replaced them. Most things I can do alone; it just takes longer."

"How do you capture a mooring buoy or release and secure the anchor alone?" I asked.

"Good question, and something I forgot to cover. Let's go back to the bridge."

On arrival, Fletcher explained how to implement the "hold station" feature on the autopilot. "It takes some time, but if I need to pull up anchor, I do what I can from here, then press the hold station button. The autopilot uses the thrusters to keep the boat in the same position while I walk down to the bow and do what I need to from there. Sometimes, I have to come up, reposition, and repeat the process several times, especially when attaching to a mooring buoy."

I looked out and saw Sam coming toward us with several grocery bags. A young man, a boy really, was training behind him, carrying several more. I met him at the gangway.

He passed his bags off to me and then took the bags from the boy. Fletcher took those bags to the galley. Sam reached into his pocket and removed a $20 bill in US currency before handing it over to the boy.

"What is their currency here?" I asked.

"I have no idea," Sam said. "But they take AMEX and recognize Andrew Jackson."

We went into the galley and put away the groceries. There were several pounds of red meat, plus bread and coffee in the bags. In Sam's world, that was all one needed to survive.

Fletcher came up the stairs from the captain's quarters with a bag over his shoulder. His orbital was fully black now. I almost felt bad for hitting him.

"Guys, I am sorry. I had no idea that they were on to me. I would have let you know. Please let Langley know what happened."

"Since we are not CIA, I am not sure contacting the Company would be a good idea," Sam said before I could. It's probably best you do that."

"I know you have a sat phone with you, so I took the one from the pilothouse. It is mine, and I pay for it." He passed over a slip of paper with the phone number on it. "I would appreciate it if you would call and let me know how this all works out. I would like to return to Venezuela and visit my daughters one day."

I responded. "Assuming we survive this, I will try to let you know what happens."

Fletcher looked dejected.

"You will tell Pancheo I am dead?"

"We will tell him we shot you in the forehead, tied a heavy chain around your neck, and tossed you overboard," I said. "It's what they would expect. Give us 90 days. You have to be dead until this is over."

With that, Fletcher walked to the fantail, across the gangway, and down the pier.

While we watched Fletcher go, I said, "We need to make a phone call and ask Daddy for a five-million-dollar transfer."

"Yep."

Sam and I slept for six hours before starting toward Caracas at a more leisurely pace of 25 knots. Manning waited a day as instructed, then wired the money from the Rolle Imports account to Pancheo's account in the Cayman Islands. Within minutes of the deposit, I felt certain that money had been moved through ten different banks in ten other countries.

Sam and I talked a lot on the return trip. We noticed several things. Most importantly, we both noted earlier that the man Diamante put us in contact with, the one we spoke to about Pancheo, had no discernable accent when speaking in English. I left a message for Manning requesting photographs of the three missing CIA agents.

Second, I wondered if Pancheo's story about owning car parts stores would check out. I thought it would, but I wanted to know. I sent another note asking Manning if he could find out.

Lastly, we still were not sure about Fletcher. Neither of us knew much about the CIA. In fact, Sam had spent the last eighteen years trying to stay very distant from them. It didn't seem logical to us that Fletcher would be left in Venezuela on a thirty-million-dollar yacht, simply providing a piece or two of intel each year. Intel that was, by his own admission in an earlier conversation, "mostly rumors about the status of the president."

It was all perplexing. Did we ask Manning to inquire about Roman Thompson? We decided no.

Twenty hours after leaving St. George's, Grenada, we returned the *Guppy* to pier number three, slip seventeen at Marina Deportiva. The docking was smooth and relatively easy, with Sam at the helm and me handling the fenders and lines.

Within minutes of tying off the *Guppy*, a woman approached and asked to come aboard. I wasn't sure of the protocol.

She wore a skin-tight white dress that barely covered her breasts and barely extended down to her upper thigh. I was certain she carried no weapons.

"Is there something I can help you with," I asked, not responding to her request.

"Yes, Mr. Thames. There is."

The use of my name settled it.

"Permission to come aboard granted," I said. She simply held out her hand, waiting for me to assist her. I stepped onto the gangway and assisted her with the five steps required to board. Sam appeared beside me a moment later.

She was a strikingly beautiful woman with a long, feminine neck, black hair just below her shoulders, and piercing dark eyes. Her skin was dark, but it was more of a natural tan than the complexion of a native Hispanic. I could not place her accent. I didn't think her native language was Spanish or any other Latin derivative.

"My employer has asked to meet with you. Will you come with me?"

"Where are we going?" Sam asked.

"To meet my employer."

We were getting nowhere.

"And who is your employer?" It was my turn.

"He will explain all," she said. I was still lost on the accent.

"We just arrived from a long trip. Let us change our clothes and lock up," Sam said.

"No problem, I will wait in the galley."

"You will wait here," I said quickly. I didn't want her inside until I knew what we were dealing with. "You go ahead and change, David. Then you can keep our guest company while I do the same."

Sam headed inside.

"What is your name?" I asked.

"My name is unimportant," she replied with a smile. She enjoyed playing the part of the mysterious woman in a thriller novel.

"Where are you from?" I asked. "I don't recognize your beautiful accent."

"I was born in Croatia, and my parents are from there. I attended university in Italy and then London. Perhaps it is now a blend, and that is why you don't recognize it."

"Perhaps," I said. "How did you end up in Venezuela?"

"My employer brought me here to help with his business. I have a degree in international banking and finance from the University of London."

"Impressive. Have you handled any five-million-dollar deposits lately?" was my next question.

"You are fishing, Mr. Thames. But that is okay." Another non-answer.

Sam returned, and I went to change. I assumed then that he would ask the same questions and get the same answers. He later confirmed that was what happened.

When I returned to the fantail, our guest rose and stated, "Your instructions are as follows. No weapons, nothing in your pockets, no money, no passport. You will not need anything, and you will be thoroughly searched. Go back inside and lock up whatever you need to. I will wait here.

Sam and I looked at each other. What were we to do? We went into the galley and removed our weapons and everything else in our pockets.

We stepped back outside and locked the door using the digital keypad. "After you, Miss. Unimportant," I said.

She smiled. It was a beautiful smile. "Call me Nadia."

We followed her to the marina entrance, where two men, bodyguard types wearing identical pale blue linen suits, stood waiting beside a pair of Range Rovers, one black, one white.

"You will go with these gentlemen; I will follow," Nadia said. "It isn't far to our destination."

Sam and I were ushered into the back seat of the black vehicle. The two men climbed into the front. Before we departed, the one in the passenger seat tossed two black bags in our direction and motioned for us to put them over our heads. They never said a word. This is what I had expected on Bonaire, and I was still perplexed as to why Pancheo allowed me to see where he lived on the island. Sam had suggested that it might be a temporary residence, a one-time rental, and I had to admit that there was nothing in the house, like photos or other personal items, to make it look like a home. It was the only thing that made sense. Perhaps he had rented it only for the meeting with us. It was a sound strategy. Who is aware of a location is unimportant if one is never returning. I guessed we were now being taken to his home or perhaps his office, a more permanent location.

After only ten or twelve minutes, the vehicle stopped, and I heard what sounded like a garage door closing. I felt queasy. The rough roads, vehicle turns, and inability to see gave me motion sickness. I never had that trouble on the boat. The hood was pulled off my head, and as my eyes readjusted to the light, the man in front of me motioned that I should remove Sam's hood as well. Again, he said nothing.

We were in a large garage with the doors closed. There were no windows, and the heat was stifling. The two exited the front seats and opened our doors. Sam and I stepped out.

The driver motioned for us to follow him while the other bodyguard fell in behind us. We walked down a long, narrow hallway with doors on either side. I could not tell if it was an office building or a residence, but the air conditioner was working well, and that helped relieve the nausea I still felt following the ride.

A set of double doors stood closed at the end of the hallway, but twenty feet before we reached them, we were ushered into a side room, probably fourteen by twenty feet, with a sofa, several plush chairs, a coffee maker still dripping a fresh pot, and a basket full of individual snacks. I saw Twix bars and recognized Rice Krispy treats, though the labeling was Spanish. There were also bananas and apples. The door closed behind us.

I placed my finger to my lips, but signaling Sam to be quiet was likely redundant. I checked a door at the back of the room in the opposite corner from where we entered and found a small bathroom. Continuing around the perimeter, I checked for cameras and microphones but found nothing. That didn't mean they were not there.

Sam was doing his own checking – checking the quality of the coffee in the pot. He sipped and nodded his approval. I circled back around to him.

Standing close to him, I whispered, "I don't see any cameras or bugs, but be careful." He nodded, then said, "You take the lead here. Unless a question is asked directly of me, you answer."

I wasn't sure why he said that, but I nodded my understanding.

The coffee sounded good after the long trip from Grenada. I started doing the math and calculated that I had slept about six of the last forty-eight hours. Not too bad, actually, and the coffee would help. As I lifted the pot and a mug from the counter, the door opened, and Nadia entered.

"I see you have found the coffee. Please help yourself, then come with me."

I poured, and then we followed her to the end of the hallway. She opened the door on the right and escorted us into a large, well-furnished room. I estimated the space to be thirty feet wide and forty feet deep. It had a beautiful, ornate wooden desk in the back right-hand corner, with three computers and monitors spread across two matching credenzas behind it, but the balance of the space looked more like a formal living room. The ceiling was high, probably fourteen feet, and four chandeliers were evenly spaced in a rectangle. There were two other doors on the side walls near the front of the room where we entered and a door near the desk on the left-hand wall. Again, there were no windows.

Nadia motioned toward a pair of wing-back chairs and asked us to have a seat.

"Where are you from, Mr. Thames?" Nadia asked.

I started to reply, 'That is unimportant,' but I thought better of it. "Mayfield, Kentucky," I said. I was pulling information from the James Thames alias.

"And how did you get in this business?" she asked.

"What business would that be?" I replied.

"Don't be obtuse," Nadia said. You want to buy weapons—several million dollars worth if the rumors are true. Are they true, Mr. Thames?"

"I will be happy to discuss that with your boss," I replied. Her beauty was being overwhelmed by her brash delivery.

"You will discuss it with me, or you will never see my boss."

She had the upper hand, and she knew it. She also wanted to make sure we knew it.

"Several years ago, a friend asked me to secure some guns for a guy he ran around with. It was off-the-books stuff. The total order was less than thirty grand. Word of mouth led another group in my direction, and the orders kept getting bigger. At first, I had a legit wholesaler I could buy through, but within a year, I ordered more than he could remove from the books. I did some research and found Docic Josovic.

She turned to Sam. "And you, David Walker, where are you from?"

"I grew up in South Africa. Just outside Cape Town in an area known as Camps Bay."

"Really?" Nadia said, her mood brightening a bit. "I spent some time near there. Do you know Callie Park?"

Sam was smooth. "I know Comrie Park. Not Callie Park." They never broke eye contact.

Nadia just grinned.

The door beside the desk opened, and an older man dressed in an impeccable suit entered the room. I recognized him at once. He shuffled his feet and held, but did not use a light cane. His hair was greying and cut close. The right eye was cloudy with cataracts; the left was also starting to cloud. He walked up to Sam this time, stopping inches from his face.

"Which one are you?" he asked in English.

"David Walker."

He looked at me.

"James Thames," I said, extending my hand. He either ignored it or couldn't see that far.

I realized that the cane was likely used to help him get around.

Nadia stood near him as he turned and sat in a third wing-back chair. She sat on the sofa, only a couple of feet from him.

"We have searched your boat," he began. "There is no sign of your captain. Where might I find him?"

"He is no longer with us," I said.

"Is he still in Bonaire?" Someone had been watching us. I just hoped they had not tracked us to Grenada.

"He is no longer with us," I repeated. "We learned some things and took the appropriate steps."

"Very well," he said. "Have you had fun chasing the ghost of Victor Pancheo?"

"We have found two Victor Pancheos. You and another gentleman we met in Bonaire."

"I have news for you, young man. Victor Pancheo does not exist."

"Then who are you? You told me you were Pancheo when I saw you near Campo Mara."

"I was Victor Pancheo because that is who you were looking for. I own that land under the name Victor Pancheo. I also own other land, other homes."

"And the man we met in Bonaire?" I asked.

He shrugged. "Also a ghost. Certainly not Victor Pancheo. Once again, you were allowed to find what you were looking for. I suggest you be more careful."

"You have watched us since our arrival." It was a statement, not a question.

"It is how I survive. You spoke to my granddaughter in Miami. We tracked you from the airport to the beautiful yacht at the marina. We knew the owner was CIA, so we were very suspicious of you after that."

"I assume we have passed some type of test, or we would not be here," I offered.

"You have passed nothing."

"You said we spoke to your granddaughter in Miami. Who is Artura Simonyan?" I asked. It wasn't adding up. She had said her father was Artura Simonyan.

"I am sometimes called that. Sometimes, I am Pancheo. But I was born Adolph Finn Weber seventy-seven years ago in Germany. My parents were followers of Hitler. I was ten when my parents smuggled me out of Germany and into Armenia. I was raised by a family sympathetic to the plight of children displaced by the war and unsympathetic to the Nazi regime. My parents knew the war would be lost, but they stayed behind in

Germany. I am told a Frenchman, of all people, shot and killed my father. My mother took her own life when she heard of Hitler's death. For obvious reasons, I dropped Adolph from my name and became Finn Weber. I still use that name on occasion. The family in Armenia wanted to erase my German name and heritage, so they baptized me in the Armenian Apostolic Church as Artura Simonyan."

"Thank you, that explains a lot. Why come to Venezuela?"

"Let me just say that the situation here is conducive to our business."

In short, the government, meaning Chavez, was getting paid.

He turned to Sam. "Mr. Walker. I believe you have met one of my associates in Argentina?"

"Yep." Sam was being talkative again.

"You placed an order but never followed up."

"I don't like dealing with middlemen who can't help me. He couldn't fulfill my order without going to others. He told me he would have to speak to his supplier in Venezuela. Mr. Thames and I asked around and got two names. Victor Pancheo and Artura Simonyan. We came looking for them."

"Well, here we are." He smiled.

"And which of those names shall we call you?" I asked. "Or is there another name we should use?"

He waved a hand. "It doesn't matter, but I have always preferred Weber. It is simple."

"Okay, Mr. Weber. Since we are sharing, will you tell me who I spoke with in Bonaire?

"That was my son; I am Artura Levon Simonyan. He is Artura Gayane Simonyan. Armenians have not adopted the American practice of naming their children with a junior or a number. We give them a different middle name."

"So, he is Victoria's father," I stated for clarity.

Nadia spoke for the first time. "I think we are done with this. Convince me you are not CIA."

"I can't prove a negative," I said. "I am sure you have dug into my background, Walker's, as well. We have been chasing our tails for the last four weeks, and you could have made contact anytime. You used that time wisely, I am sure."

"May I ask again about Roman Thompson?" Nadia said.

"He is at the bottom of the Caribbean. After Mr. Panc..." I paused. "After your son told me he was CIA – please thank him for that information – I got him back to the boat and, after his head cleared from whatever your men shot him up with, told him to head toward Grenada. About a hundred miles out into the Caribbean, Walker put a gun to his head. We stopped the boat and questioned him. He lost a few toes before admitting he reported to the CIA. He said we were just another charter for him, part of his cover, and he didn't care what we did. He said gathering information about Chavez was his only mission. The bottom line: we had to decide. Eliminate him and possibly draw questions. Or trust him to keep his mouth shut. I trust no one. He is resting peacefully about a hundred thirty meters below the surface."

"So, there is no body to verify his death?" Nadia asked.

"There may be, but it is going to be hard to find. It has probably been consumed by now. That was over a day ago."

Nothing was said for a while. The three of us all looked at Weber. It was his move.

"I will leave you with Nadia. We have the jump drive you gave my man in Paraguiapoa; she can tell you what is in our inventory. You will find it almost 100 percent complete. I don't have to go to other suppliers for orders of this size," he added while once again looking in Sam's direction.

We all rose as Weber struggled to his feet. Nadia walked along beside him as he made his way back to the door through which he had originally entered. He was frail and likely legally blind, but perhaps that was all a show, too.

Nadia indicated that we should sit in front of the desk while she took residence behind it. She began typing on the computer to her right, and a laser printer that I could hear but not see began spitting out pages.

She turned to us. "You can look this over, but the paper must never leave this room. Just so we know, to whom will these arms be delivered?"

Sam spoke up on this one. "I own an import and export business in the Bahamas. I have a process for receiving the goods in the Bahamas that I will share at the appropriate time. We will handle all distribution from there."

"That isn't my question. What is the ultimate destination?"

"Why does it matter to you? You get money; we get goods to sell."

"It matters because we don't want to end up like your previous supplier. Josovic sold to many people, so there is no way to know who sold him out. But if you are selling to guerillas in some African nation, for example, and word spreads about the arms being supplied from Venezuela, then we know to be concerned and take certain steps."

I decided it couldn't hurt. It was all made up anyway. "Most of my sales are inside the United States. That is why my clients have a preference for American-made weapons. Several large anti-government militias have been recruiting and procuring weapons for years. I sell to them."

"But you are an American. Why would you supply people who will fight against your government?"

Luckily, it was a question Sam and I had expected, so I was prepared.

"The militias pose no threat to the government in the United States. They talk big, and they recruit and raise money. But a single company from the National Guard could wipe them out in hours. A few employ mercenaries to help with training and tactics, but even five thousand beer-drinking rednecks pose no real threat."

Nadia looked at me. "Their necks are red?"

"Sorry, just a term we use for uneducated country folk like me."

She still didn't understand.

"And you, Mr. Walker?"

"I have an outstanding order with the government of Chad that must be filled soon. It is the order I tried to fill in Argentina, and they have grown impatient. I have also sold to Libya and Algeria in the past, but they are getting tight with Russia and are buying directly from Putin now. Ukraine and Georgia are good customers. Citizen militias in Ethiopia, Sudan, Uganda, and Ivory Coast place small orders, but they all add up."

"Why have we not heard of you before?"

I took the question. "In the past, I have only bought from Josovic. No one else needed to know."

The printer had stopped, and Nadia reached below the desk and removed a stack of probably twenty pages.

"I need to catch up on some things. Return to the sitting area and look this over. Let me know if it is satisfactory." She flipped to the end before continuing. "The last page shows 13 items we do not currently have in our inventory. They are mostly small-volume items. We have 157 of the SAM-7 man-portable missiles in stock today. You ordered 200. Also of note, Claymore Anti-Personnel Mines, the M18A1 version, are hard to come by. They haven't been manufactured in years, but the US government still has a huge stockpile. We can procure them occasionally. As of now, we are out. We can replace it with a Russian equivalent if you wish."

She handed the pages to Sam, and we returned to the wing-back chairs. Sam gave me half the stack and began flipping through the remainder. Conscious of listening devices, we didn't say much. After ten minutes, we switched stacks and started over. When we were finished, Sam looked at me and nodded.

"You have five million dollars; how much is the balance?" he asked, looking toward Nadia.

"I will round down to sixty-one million dollars, half now and half on delivery. You will be allowed to open the containers and look everything over on arrival if it is safe to do so, but the containers will not be offloaded until the balance is paid in full."

"Have you calculated the number of containers," Sam asked.

"Shipping to the Bahamas is included in the price. We estimate six full-size containers and perhaps another half-size one. You have over forty metric tons total."

"And you will have no problem getting this out of the country?"

"As we stated, there is a good reason we are in Venezuela."

"It will take a few days to consolidate that much money. Plus, we will need to know how much each item costs so that Mr. Walker and I can each pay our share."

"You will get itemized costs on delivery. How you split everything is not our problem."

"Before I sign off on sending you thirty million, I want to see that you actually have the merchandise," I said.

Nadia hesitated, then said, "Keep your seat." She exited through the door Weber had used.

She was back in thirty seconds. This time, she sat by us instead of returning to the desk.

"Today is Monday. You go and get the money ready to transfer. On Friday morning, we will pick you up at the marina. Again, bring nothing. You will be bagged again. Just so you are aware, as you walked down the hallway, you were x-rayed. You passed through a metal detector. You were scanned for explosives. You were checked for electronic transmissions. Searches don't have to be invasive when one employs the right technology. The same thing will happen on Friday. Mr. Weber says you can view one of the smaller warehouses at that time."

Nadia pulled out her cell phone and pushed buttons for a few seconds. The door to the hallway opened, and our driver stood there.

"Thank you for your business," she said, taking the documents and moving her hand toward the door. That was our notice that it was time to leave.

When we reached the garage, we were bagged again. The trip back was hot and rough, and I was feeling ill again when we stopped.

Sam and I walked back to the *Guppy*.

"Say nothing when we get back," I told him. "I will get the scanner and check for bugs."

"Check, but don't remove any. Maybe we can use them. We will have all private conversations here on the pier, or we can take the tender to sea. That should be safe."

"No windows, no sounds in the building. Any clue where we were?" I asked.

"No, they orchestrated that well. All I know is that we are likely within three to five miles, given traffic and travel time. Three is more likely."

"The heart of Caracas is fifteen kilometers from here, so we didn't enter the city. We had to be within a couple of miles of the airport. I hear jets taking off all day from here, but I heard nothing during the visit."

Sam thought for a minute. "Underground? Maybe a basement?"

I had not considered that. "It would explain the lack of windows and the lack of external noise. It also creates problems for us."

"And problems for others, which is why I think it is accurate."

Sam and I continued walking toward the *Guppy* when something caught my eye.

"On our left, sitting on the jetty. Our watcher is back."

"Yep."

Chapter 24

Back aboard the *Guppy*, I pulled the scanner from one of Fletcher's 'hidey-holes' and spent almost an hour scanning for any listening devices. I found none. There could be several reasons for that, but the most likely was that none were aboard. We were not going to risk it, though.

Sam spent most of the time in Fletcher's small captain's office adjacent to his quarters. I had given it a cursory look on the return trip from Grenada, but Sam was digging deeper.

He emerged with several items in his hands. We made eye contact. I shook my head and shrugged, indicating I had found no bugs. Sam thought a minute and passed me two of the sheets of paper. The first was a receipt for the space at the marina, pier three, slot seventeen. It was paid through the end of the year. He also passed over a photocopy of Fletcher's Master Captain's License issued by the US Coast Guard. It was issued to Roman Steed Thompson.

"We need to arrange to move some money," I said in my normal voice. "I would also like to do some fishing and diving, so let's take the *Guppy* out for a few days. We will be back to meet Weber's crew on Friday."

"If you can get the lines, I will drive us out of here," Sam replied.

"Yes, sir, Captain," I replied with a mock salute.

The water in the marina didn't move much, but the breeze did rock the *Guppy* a bit. I removed all but one line I had placed mid-ship and allowed the wind to hold the *Guppy* in place, softly bumping against the fenders. Sam had the engines running and warming up. On my signal, he used a small joystick to control the thrusters and move us a few feet from the concrete pier. I jumped aboard during the move and began pulling fenders over the side. Moving the throttle forward about an inch, the *Guppy* began slowly creeping forward until it was clear of the slip.

Sam again used the bow thruster to turn the vessel toward the marina's mouth and along the protective stone jetty.

After we were clear, I began stowing fenders and ropes. It was mid-afternoon, hot and humid, but the wind sliding across the deck felt good. I guessed our speed at ten knots. There was no need to hurry.

Sam picked a spot in the middle of the Southeast Caribbean, halfway between Bonaire and Caracas, and entered it into the autopilot. The location was also about 60 kilometers from the Venezuelan coast to our southwest and the Venezuelan island of Grand Roque to our northeast. It would put us right in the middle of our little piece of the Caribbean.

After checking the radar to ensure nothing was nearby, I motioned for Sam to follow me below. I opened the hatch to the engine room, but we didn't enter. I just wanted the noise.

"The sweep was negative, but there are tons of electronics on a boat this size, so there was a lot of electronic noise," I told him. "I am ninety percent sure we are clear. I am certain there is nothing on the foredeck or the sundeck up top."

Sam nodded.

"What will Manning say about another thirty-one million that he will likely never see again?" I asked.

"I don't know," Sam replied. "He has never hesitated as long as I had a plan, but I have never asked for anywhere close to that. I had never asked for five million until two days ago."

"When we reach your spot in the middle of nowhere, let's call Manning from the sundeck and update him. Assuming he can and will get that much money, that will give him several days to prepare for the transfer. Then, we can come back inside and have some fake conversations with some banks, just in case."

Sam gave me a thumbs-up, checked his watch, and signaled me to close the hatch. "I am going back up to the bridge. Fix us some sandwiches. We should arrive about dark."

It was 7:05 p.m. Venezuela Mean Time when we climbed to the sundeck above the salon to call Manning. The rainy season was still two months away, but dark clouds were building to our south and west in the fading light. On occasion, I could see the sky light up from lightning strikes over the horizon. I hoped the easterly winds would keep the storms over land.

Sam gave the Iridium unit a moment to connect to a satellite, plugged in earbuds so we could both hear and pushed his preprogrammed number for Crumby, our pilot.

"Air Crumby," he answered after a few rings.

"This is Jackson," Sam said. "You are free until Friday morning at nine a.m. After that, you need to be back at Simon Bolivar Airport. I figure you guys need a break from the boredom. Go do something. Anything. Also, know that the jet is likely being watched."

"I will talk to Cruz. Maybe she would like a couple of days in St. Lucia. Just over an hour away for the bird. We will be close by if you need us."

Next, he dialed Manning, who answered on the first ring.

"Please tell me you have good news," he said instead of hello.

"I have news," I said. "You can decide if it is good or bad."

"It always scares me when you call in,"

"Sam is on with me. We had a productive day in that we met with Victor Pancheo, Artura Simonyan, and Adolph Finn Weber today. All at the same time." I waited for him to say something, but he remained silent. "They are all the same guy. It seems Finn Weber is his birth name, Artura Levon Simonyan is an adoptive name, and Victor Pancheo is simply an alias. He uses all three depending on need. The Victor Pancheo I thought I spoke to a few nights back was his son, Artura Gayane Simonyan."

275

"Where did you meet Weber?" Manning asked.

"Don't know. We were told to bring nothing with us, and we were told that we would be thoroughly searched, so we didn't take a tracker dot. When we were in the car, they told us to put black bags over our heads. The bags were removed after we were securely enclosed in a parking area like a garage. There were no windows and no sounds from outside. Sam thinks it was a basement."

"And what did you learn?"

"Weber is old. Seventy-seven is what he told us. Cataracts. Almost blind if it isn't a show. He seems very smart and articulate, in any case. We were summoned by a woman: tall, trim, dark hair, maybe thirty to thirty-five years old. She said her name was Nadia, and that is what Weber called her. After we spoke to him, he turned us over to her to work out the money and details. According to her, they have the entire order in stock with only a few exceptions."

"They want another payment?"

"Half of the balance is thirty-point-five million."

I waited again. Nothing this time.

"We negotiated for a look at the merchandise before the next payment. Nadia said we could view a sample in one of the smaller warehouses this Friday. Then, after they receive the $31 mil, they will put everything in shipping containers and send them to the Bahamas. We will be able to check the shipment onboard before the final payment. After the balance of the funds is wired and verified, the containers will be offloaded."

I waited again. Finally, Sam spoke up. "Manning, you there,"

"I am here." Another long pause. "Do you have a plan to resolve this?"

Now, it was our turn to pause. Sam and I looked at each other. "Working on it," I told him.

"I will arrange for the first payment," Manning said as if it were no big deal. "At worst, we will work with the Bahamas to confiscate the shipment. Maybe we can pass it all along to some friendly government in need. At best, you will resolve this before the transfer is made. Make that happen. Anything else?"

"Yes," Sam said. "Do you remember when I was in Ukraine, and you were going to track me by satellite, but they fooled us with the identical Sprinter vans?"

"I do. Not our finest moment."

"Yep. But I think we need to try again. Can you arrange that?"

"Tell me when and where."

∞

Sam and I traded watches overnight, and each of us managed about six hours of sleep. Feeling refreshed, we resumed planning and plotting over coffee as the sun rose the next morning. The rain had remained to our southwest, but I could still hear thunder on occasion. With the *Guppy* floating on still-calm seas far from land, we again brought the equipment we had smuggled in, plus everything Fletcher had secured for us, to the salon. I continued staring at the Semtex. I had some ideas, but it was useless without a detonator.

I went to the storage locker near the engine room and looked through the dive equipment Fletcher kept on board for his charters. There were racks with tanks, masks, fins, regulators, and a 3,000 PSI air compressor for filling the tanks. It looked like a collection cobbled together over time. Buried in the corner were three older model Draeger rebreather units. Special forces often prefer Draegers because they can be used in a closed circuit configuration at shallow depths, which means no tell-tale bubbles. But I didn't know if the units worked or if the CO_2 scrubbers were still functional. Have I mentioned that diving isn't my favorite thing? I hoped we wouldn't need this equipment.

Manning called at around noon to let us know two things. First, he had the money and would transfer it through the Rolle Imports accounts if needed, and the satellite coverage for Friday morning was set. Hopefully, they could follow us to see where we were taken. Second, Manning had received photographs of the three missing CIA agents—no names, just photos. The CIA wanted our help, but they didn't want to share. It was nothing new.

Manning said he had attached the digital photos to a draft email in our shared Hotmail account. We would have to find an internet connection to view, download, and print them.

Sam and I decided to make a quick run to Bonaire. We doubted anyone would be looking for us. I remembered passing an Internet café on the ride to the house where I met Artura Simonyan, the son. Plus, I wanted to drive by the house where I had met him. I was curious to see if he was still there.

I radioed the marina and arranged for a mooring. Catching it, with Sam using the thrusters and me giving hand signals from the bow, proved to be more difficult than expected, but we managed it.

We considered using the tender but decided it would be best to just call for a ride. The harbormaster sent a small boat out to fetch us. He dropped us at the gate and then called for a taxi, which arrived after thirty minutes of standing and waiting.

Climbing into the small, four-door pickup, I pointed to the north and said, "I don't have an address, but I can tell you where to go."

Two minutes later, we dropped Sam off at the retail strip mall with the Internet café. I continued with the driver, giving turn-by-turn directions until we passed the house where I had met Simonyan. There were two identical trucks parked in the driveway. Each had "Dive Bonaire" and a phone number on the side. I wanted to sit and watch, but I preferred the driver not to know what I was interested in. After another block, I told him to turn around and reverse course. When we passed the house a second time, a man and a woman were loading dive tanks into one of the trucks. Neither looked familiar.

When we returned to the strip mall, Sam was waiting near the road. He jumped in, and we were back at the marina within two minutes and aboard the *Guppy* in fifteen.

In the salon, Sam pulled three folded sheets of paper from his pocket and passed me one.

"Look familiar?"

He did. He was the man Diamante introduced us to—the one who worked for Pancheo, a.k.a. Simonyan and Weber.

He passed over two other photos, but neither one looked familiar.

"I was afraid we would see Fletcher's face," I told him.

"Yep, I had the same thought. What did you learn?"

"The house is a rental. Pretty sure about that."

"Let's head back to Caracas. At 30 knots, we can get there before dark."

∞

As soon as we arrived, I caught a ride to the airport and was lucky enough to rent a North Korean-made minivan. It was old and ugly, but I didn't care; I would probably never return it. I parked it in a lot near the Marina.

Now, to deal with another problem.

Sam and I waited for darkness – not that it got that dark under the lights of the marina – and we headed out. He took off down the pier while I, dressed in a wetsuit from the locker on the *Guppy*, slid quietly over the side. I used standard snorkeling equipment to slip away from the boat, hopefully unobserved. Sam walked around under the lights on the pier with a cell phone to his ear, hoping he would be observed. We wanted anyone watching to focus their attention on him. I swam slowly and quietly to the unprotected side of the jetty and stuck my head out of the water.

About 60 yards away, I saw something that didn't match the outline of the huge rocks used to build the jetty. I submerged and swam thirty strokes, which I knew was about 40 yards, before slowly lifting my head above the surface.

There was our watcher. He was lying on the boulders, with the camera lens pointed through a space between two rocks. I submerged and swam another 20 strokes before coming up – quietly this time. I silently swam up behind him and pulled an EVO titanium diving knife from its sheath. The sound of the surf covered any noise I made as I climbed the short distance up the rocks.

I placed the knife's point against the base of his skull and said, "Tranquilo." 'Quiet.'

"Who are you?" he asked in perfect English.

I pulled a small flashlight from inside the wetsuit, pointed it toward Sam, and flashed it three times. I got three flashes back. He was on his way.

The man kept asking me questions. Who was I? What did I want? I said nothing. That approach is often unnerving, and I could tell from the man's tense body that he was becoming increasingly distressed.

It took Sam about ten minutes to circle the marina and climb over the rocks to my position. He brought my trainers and placed his knee on the neck of the still-face-down man while I pulled them on.

After I tied the shoes, I took a rope from around my waist.

"I am going to tie your hands behind your back, but I will leave some slack. If I see you trying to untie them, I will kill you. If you try to fight, I will kill you. If you scream, I will kill you. If you run, I will kill you. Are we clear?"

I heard a grunt from under Sam's knee. It sounded like a yes to me.

"We will all walk back to the boat side by side. Do you understand?"

Again, I got a grunt. By this point, his hands were tied with about two feet of slack, and the rope ran through his belt and belt loops on the side, further limiting his ability to resist but giving him the ability to walk rather normally.

In ten minutes, we were back on board *Guppy Love*. Sam sat before the man and held up two photos. One was a match. This was the second CIA agent. One to go.

"I am David," Sam said. "David Walker. What is your name?"

"Alonzo Moreno," he said.

"Alonzo, my friend over here is going to run a name through the CIA database. If we run Alonzo Moreno through the database and it isn't found, I am going to be really mad. Is that the name we need to run?"

"Yes," he replied. "But you may not find it. I was sent here to infiltrate Artura Simonyan's operation. I am guessing you know that. I haven't communicated with my contacts in almost a year, so they may think I am dead or turned."

Sam nodded at me. I typed the name into the computer but had no connectivity or access to the CIA's systems. It was all for show.

"Why no communication?"

"The CIA sent me here to infiltrate Simonyan. I got in, to some degree, but I was sent to a damn warehouse in the middle of the damn jungle for nine months. I have no idea where it was. It might have been in Columbia or Brazil, for all I know. Simonyan is moving more than guns, I can tell you that. There were no phones, no electricity other than what a couple of Honda generators could produce, and I had no way out. Four weeks ago, they brought me back here. They handed me the damn camera and told me to watch the airport for a specific jet. When it landed, I followed you here. Simonyan's men told me to keep watch and take pictures of anyone who visited the boat."

"And why didn't you call your contact after you arrived back in Caracas?" Sam asked.

"I only have a phone that Simonyan owns. He would know. His men pick me up and drop me off each day. I am close to getting in, though. I just have to continue to build trust."

"What does Simonyan look like?" I asked.

"Tall, thin, distinguished. Light brown hair going gray."

It sounded like the man I spoke with on Bonaire.

"Who is Finn Weber?" Sam asked.

"I have heard Mr. Weber mentioned. But I do not know him. I assume he works for Mr. Simonyan."

"When are they supposed to pick you up?" I asked.

"Tomorrow morning. They told me to watch overnight and let them know if anyone else came aboard. I report in again at midnight—just a phone call. I will tell them there is nothing to report. Then again at four and eight."

"What do you know about this boat and its captain?" Sam asked.

"Nothing, but I haven't seen the captain since you returned."

"Did you follow us to Maracaibo? Someone was watching us there as well."

"It wasn't me. After you left, they sent me back here day after day. Cooking in the sun. I was here earlier this week while you were away as well. Where is the captain?"

"Dead," I told him. He simply nodded.

Sam and I walked away and stepped outside the Galley onto the fantail. There was only one way out, and we could see him, so he wasn't going anywhere.

"What do we do?" I asked.

"Grab the sat phone and wake up Manning. Tell him to call his CIA contact and ask if the name Alonzo Moreno rings a bell. Tell him to call Landry if he has to. Tell him you will hold for an answer."

With that, Sam turned and went back into the galley. I grabbed the satellite phone and a change of clothes. By this point, the wetsuit was very uncomfortable and hot.

I climbed to the sundeck, called, and explained the situation to Manning. He placed me on hold. I turned on the speaker and changed while I waited. After about five minutes, he came back on the line."

"They confirmed the name. He was sent to find and infiltrate Simonyan. They want him brought back for questioning."

"This presents a problem. I had hoped he was one of Weber's men so we could just eliminate him."

"If he is a threat, you can still do that. Again, locating and repatriating rouge CIA agents isn't your assignment."

"We'll try to find a way around that," I told him before hanging up.

Returning to the galley, I saw Sam was still asking questions. I tapped at the glass.

"That is him, and that is his name," I said when Sam stepped out. "The Company wants us to bring him home; Manning said to do whatever we need to do to ensure the mission."

"Yep."

Chapter 25

When Friday morning arrived, we still had more "if-then" statements than a computer program. If this happens, then we will do this. If that happens, then we will do that. Sadly, we had no clue what would actually happen.

At six a.m., we made a final call to Manning, who was already in a strategic command center near Washington, D.C. He had eyes on the *Guppy* from space.

"As of now, the picture is a bit grainy," he said. "But as soon as the sun comes up, we will look on in high definition. We also have some new thermal imaging technology at our disposal, just in case you get switched around like Sam did in Ukraine. Hopefully, we can identify which vehicle has multiple passengers. If you can just reach up and press a hand against the roof of the car for several seconds, it will leave a heat signature and we will be able to pick that up easily."

"Assuming everything goes well this morning, we will have to act fast. Be ready with coordinates and any other information you can share," I told him.

"Your pilots and jet just landed at the airport. We can transmit documents, maps, and other images to them if needed. Remember, as far as Weber is concerned, that is your Jet, and you know they know. No reason not to visit it."

"If we fly out of here, what about the *Guppy*," Sam asked.

"Let's talk that over when the time comes," Manning replied. "Just fly away to somewhere safe. Then we can discuss options if needed."

"I am just concerned about all of the equipment we have on board," I explained.

"You don't have anything Weber needs. He already has all of that. We will deal with it."

"Do you think our pilot and copilot would take on a little mission?" I asked.

"As I told you, they are both combat-tested, but I don't know about them doing anything on the ground. As far as I know, they are just airmen."

"After we leave for the meeting, ask them to rent a car and visit the *Guppy*. She sits in slip seventeen on pier three. Moreno will be tied up and locked in the hold near the engine room. I'll leave the key taped to the door. The door to the galley can be opened with a touchpad. The combination is 9731. They can escort him back to the jet and hold him for our arrival. If anyone seems to be watching, tell them to turn around and head back to the jet. Get it done between 9:30 and 10 a.m. if possible. Have them walk him onto the plane like a guest, then tie him up."

"I will ask, and happy hunting." And with that, Manning broke the connection.

∞

At 8:00, we told Moreno to make his final call to his contact before tying him up and locking him in the equipment room. He just said, "Moreno. All is clear. They are on the boat. No visitors." It was the same as the 4 a.m. message. We had no way to know if that was his typical report or a red flag phrase.

At 9:05, one of the blue-suited bodyguards turned down pier three, walking our way. Sam and I wore golf shirts and chinos instead of our suits. We didn't expect any trouble during this meeting, but we were still unsure about Fletcher, Vasquez in Argentina, and Moreno. If one of them ratted us out, we were likely dead men walking.

We stepped onto the pier and headed his way.

He motioned for us to follow him. His partner was already in the driver's seat. This time, he gave us a cursory pat down before directing us to the back seat. The black bags were on the seats waiting for us.

"Please go slowly," I said before pulling the bag over my head. "I almost threw up last time."

As we pulled out, I placed my palm on the car's roof to ostensibly brace myself. It wasn't necessary, but I wanted to set a precedent. I just hoped Manning was watching.

There was no double switch on the vehicles, and shortly after departing, we arrived at the same garage we had visited four days before. The bodyguard again escorted us down the hallway and into the waiting room. Having nothing else to do, Sam and I each poured a cup of coffee. After 20 minutes, he returned and walked us back to the garage. I guessed we had been scanned again.

Back in the bags, we rode for what I guessed to be thirty minutes. I kept my hand on the roof part of the way. The roads were rough, so it looked like I was bracing myself. I was sick by the time we stopped and wondered if I should vomit on my host when he pulled the bag from my head. I decided a badass arms dealer wouldn't do that, so I fought it. We were once again inside a building, but it was a warehouse this time. It was at least 100 feet wide, and I didn't know how long because I could not see the back wall beyond the tall steel racks stacked 20 feet high with crates and boxes. Dirty skylights and halogen fixtures lit the space, which smelled of solvent and oil.

It looked more impressive than any of the armories I had visited in the Marines.

Nadia appeared from behind a stack of wooden crates along the right wall. Looking at the sun through the skylights, I could tell that wall was on the east side of the building.

"Is there anything specific I can show you, gentlemen?" she said.

"I have clients specifically interested in American-made AR platform rifles in 5.56 NATO. I believe I had 400 of those on the list. Can I take a look at those?"

"Not a problem. And Mr. Walker, what about you?"

"My contacts in Chad, the impatient ones, need the M134 minigun and Type 80 machine guns yesterday," Sam said.

Nadia consulted an iPad for a few moments, tapping buttons and scrolling down a long list.

"Follow me. All of the M134s and Type-80s have been loaded into a container for shipment. We will start there."

Sam and I followed her through the warehouse, with the two bodyguards bringing up the rear. As we walked, she asked us several questions about nothing important. After a couple of minutes, we reached the back of the warehouse. Before me were a dozen loading dock doors with full-size shipping containers inside each door. Near the east end was a huge forklift that I assumed could move the containers around and load them on trucks.

Two men were driving smaller forklifts, and another pulled an empty pallet jack. Nadia called him over and pointed to the iPad. After a moment and a short conversation, she resumed walking. We continued to the last container. The doors were open, and we entered. The worker she had consulted with returned with a crowbar, drill, and a hammer.

"Pick a crate, Mr. Walker," she said.

Sam walked up and knocked on a crate with Chinese writing. The worker struggled to pull it from the stack before placing it on the floor. Using the drill with a driver bit, he unscrewed the 12 screws holding the lid in place. After he removed the lid, he stepped aside and motioned to Sam.

Sam pulled aside some packing material and lifted a barrel and receiver from the crate. Each was packed in thick plastic and soaked in oil. They appeared to be new. He also looked at the stock and bipod that were packaged separately. All were in good shape.

"The M134s?" he asked.

We repeated the entire show with a crate pulled from another stack. I had to help the worker set it down since the gun alone weighed in at 85 pounds, probably over 100, with the packaging. Again, all seemed in order.

As we moved down to a container near the middle of the row, it once again hit me that I had lost friends in Afghanistan, and it was likely that this operation had a hand in supplying the arms that led to their deaths. Much of what the Afghans used was left over and captured from the Russian occupation and the arms the United States had supplied the Afghan resistance in its fight against the Russians. But, we occasionally found newer American, Italian, Czech, and even Israeli-manufactured weapons. I was becoming enraged, but I managed to bury it inside. Eventually, I would release that pent-up pressure, and it wasn't likely to be pretty.

I also began paying attention to other crates in the building. Many were marked in Russian, Chinese, and Korean characters, others in languages I couldn't identify, and still others clearly labeled in English.

The next container was only one-fifth full yet stacked floor to ceiling with crates. We placed one of them on the floor, and the worker again removed the lid, this time with a crowbar since it was nailed on.

Inside were six AR-15s built by Daniel Defense.

"According to the manifest," Nadia said, "216 of the AR-15 rifles are made by Daniel Defense, 24 are Colt, 48 are from Palmetto State Armory, and the balance, 12 are M16A1 rifles."

She smiled. I smiled.

"A bonus," she told me. "Anything else?"

Sam and I just shrugged.

"Quite an operation you have here," Sam said.

"Mr. Weber is proud of it. He has been building the business here in Venezuela for over 15 years."

And it ends tonight, I thought.

"I am satisfied," Sam told her. "What about you, James?"

I shrugged. "Honor among thieves and all that."

"When can we expect the payment?" Nadia asked.

"It will probably be wired on Monday," I said. "I have to move some of my share from an account in the United States. I can do it, no problem, but it takes time with all the regulations and the weekend. The money in European and Caribbean banks will be easier."

She handed over a business card; it said, 'Jolly Auto Parts.' There was a number but no name.

"Call me as soon as we get the transfer confirmation and provide the delivery details. Assuming the delivery plan is acceptable, we will have the containers going out on Tuesday morning. They will be in Bahamian waters on Friday morning."

We nodded.

"Do you wish to return to your boat or your jet?"

"Take us to the boat for now. We will contact the banks, then pack and fly out after we know all is in order," I told her.

She pointed to the bodyguards. "Gentlemen, please return our guests to the marina, and David, James, if you need us again, just call the number."

Chapter 26

When we stepped aboard the *Guppy*, I heard the satellite phone buzzing, but I didn't answer. First, I confirmed that Alonzo was gone. I assumed Crumby and Cruz were babysitting him on the jet.

Sam checked the rest of the boat and reran the scanner to look for listening devices—still nothing.

Back up on the sundeck, we called Manning.

"You were driven eight kilometers due west to a warehouse near the shipping port. It appears to be about 40 meters by 50 meters. I am having that analyzed. There are no windows on the sides, but it does have skylights. Only one door on the west side and a roll-up door on the south side. The north side has twelve loading docks."

"That is the warehouse," I said, "where did we go first."

"There is also what looks like an addition running the full length of the building along the east side. On the first stop, you entered one of two roll-up doors on the south end of the addition. Then they drove you around for half an hour and brought you back to within a hundred feet of where you started. You entered through the roll-up doors on the south side of the main building. And jot this down. Ten degrees, 35 minutes, 4 seconds north by 66 degrees, 57 minutes, 14 seconds west. That is your target location."

"Could you see security?" I asked him.

"We identified six live humans outside, but there doesn't seem to be a perimeter fence or anything. What did you find inside?"

"Probably a couple of billion in guns and ammo," I told him. "Nadia mentioned we would be allowed to visit one of the smaller warehouses. I hope that was just to impress us. Unless the crates were empty, and I don't believe they were, a war could be waged from that one warehouse."

Sam picked up the conversation. "Do you have any pictures?"

"We recorded the video. Great quality, too. What do you want to see?"

"Pictures of everything, wide and close-up shots all around the warehouse. Can you send them to the jet?"

"Give me an hour."

"You have two hours. We will call back later if we need you." I ended the call and looked at Sam. I knew we were thinking the same thing.

We carried a bag and a couple of cases to the rented van. We drove a zig-zag route from the marina through the Caracas traffic before entering the coordinates Manning had provided into the handheld GPS.

By this point, we were confident that no one was following us. Ten minutes later, we passed the warehouse. There were containers stacked outside the building and on vacant lots for a quarter mile in every direction. As Manning had indicated, we saw no fences or other perimeter protection. The warehouse space was probably thirty-five feet tall, but the add-on along the east side was only half that.

I drove part of the way around the building, but a guard house controlling access to the cargo dock prevented me from making the block. We each made mental notes and pointed out items of interest. I parked for 20 minutes just to observe. Sam pulled binoculars from the bag and noted that he could see no cameras. We saw little activity other than one of the guards seemingly making circles around the building.

From there, we drove to Simón Bolívar International Airport. Crumby had printed eight photos for us. All were in black and white but high resolution. Moreno was sitting quietly halfway back with dried blood on his lip. Cruz was beside him, reading a book. He just looked at us and never said a word.

"He give you any trouble?" I asked Crumby, nodding toward Moreno.

"Not really. He was a little spooked when we opened the storage room. He tried to run, but he accidentally hit Cruz's elbow with his mouth. They are friends now." Crumby smiled. He was loving this.

"Okay, your time here will soon end. If all goes as planned, we will see you sometime between three and four a.m. We will give you a call and probably come in hot. Get everything ready and get clearance for somewhere like Cancun. We will change it once we are airborne and over the water."

"Ten-four, we will be ready."

Sam and I returned to the *Guppy* to study the photos. Our plan was falling into place. The basis of the plan was that everything we needed to destroy the warehouse – was in the warehouse. The problem would be figuring out how to destroy Weber. I had a thought about that as well.

That afternoon, we walked to a chandlery near the marina and bought rope and several other items. Then we moved on to a hardware store where we purchased a small 12-volt screwdriver, charcoal starter fluid, and a small crowbar. Just before dark, we walked back to the van with more equipment. Assorted guns and other munitions were in one bag and dark clothes, protective vests, and equipment like night vision goggles and radios were in the other.

We ate dinner aboard the *Guppy*, then, hopefully, slipped away from the marina unnoticed just after midnight. We were concerned that since Mareno was missing, he had been replaced.

There was little activity in the dock area and around the warehouse at night, which was good. But there were a lot of bright lights, which was bad. Darkness was our friend. The dock itself was 400 meters away, but even the shadows around the warehouse caught some of the light, which afforded us little cover.

Sam and I found a dark place about two hundred meters from the target to park the van and change into our BDU pants and bulletproof vests with attached tactical gear. I also threw a backpack over my shoulder, and Sam carried a small tactical bag plus a longer case with the sniper rifle. That done, we walked along the buildings, using the few shadows we could find until we were across the street from the south end of the warehouse. We located a row of shipping containers stacked three high and locked together about a hundred meters away. The cross bars allowed Sam to scale the side with the AWM sniper rifle slung over his shoulder. When he was in place, we turned on our comms. Everything seemed to be in working order.

I remained in the shadows for several minutes until I heard Sam report.

"I have three targets on the south end—all with poor tactical discipline. One is smoking a cigar and standing near the roll-up doors at the office. One is sitting at the southwest corner of the building with his legs stretched out. The third one is walking around but looking at his phone. Make your way around to the west side of the building near the southwest corner. If you can take out that target quietly, I can take care of the other two without raising an alarm."

"Affirmative," I replied before heading off into the shadows. I moved a block west before turning north to cross the main highway. There were sporadic cars, and now and then, a truck hauling a container would come by. I timed it well and crossed the road without being seen, keeping other buildings between me and the target. After twenty minutes, I was in place. I clicked the radio twice and got two clicks in return. We were set to go.

The door Manning had mentioned on the west side of the warehouse was about twenty feet behind the man on the corner. I was actually behind him but could see his legs and right shoulder. He had not moved. I waited five minutes for a truck to drive by, which created a little ambient noise, then I quietly walked to the doorway behind the man. It was recessed about two feet into the wall, providing concealment. I checked; it was locked. When I heard the next truck, I moved my H&K VP9 with a suppressor to my left hand and pulled my Ka-Bar combat knife with my right. As I moved along the building to approach the man from behind, I heard snoring. There was no noise as the blade slid into his neck, severing his carotid artery. A quick twist moved the blade through his esophagus, eliminating any screams. He was dead in seconds. I moved back around the corner.

"Walking man headed your way, maybe fifteen seconds from you. Still staring at his phone. When he gets close, eliminate him before he sees his friend. I will take care of number three. A fourth target is on the east side but near the back."

I gave Sam two clicks in acknowledgment. Ten seconds later, I swung around the corner and double-tapped the guard. I also heard something hit the side of the warehouse and realized it was the .300 caliber Hornady boattail bullet that had passed through the third guard's head. The suppressor did its job. I never heard Sam's shot.

I had two options for entering the building. One was to use the rope and hook in my backpack to scale the side of the building. I could climb to the top of the office first, then repeat the process to get to the roof, where I planned to gain entry through a skylight. The second option was to use containers stacked along the back of the building to access the roof. My problem with that option was two-fold. First, the guards near the rear would have to be eliminated. Second, the containers were not right against the building. From the photos and earlier recon, we estimated that there was a seven-foot gap, and the top of the containers was still ten to twelve feet short of the roof.

"Give me a few minutes to reposition," Sam said. Are you going up and over or headed to the back?"

I peered around the corner at the dead guard, and something caught my eye.

"Start this way and let me know when you get across the road," I told him. "There may be a better way." I heard two clicks.

After checking for traffic and movement, I moved to the dead man in the parking lot. There was a keyring clipped to his belt. I removed it and found six keys. One was a car key, and two looked like they fit padlocks. The remaining three could be door keys, though the tooth pattern was unlike anything I had seen before. I moved back to the door.

I would like to tell you I channeled my inner Jason Borne and quietly tossed the grappling hook over the roofline thirty-five feet over my head, catching a ventilation pipe on the first toss before scaling the side of the building like a spider and climbing silently onto the roof just seconds before the ventilation pipe broke off sending me to certain death. But as Sam told me, real life isn't like books and movies.

The first key I tried unlocked the side door.

"Status?" I whispered.

"Give me two minutes."

"I have entry. Door. Southwest corner."

Two clicks.

We knew that everything we needed to destroy the warehouse was inside. The challenge would be finding it and creating a detonation system that would allow for our safe escape. Thankfully, MARSOC put a lot of effort into training its members for fluid situations just like this. We called it MacGyvering, but I didn't know why until someone filled me in later. As I have said, we didn't watch much television.

I turned the knob and cracked the door, immediately checking for an alarm contact. Sure enough, I spotted one at the top of the door. I heard nothing, but Sam and I had discussed this. Would an arms dealer's alarm notify the police or the dealer? We guessed it would not call the police, but this was Venezuela, so who knew? I moved forward, trusting Sam to let me know if there was trouble on the outside.

Light from the dock poured in through the skylights. There was plenty of light to move around, but not enough to read labels in the shadows.

Pulling a small flashlight from a pocket on my vest, I began to look around. Most of the crates had Chinese or Russian characters on the side, but a few were from American, French, and other manufacturers.

After ten minutes, I was frustrated. I had found nothing that I was looking for. I wondered if the high explosives were in another warehouse.

Sam's voice interrupted my thoughts.

"I have two men circling to the front of the building, and two cars just pulled into the parking lot."

Apparently, the alarm was active.

"Four additional men," Sam said. "And what I guess to be Nadia."

"I am coming back out," I said.

"No, I will keep them busy. Get it done...quickly."

Taking a different tack, I ran along a row of racks to the containers Nadia had shown us. We had ordered C-4, and it was on the manifest. I just had to find it. The containers were stacked almost full, but I got lucky when I entered the third container. There were two cases clearly labeled M112 Demolition Block, military-grade C-4. The cardboard boxes were sixty pounds each, containing 48 of the 1.25-pound bars of the material.

I grabbed the first case and headed toward the middle of the warehouse. Along the way, I heard shots fired outside.

I dropped the box of C-4 near a rack stacked high with wooden crates, and then I keyed the mic. "Sam, are you okay?"

"Yep, keep going."

I heard more shots as I returned to the container. This time, I stepped into the fourth container, where I had spotted a shrink-wrapped pallet of .50 caliber ammunition. Using the Ka-Bar, I cut through the wrap, opened the first box, and pulled out four of the five-and-a-half-inch long cartridges. I dropped them into my pocket before grabbing the second case of C-4.

As I made my way to the center of the warehouse again, the lights came on. There was still gunfire outside. This wasn't good, but I was hidden, for the moment at least, by the racks and crates.

I quickly dropped the case of C-4 on top of the other and removed the .50 cal cartridges from my pocket. I used the tip of the kbar to puncture deep into the C-4, and then I began prying the primers out of the cartridges, exposing the powder inside.

A couple of notes about C-4: one can hit it, drop it, shake it, burn it, and cut it, and nothing will happen most of the time. It takes a huge shockwave to produce detonation. I had been told a .50 caliber cartridge was enough to set it off, but I had never tested the theory. I was going to find out.

By removing the primer, I exposed the powder in the cartridges. My plan was to start a fire around the perimeter and be long gone by the time the fire, ash, or a piece of hot coal found a small primer hole and ignited the 220 grains of rifle powder inside.

I shoved the cartridges, bullet first, deep into the top box of C-4. Then I started climbing the nearest rack. The highest crates were probably 12 to 14 feet above the floor. I removed the backpack and took the half-liter of charcoal starter from the side pocket. I also quickly unscrewed the suppressor from the H&K pistol. Stealth was no longer needed. I stood and threw the suppressor as far as I could toward the door I had entered. Maybe it would serve as a distraction.

I made my way along the rack, probably 20 feet, before spraying the starter fluid onto the wooden crates. I pulled the lighter from my pocket and lit them as I went. So far, I had seen no one inside.

Climbing down to the floor, I emptied the bottle onto a series of crates along the bottom shelf of the rack and ignited the fluid. Looking back toward the middle of the warehouse, I saw that the first crates were burning faster than I had expected. I needed to evacuate.

"Sam, I am going out the back." I got no response but still heard occasional gunfire from the front of the building. Hopefully, he was just busy.

As I approached the containers in the rear, several shots rang out from inside the warehouse. One round ricocheted off the steel container and hit my vest. It hurt, but it didn't penetrate. I continued to the back of the container and used it for cover.

"Mr. Thames, you are a dead man if you leave. We have the building surrounded. Talk to me, and perhaps I will let you live." It was Nadia.

I reached up and punched the button to raise the roll-up door. Nothing happened. Damn.

I sprinted back toward the west, punching several roll-up door buttons and getting the same result each time. The fire was growing, and ash could hit one of the primer holes at any moment. I wasn't sure if my system would work, but I wanted to be at least a quarter mile away when I found out.

"Sam, I don't know where you are, but evacuate. Now. I will meet you at the rendezvous," I said, hoping Sam was still in the fight.

Two clicks.

"101?" Sam asked, using the 10-code to ask my status.

"Northwest corner. Heading south. Inside."

Two clicks. I knew Sam wasn't evacuating.

I saw Nadia just before she fired at me from 50 feet away. She missed again, but debris from the block wall stung my face. She had a submachine gun, likely an MP5, with multiple 30-round mags. I had a handgun with 13 rounds remaining and one spare mag. She had the advantage, but now I knew where she was. I headed south along the western wall and took cover behind the huge forklift. I climbed and peered over the top but didn't see Nadia. I fired two rounds in her general direction, not expecting to hit anything. I was simply buying time. I had found my way out.

I climbed into the driver's seat of the Toyota brand forklift, which I immediately dubbed "The Beast" in my head. I had never driven one of these monsters before, but thankfully, the fine folks at Toyota use many arrows on their controls. I turned the key, and the propane engine came to life. The fire was raging now, and smoke was filling the building. This was my only shot.

I moved every lever with a forward arrow, and the beast began to move. I pointed it at the nearest container and pressed the accelerator. Seconds later, the long forks pierced the container. The machine continued pushing forward until it met the container, pushing it into the roll-up door and ripping it from its tracks. I followed it out as bullets tore through the tempered glass enclosure. One caught me just below the armpit. Since it was fired from behind me, it took a little flesh and then became trapped inside the vest. Later, I would find a serious burn where the bullet came to rest. But again, it was outside my body where all bullets should stay.

"Evacuate. Evacuate," I screamed. "I am clear of the building."

"I am pinned down," Sam said. "Get out of here."

I wasn't going anywhere, either.

I turned The Beast around, dropped the container still skewered by the forks, and backed out, leaving the container behind.

The front glass had spiderwebbed, making it hard to see. I kicked it out and then stood on the accelerator. I drove down the east side of the building. Ahead, I saw several men covering behind the corner. They must have been focused on Sam because they never saw me. I slowed a little and took careful aim, firing six rounds in quick succession. Three of them dropped, but two turned and started firing back. I squeezed the trigger three more times, and the return fire stopped. One of the men had sheltered on the south side of the building, but that exposed him to Sam. Soon, he fell as well.

"Where are you, Sam?" I yelled.

"Two more."

"I am in the forklift; don't shoot me."

I rounded the corner and saw two men Sam had pinned down behind a white Range Rover. I ducked below the heavy metal framework and drove straight toward them. A second later, I heard a shot; then, The Beast crashed into the vehicle.

"Keep driving," Sam said. "I am 70 yards at your twelve o'clock."

I peered over the dash and saw Sam emerge from behind a small concrete block enclosure with a trash dumpster inside. I drove straight to him. He leaned against the building before slumping to the ground. I stopped The Beast between Sam and the warehouse. The fire was raging now, and there was a series of small explosions. I heard sirens in the distance.

Upon reaching Sam, I jumped down eight feet to his side. Blood was running steadily from his leg, just above the knee. Sam had used his web belt to fashion a makeshift tourniquet, but it wasn't enough. I reached into the lower pocket of my BDU pants and pulled out a CAT combat tourniquet. It was in place, and the bleeding had stopped 15 seconds later.

Sam grunted during the process.

I helped him stand and heard rapid gunfire but realized it was just rounds cooking off inside the warehouse. I sat Sam on the lowest step of The Beast, and I climbed back into the cockpit. "Hang on," I screamed.

We were back at the van in just over a minute.

I stopped The Beast, and Sam was able to hop to the passenger door. I climbed down and helped him get in. Then I jumped into the driver's seat and called Crumby.

"Ten minutes out. Fire it up. I will need help loading. Walker has been shot."

"I will taxi near the vehicle gate he said. Cruz is a qualified combat medic; she will fix him up."

We were pulling back onto the road when the night sky lit up. Just a second later, I heard the explosion. It rocked the van. I hoped the first responders had not yet arrived on scene.

I pulled into the private aviation area of the airport and placed Sam's door near the gate. Crumby was holding a gun on the security guard, who was sitting quietly in his chair with a frightened look on his face. Cruz helped me get Sam from the van, and we walked him to a small utility cart.

"I got us a ride," Cruz said before moving over to drive. We wedged Sam into the passenger seat, and she took off toward the jet parked sixty yards away. I could see the heat waves coming from the engines.

I ran back to the van and grabbed the gear we had left behind. Crumby took the guard's radio and told him to sit still and be quiet until the jet was off the ground. He nodded, and Crumby and I ran toward our getaway.

Sam was unconscious when I reached the jet. "Get him on board; he needs blood," Cruz screamed over the sound of the engines.

I threw him over my shoulder, bounded up the stairs, and laid him on the sofa along the starboard side. I heard the door close, and the engines increased their pitch seconds later. Moreno was asleep in the corner. Cruz saw me look over at him. "He got on my nerves," she said. "He will be out for several hours."

"Can we ignore customs?" I shouted to Crumby.

"We are going to. We are also going to ignore air traffic control."

I heard him on the radio.

"They have shut down the airport due to terrorist activity in the area," Crumby shouted. "But I told them I was transporting a medical emergency and had to leave. Hang on."

With that, the jet accelerated and was airborne within seconds.

"I am headed north. Where shall I go?" Crumby asked.

"Nearest military hospital?" I shouted.

Sam was conscious again and weakly answered, "Gitmo."

Crumby said, "I can be on the ground in Puerto Rico in 55 minutes."

"Go," I shouted, "Wide open."

"You did good," Sam whispered weakly. "Tell Lucy I love her."

"No. You're going to do that," I replied.

I had not noticed Cruz as the jet climbed, but she placed her hand on my shoulder and moved me out of the way. She had unzipped and stripped out of the top half of her flight suit.

She passed me scissors. "Cut his sleeves off."

I did as told, then watched her insert a needle into Sam's arm and taped it down. She then attached a syringe and pressed the plunger.

"Just a touch of painkiller," she said.

She then inserted a needle into her own arm and attached a short tube. She watched the blood flow out the end before attaching it to the needle still in Sam's arm. "I am O-negative," she told me. "He will be fine to Puerto Rico."

Crumby used the intercom this time. "Manning is on the phone. He wants to talk to you."

I stood. Sam was out again.

Crumby handed me a headset when I sat in the right-hand seat. "Can you hear this conversation?" I asked.

303

"Only your end, unless you can fly the bird. If so, I can step to the back."

"Keep your seat."

I put the headphones on.

"Thames," I said.

"Are you okay? We were watching the satellite—quite the explosion you set off there."

"Walker was shot. He is aboard and alive. But not in good shape. We are headed to Puerto Rico. Can you pull some strings there?"

"Hold one."

I held for three frustrating minutes.

"Tell the pilot to fly to Isla Grande Airport. A military ambulance will be waiting to take you to Fort Buchannan Army Base. They have a hospital there."

I passed the message to Crumby, who entered the information into the flight computer.

"Get some rest when you get Sam situated, then call me tomorrow. There have been some significant developments in the last 48 hours."

And with that, he broke the connection.

I handed the headphones back to Crumby.

"Wheels down in thirty-four minutes," he said. "How is Walker?"

"Cruz is taking care of him. Thanks."

I walked back to where Sam lay. His color was a little better. He had a battery-powered blood pressure cuff on his wrist.

"Pressure is back up a little," Cruz told me. "Who applied the tourniquet?"

"He self-applied the web belt. I added the CAT."

"You saved his life," she said.

"I owe him that and more."

Chapter 27

When we arrived at Fort Buchannan, Sam was taken straight into surgery. The bleeding from getting grazed beneath my armpit had stopped, but the burn from where the bullet came to rest between my skin and the vest was painful. A nurse injected local anesthesia and cleaned the wounds. I was exhausted and fell asleep as soon as she finished. Cruz stayed with us at the base hospital, and Crumby stayed with the jet. Two hours later, I was awakened by a nurse and a surgeon who still had blood on his army-green surgical scrubs.

"Your friend will be fine," he said. "The artery was badly damaged, but we used a cadaver artery to repair a two-inch section. I think the knee is okay, but there is significant muscle damage. It will require extensive rehabilitation. He seems to be in great condition for a forty-something American."

I nodded in confirmation.

"We were told not to ask for names, but I need something to call you."

"Call him David," I said, sticking with the names we had used in front of Crumby and Cruz. "I am James. I wearily rose from my chair and shook his hand. "Thank you."

He looked at Cruz. "You're a military medic." He said it as a statement, not a question.

"I was military. Tactical combat certified, but later a pilot before I retired. I just fly folks around now."

"You did a great job."

He turned and left the room.

A nurse entered and escorted us to a room with four bunk beds. She told us to rest and that they would wake us when Sam was alert. It seemed like only seconds before I felt a tap on my shoulder.

The same nurse whispered, "Come with me." I looked at my watch; I had slept three hours.

Sam was awake but groggy.

"Thanks, but I told you to go on without me," he said.

"I seem to remember telling you the same thing," I replied. "Don't remember us discussing rank or who gave the orders."

Sam smiled. "Call Lucy, let her know I will be home in a week or so."

I nodded. "I need to call Manning, as well. Is there anything you want me to pass along?"

"Tell him that I am done."

I spoke with Lucy first. I told her about the injury and that Sam said he was done. I also passed along that I thought it was for the best. She urged me to get out as well but understood when I said I had made a commitment and I intended to honor it.

Manning didn't answer but called back four hours later. After checking on Sam, he got down to business, and I gave him the Cliff's Notes version.

"The Venezuelan government is saying that there was an explosion at a military storage facility and that no one was injured," Manning began. "I need the details. This will be a long debrief."

"There are at least seven dead, probably ten or eleven. But they may have problems finding the body parts. The explosion was bigger than I expected."

"That is what I guessed," he said. "You lit up the night on the satellite image."

"I am going back," I told him. "Today, if I can figure out how to get into the country with some equipment. I think I know where to find Weber."

"I don't think that's wise," Manning told me. "The warehouse and everything in it was destroyed, and many of his people are dead. He is out of action, for a while at least."

"The mission was to eliminate Weber. I need to complete the mission."

Manning was quiet for a while before saying. "I am coming down there. We will discuss it. Give me six hours."

I sat with Sam while I waited for Manning to arrive. I jotted some key information about the mission on a notepad so I would be sure to remember it while talking to Manning. Sam provided details about what he had done and seen. In total, we came up with eleven dead, but we only assumed Nadia was dead since we never saw her leave the warehouse.

∞

It was early evening when Manning arrived at Buchannan. We were both hungry, so we ate fried chicken in a quiet corner of the base commissary.

"I told you a lot had happened," he began after starting to work on his chicken. "ACXN has been shuttered, at least in its current form, but it will be reborn as something bigger and hopefully better. ACXN began as an idea of the Senate Intelligence Committee Chair, Landry's predecessor, and, it has now been confirmed, was coordinated anonymously through that seat and the CIA, which is what we suspected all along. I have also learned that our current President doesn't think what we do is legal. Strictly speaking, he's right. Apparently, however, he also sees and understands the need."

"So, what is the problem?"

"Same problem as always: politics. ACXN has always worked quietly. Most of the time, what we did either never made the news or was so obscure that it was a small story in some distant country. The explosion made the news. He wants more oversite."

"More red tape. More bureaucracy," I said.

Manning nodded. "Maybe not."

"Not what I agreed to."

"He wants to remove the CIA and, for the most part, DHS. The sitting President and then-current chair of the Senate Intelligence Committee will provide oversite, and the Secretary of Homeland Security will be told to do whatever I, or perhaps a middleman, tell them and provide whatever I ask for. The good news is that we will continue to operate much the same way; the bad news is that we will likely have bigger, more long-term missions. What you and Sam undertook here, working as a team, was not our normal way of doing things, but you made a serious dent in the supply chain, and the President and Landry are impressed. American lives will be saved because of it."

I changed the subject. I could think about that later. "I still want Weber."

"You said you can find him."

"Assuming he wasn't at the warehouse, I think he will be hiding out in the country near Campo Mara. That is where I first met him. I have a feeling he lives there most of the time and comes to Caracas to do business if needed."

"What is your plan?" Manning asked.

I explained, but Manning didn't respond.

Manning asked to visit Sam, who was awake and seemingly more rested. We agreed to do the debrief in Sam's room the next day.

When we walked back through, Cruz was in the small waiting room. I introduced her to 'Mr. Smith' and asked if she and

Crumby might be up for another mission. She said they would be awaiting instructions.

∞

The debrief the following morning took over four hours. We talked through every aspect of the operation. There were loose ends we needed to tie up, and Weber was one of them.

Afterward, I discussed my plan to hopefully eliminate Weber. Sam was pissed that he couldn't participate. Manning asked what I would need and then disappeared to call the DHS secretary. Someone else called him back an hour later, and we had a plan by six o'clock that evening.

"DHS is flying an asset into Caracas. He is a retired Coast Guard captain named," Manning looked at his notes, "Marlin Garrison. He and someone he is bringing with him will land at Simón Bolívar International Airport and proceed to the Marina. They will move *Guppy Love* to Aruba and pick you up there. You said everything you need is aboard the boat."

"We left the rifle Sam was firing behind, but two were on the boat. If no one has stolen it, the backup should still be there. There is also some diving equipment and several dry bags. I should have what I need."

∞

Three days later, the Zodiac picked me up at Aruba Surfside Marina. A short, stocky man with a huge red beard and bushy hair greeted me.

"I'm McCale," he said in a voice and accent that matched his build and Irish name. "Let's get you going then."

We made our way back to the *Guppy*, where I met Marlin Garrison. He was in his mid-fifties but fit, with close-cropped hair and a strong military bearing. At only five foot six and about a hundred and fifty pounds, he wasn't very intimidating physically, but I sensed he had been a successful commanding officer before retiring.

"I understand we need to drop you in Maracaibo for a while."

"Not exactly. I need to get to the coast somewhere just north of San Rafael de El Mojan, but this boat can't be seen there. The people we have been dealing with know it." I pointed to a map of the Caribbean I had purchased at the airport. "I would like to move the *Guppy* into the Gulf of Venezuela after dark, about here, then either take the Zodiac to shore and try to hide it in this area or have one of you drop me off. Then you can head back into the Caribbean until I call you. There is a sat phone on board. The third option is to swim in."

"How hard will it be to hide the Zodiac?" Garrison asked.

"There isn't much cover along the waterline. It is a narrow beach and then almost a kilometer of tidal flats. I probably need to enter at low tide to get across the flats. I don't think we will have enough water to get the Zodiac past the flats."

"Then McCale will drop you off. This monster of a yacht moves along pretty fast. We can get in and back out under darkness. I will disable the transponder and hope no one pays much attention. If we plan right, we won't be stopped long, and we will keep *Guppy Love* several miles from the shore. McCale can take you ashore in the Zodiac and be back here in fifteen minutes. We will head back into the Caribbean until we hear from you. Tonight?"

"At low tide."

The insertion went smoothly. I made it about four kilometers inland before the sun came up. This was an agricultural area, so I had to go out of my way to avoid open fields. I stuck to tree lines and ditches as much as I possibly could. At sunrise, I found a place to hide in the woods. I carried four liters of water and high-calorie energy bars in my backpack, so I ate and drank before resting all day.

When it became dark again, I used the GPS to continue toward Campo Mara to coordinates I had previously marked. At four a.m. I arrived and circled the property where I first saw Weber. The driveway to the small house where I had first encountered Weber continued behind and beyond through a stand of trees and cacti, so I followed it for almost half a mile. The sun was coming up again when I spotted a twelve-foot-tall stone wall with a solid steel gate. I had little doubt that Weber's house was somewhere beyond.

An area fifty feet wide had been cleared outside the stone wall for as far as I could see around the perimeter. I assumed there were cameras, so I stayed inside the tree line and searched for higher ground. I found it about six hundred yards from the house where a ridge rose fifty meters higher than the house. I stuck to the densest foliage until I found an opening that gave me a view of two sides of the house.

The house was not huge, maybe three thousand square feet, but the grounds were immaculately maintained. There was a green lawn in front and a vegetable garden on the west side. I assumed the east side held a garage or carport, but I was unable to see that.

I assembled the sniper rifle and loaded a round in the chamber. I then built a blind to provide camouflage.

The plan was three days maximum. If I didn't see Weber in that time, I would return to the coastline and call Garrison for a ride.

But I got lucky.

At around ten that first morning, Weber stepped outside and started toward the garden. He was wearing the same ragged-looking clothes as when I first saw him, a straw hat, and he was carrying a basket and the thin cane.

He was slowly walking toward my position, so I waited a moment with the crosshairs pointed at his center of mass. When he stopped near a cluster of tomato vines, I checked the range: 650 yards. There was some wind, but it was coming from straight behind me. I performed some mental math regarding range, wind, and elevation, adjusted the scope to allow for a 63-inch drop, steeled the crosshairs on his right temple, and slowly squeezed the trigger. I slid the bolt back and forward again, ready to fire a second round, but when I found him through the scope, he was face down in the dirt, unmoving. Blood pooled near the base of his neck. I fired a second round into him just to make sure before breaking down and stowing the rifle. Perhaps his son would rebuild the empire, but Weber was no more. I was headed out.

It took three days to get back to the shoreline. Gun-toting men in pickups constantly drove the roads but never got out to search. I assumed they were looking for me, so I took extra time.

At two a.m., almost exactly five days after I returned to Venezuela, McCale arrived at the shoreline in the Zodiac. I was headed home, but it would take longer than I expected.

Chapter 28

"The President told DHS Secretary Halen he was to do as I say and ask no questions," Manning told me over the satellite phone. "You should have seen his face."

"I imagine he was thrilled,"

"And here is the plan for you. It comes straight from the President. He wants a small team, probably three or four operators, including you, plus a small support staff, to continue to operate from *Guppy Love*. I think Landry provided some input into that decision."

"I don't understand that. I like being a lone operator unless I can work with Sam, of course."

"I should have some more information when you get back stateside. Garrison may be able to fill you in on whatever has been discussed with him. I asked him to swing by Grenada and pick up Roman Thompson. The guys at the Company say he has been a good resource over the years, and they want to keep using him, just not in the South Caribbean. Then, you need to spend a day in Grand Cayman. Open a bank account there. Rolle Imports has nowhere offshore to send you your pay, and it is building up. You, Garrison, and Thompson will bring the yacht to Newport News, Virginia. We have a shipyard set to retrofit her with a new paint job and a new name; plus, they will change the superstructure again, so the profile is a little different. At thirty-plus meters, that vessel has the range and stability to cross oceans and the speed to get out of harm's way. It is already a great asset. Garrison has made some suggestions that will enhance its capabilities. Spend that travel time learning. We will find a qualified captain, but you need to learn everything you can."

"This isn't what I signed on for," I told him.

"Joshua," he said. "I don't know what to tell you. As you know, our independence and anonymity have been eroding anyway. In this new role, you will likely lead a team. One that you will choose. I will still coordinate, but I should have the resources of DHS when I need them and the President to back me up if I don't get them. I believe we can do some good."

I changed the subject. "How is Sam?"

"He left for Lexington airport at about eight this morning. Abercrombie and Cruz are flying him in. He will be back home by mid-afternoon. I need to go. Talk to Garrison and learn what you can about taking care of a big, expensive yacht. I will come to visit you soon. Landry said they already have some things that need to be addressed."

With that, he broke the connection.

∞

Two days ago, I had a plan. Return to Rachael's Ridge, ask Lauren to marry me, build us a house, and occasionally work for Manning. Now, things were in limbo again. Would Lauren understand? Could Lauren understand? Could I even ask her to understand?

Perhaps if I ever decide to tell you about another of my adventures, I will let you know how that turned out.

About The Author

R. Willis Smith has spent most of his adult life living in two worlds. The first is the professional world, where he worked in business development for a software company and later as a soft-skills trainer. The second world is a world of fantasy, where great writers like Tom Clancy, Daniel Silva, Steve Berry, and others took him on adventures filled with intrigue, adventures where the good guys ultimately win, and the hero may - or may not - get the girl.

After years of starts and stops, Operation Hoplon is Smith's first full novel. He hopes you enjoy reading it as much as he enjoyed researching and writing it.

No project would have been finished without the loving support of his wife Lisa, who, 36 years ago, made him the happiest guy on earth.

Acknowledgment

I want to thank many people, but I have neither the space, cognitive recall, nor the time to list them all. A few people, however, stand out.

First, thank you to my wife and proofreader-in-chief for your support and encouragement. You will never know what it means to me.

To my parents, John and Delores, your unfailing faith in me is noticed and will never be forgotten. Thanks for instilling a strong work ethic in me.

Thank you for your valuable input to Richard Barkley, Teri Brinkman, Tom Pitts, and other beta readers.

I also want to thank Carolyn Jackson (10th grade English) and the late Marilyn Monroe (12th grade Journalism and English) for inspiring me to write and hopefully to write well.

Made in the USA
Columbia, SC
26 November 2024